BOUND
BY
HONOR

CENTALLIAN GUARDIANS

VOLUME I

BOUND BY HONOR

CENTALLIAN GUARDIANS
VOLUME I

ROSE SARTIN

LAGAN
PRESS

an imprint of
OGHMA CREATIVE MEDIA

OGHMA

C R E A T I V E   M E D I A

Lagan Press
An imprint of Oghma Creative Media, Inc.
2401 Beth Lane, Bentonville, Arkansas 72712

Library of Congress Cataloging-in-Publication Data

Names: Sartin, Rose, author.
Title: Bound by Honor/Rose Sartin. | Centallian Guardians #1
Description: First Edition | Bentonville: Lagan, 2017
Identifiers: LCCN: 2019950129 | ISBN: 978-1-63373-200-1 (hardcover) |
ISBN: 978-1-63373-201-8 (trade paperback) | ISBN: 978-1-63373-202-5 (eBook)
Subjects: | BISAC: FICTION/Romance/Science Fiction
FICTION/Romance/Action & Adventure | FICTION/Science Fiction/Space Opera
LC record available at: https://lccn.loc.gov/2019950129

Lagan Press trade paperback edition November, 2017

Cover & Interior Design by Casey W. Cowan
Editing by Gil Miller

To the memory of my husband, Gary Allen Sartin, the hero of my life's story.
And to our children, Melissa, Angela and Eric.

My thanks to Eric Sartin, my scientific advisor, Honnah Sartin, my computer tech, my daughters, Melissa and Angela, for believing in me, Mark Whittemire, my moral support, the Mid South Writers Group, Barbara Warren, Susan Eschbach, Prix Cautney, Sherri Akers, Matthew Eschbach, Kelly Henkins, Dona Fellows and Juanita Waxelman. You've been with me from the beginning. With a special thanks to my publisher, Casey Cowan, my advisor, Venessa McDaniel Cerasale, and my editor, Gil Miller.

PROLOGUE

Massive spears of jagged stone breached the meadow's surface, spewing clods of dirt and grass as they lunged skyward. The ground buckled under Amber, flinging her onto the sharp stones, shredding the skin on her palms and knees. She covered her ears to muffle the shriek of tearing rock.

Boulders, tossed like dice, lay askew. Imploded, smoking holes pockmarked the ground and gaping rends slashed across the meadow. Trees smoldered, and here and there were small, blackened mounds her mind refused to identify. The stench of singed hair and charred flesh pervaded the air.

An old woman staggered out of the smoke, clutching a large bundle of rags to her chest. Blood oozed from scratches etched across her pale, oval face. One gray braid drooped from the coronet on her head. She shuffled along the edge of a fresh chasm, her feet inches from the brink.

"Stop," Amber cried, scrambling to her feet. The ground erupted and a thunderous roar muted her shout.

The woman turned, then stumbled to her knees and fell forward. The bundle rolled from her arms and came to rest at the base of a splintered sapling. A baby wailed and the woman crawled toward the heap.

Low, shuddering rumbles vibrated the air, increasing in intensity until the trees shook. Terror contorted the aged features as the ground crumbled beneath her. Her fingers clawed furrows in the dirt as she struggled to keep from sliding over the rim.

Amber swayed with the rolling ground as she closed the distance between them. She lunged in a desperate attempt to reach the woman in time, her stomach slamming the debris-strewn loam, forcing the air from her lungs. She caught the woman's wrist with both hands and held tight.

The woman's weight gradually pulled them over the edge. "Let me go. You'll fall with me!"

"No." Amber dug the toes of her shoes into the dirt, slowing their progress into the abyss. "Try to get a foothold. Give me your other hand."

Gnarled fingers closed around her wrist and the strain on her arms eased as the woman obeyed. A whimper of relief caught in Amber's throat.

Pebbles clattered, and the woman's feet swung away from her unstable perch. She lurched downward, her body slamming into the rock face. The force jerked Amber's head and shoulders over the edge.

The baby howled behind her, but Amber dared not spare the child a glance. The weight on her arms was drawing her into the pit.

"Release me," the woman's pain-filled whisper pleaded. Tears mingled with the dirt and blood on her weathered face.

Amber's own tears spilled down her cheeks. She remembered now…. This woman was too precious to lose.

"I can't let you go," she sobbed. "I love you too much."

"Do you think only of yourself? Can't you hear Dzang cry? You must save my granddaughter, and find your sister. Saing cannot protect them. He was the first to fall." Her stern features softened to a sad smile. "I love you, too," she whispered, and as that love washed over Amber, the woman twisted free.

"No! Mother…."

1

✧

Amber bolted upright in bed, her hands reaching out to grasp...

What?

She glanced around, confused, and recognized her room. A dream. She pushed the hair out of her eyes, leaned back against the pillows, and waited for the nightmare to fade. The tension slowly eased from her body, but she couldn't shut out the images. Everything had been so vivid.

She couldn't shake the feeling of not being altogether alone, as if the person she'd been in the nightmare followed her into reality. She half expected to discover her alter ego lurking in the shadows.

She shook her head over the ridiculous notion. This was home, her sanctuary since childhood. She was secure in this room, comforted. Yet tonight she ached with an inexplicable sense of loss. What made the dream so painfully real? She kicked free of the sheets and swung her legs over the side of the bed.

Moonlight streamed through the window, bathing the room in a brilliant, blue haze that illuminated all but the alcove beyond her bed. Its brightest streamers slanted across the bed to light the wall and the doorway to the hall. The cut-glass bud vase on the corner of her desk caught and refracted the light, dappling the opened sketchpad in kaleidoscopic shades of blue and gray.

The glowing red numbers on the digital clock read 4:42. She climbed out of bed and moved to the open window, her shadow flitting like an ebony ghost over the cabin's varnished log walls.

The room was warm, almost stuffy. She raised the window, and cool air drifted through the bottom screen. A light breeze rustled the newborn leaves of her favorite old oak. The sound soothed her, reminded her of gentle rain. She leaned against the window jamb and breathed in the cool night air. It was easy to understand why Grandpa chose to make their home in this remote area. The peace it afforded was a balm to the soul.

At least it usually was.

A cricket chirped somewhere in the room. Its raspy song mimicked the high-pitched croaking of the tree frogs in the surrounding woods. She'd grown used to the insect's nightly serenade. Tonight she welcomed its affable companionship, a friendly voice in the dark.

She pressed her forehead to the cool windowpane. Who was the woman in her dream? Why had she called her mother? She wasn't Mom. Mom never had a chance to grow old. Neither had Dad. The woman in the dream was a stranger. So why did her death seem so personal, so devastating?

A whippoorwill's song pulled her from the disturbing thoughts. Another haunting call echoed the first. She closed her eyes and let her troubled spirit follow as the small nighthawks soared above the Ozark valley floor.

But the peaceful night didn't ease her melancholy, or dispel her anxiety. She still felt it, the sense of not being altogether alone.

Disquiet, like static electricity, raised the hair on the back of her neck. She rubbed the gooseflesh away, and shook her head, denying her imagination the power to frighten her. She was too old to be frightened by monsters in the closet, or ghosts lurking under the bed.

The tree frogs stopped croaking. In the same moment the whippoorwills' calls died away. Even the cricket quit chirping. She lifted her head at the unexpected cessation of night sounds.

Nothing moved. Her smile wavered. Too old to be afraid of the dark? Tell that to her pounding heart. The pain in her chest reminded her to breathe.

She waited for the insect to renew his chant, but all she heard was a faint,

undefined noise, like the little creaks and groans a house makes when it's old…
or like the sound of an aging floorboard under a person's weight.

A breath, warm and real, touched the top of her head, fanned her hair. Her
stomach knotted. She eyed the ground fifteen feet below.

Escape!

The word burned in her mind. Her hand moved to the screen, the pressure
of her fingers stretching the thin, metal strands. The old screen was loose. One
good shove and—

"You'll break your neck."

She spun, and her knees nearly buckled. He was so close their bodies almost
touched. Pivoting, she slammed the screen with both palms and sent it flying,
but powerful arms circled her waist and dragged her away from the window.

She slashed at his hands with her nails, twisted around, and drove her
knee between his legs. He grunted, but didn't crumple as she'd expected.
Instead, he spun her back around, hooked an arm under her breasts, and
lifted her from her feet. She screamed, but he clamped a hand over her mouth
and propelled her toward the bed. She squirmed and kicked in a frantic effort
to free herself. She didn't stand a chance of matching his strength. He was
going to rape her and she couldn't stop him. Desperate, she sank her teeth
into his callused palm and held on.

Her captor flinched and tightened the arm around her waist until breathing
was nearly impossible. "Let go. Now."

She had no choice. He could crush her ribs with a flex of his forearm. She
relaxed her jaw and the pressure eased.

"I'm not here to hurt you," he said. "Calm down." His lips touched her
ear. His husky baritone voice shivered over her senses. "No one can hear you
scream. Promise to be quiet and I'll remove my hand."

She nodded.

His hand fell away. When she didn't make a sound, he turned her loose.

"Sit down."

She lunged away from him and scrambled across the foot of the bed on
hands and knees, determined to reach the door and freedom.

He beat her to the other side, and stepped into a shaft of bright moonlight.

She sat back on her heels and stared up at him. The sheer size of the man was daunting.

The lacings of his black shirt must have loosened during their struggle, exposing his rock-solid chest and ridged abs. The shirt still concealed his arms, but they were no doubt massive, and unbelievably strong. She'd felt them. His long, sleeveless vest was also black, as were the pants that fit snug enough to reveal thick-muscled thighs.

Long hair, dark as a lunar eclipse, framed his sharp-angled face. His equally dark eyes burned with an intensity of purpose that terrified her. He looked like the dark incarnation of some unrelenting primitive god.

"Who are you?" she whispered.

He didn't answer. His gaze swept her body, making her aware of the thin nightgown she wore. Approval tempered his iron-cast features.

She folded her arms across her chest and glared at him to hide her fear. "I asked who you are."

He looked up, and his gaze locked with hers. "I am Rhyel. And you, Amber, are not what I expected."

"How do you know my name?"

He shrugged. "It is easy to discover a name."

He hadn't hesitated to give her his name. Her heart pounded in her ears with that realization. He hadn't worn a mask to hide his face either. He wasn't worried about hiding his identity. Why?

"If it's money you want," she blurted out, "what I have is in my bag." She nodded toward the dresser. "There's over two hundred dollars in it. Take it all. Just leave."

Rhyel reached into his vest pocket. "I have no use for your money."

Amber watched him remove and unfold a white cloth, revealing a slim, capped hypodermic needle.

The air was suddenly heavy. "What's that?"

"Nothing to harm you. I promise."

Was he after drugs? Addicts were desperate, unpredictable—and dangerous.

"This is our home," she said carefully. "You won't find any drugs here."

The stranger's eyes hardened. "Drugs hold no interest for me."

She couldn't drag her gaze from the hypo. "Then why are you here? We have nothing of value."

"You belittle yourself." He uncapped the syringe and held it up to a shaft of moonlight. A dark liquid filled the narrow tube. "I've come for you."

2

Amber fell back, rolled over the end of the bed, and bolted for the window. But her hip slammed into the corner of the desk, and she plunged to her hands and knees. The bud vase shattered on the floor in front of her. The base rolled against her hand, a long dagger-like shard of glass still attached. She closed her fingers around it.

He touched her shoulder. "Amber—"

She spiraled up to face him, and stepped back against the wall, the ominous fragment of glass held defensively before her. "Get out of my way."

Her antagonist shook his head. "Put it down."

She stifled a whimper. "Don't force me to use this."

"You are a healer, Amber." He recapped the hypo and placed it in his pocket. "It isn't your nature to hurt anything." He extended his arm, his hand palm up. "Give me the crystal."

"No." She brandished the jagged weapon, and edged toward the hall door, but the wall abruptly ended and she backpedaled into the small alcove.

He crowded her deeper into the dusky niche. He was so big, so powerful. There was barely room for them both. Her hips bumped the back wall, and she lurched forward. His arm snaked out and she pulled back, turning the shard away from him.

"Don't!" He grabbed her wrist, but not before the glass pierced her throat.

Stunned, she dropped the shard. Something warm trickled from the hollow of her neck. She glanced down. In the shadows, her blood looked like a thin, black satin ribbon trailing between her breasts. She reached for her throat.

He caught that wrist too. "Wait."

"Let me go." She fought to twist out of his grip.

He pressed her against the wall with his body. "Stop fighting me. I need to see how bad that is."

The worry in his voice penetrated her fog of panic. She stilled.

He stepped back, released her wrists, and cupped her face in both hands, his fingers gentle as he tilted her head back to examine the damage.

"It's too dark in here." He picked her up before she could protest, and carried her to the bed. He bent to place her on the rumpled sheet and she instinctively grabbed his neck to keep from falling. He sucked in his breath as if the half-embrace caused him pain, and buried his face in her hair. "*Rishka.*" She pushed away from him. He allowed her the distance and placed her in the center of the bed. "You need to be as still as possible."

The bed dipped with his weight as he sat beside her. He fumbled with the lamp and she blinked when the room brightened. He plucked several tissues from the box on her bedside table and carefully dabbed at the blood surrounding the cut on her neck. He leaned close to examine her injury.

The man's fingers were feverish against her skin. The scent of his warm body filled her nostrils—exotic, seductive, male. Her mouth went dry. She resisted the urge to lick her lips. Never before had she been so aware of another person, not even Chris—and she'd almost married him. Terror had heightened her senses, she reasoned. It was an instinctive reaction.

He sat back and tossed the bloody tissues on the stand. She couldn't read anything in his expression.

"Is it deep?" she finally asked, wincing at the pain that speaking caused.

"The puncture is shallow and I can find no glass fragments. The bleeding has almost stopped. You are most fortunate."

Fortunate? How did he have the nerve to say that?

He pulled a drawstring pouch from his vest pocket and sprinkled a dark, beet-colored powder into his palm.

She tensed. "What's that?"

"An herb we use as an antiseptic and coagulant."

"I have something better in my medical bag on—"

His palm and the red powder covered her throat, scorching her lacerated skin. She grabbed his wrist and tried to jerk his hand away.

He ignored her efforts and reached into his pocket, retrieving the syringe. He snapped the cap off with his teeth.

Before she could react, he released her throat, twisted his hand out of her grip, and caught her wrist. He stretched her arm out against the sheets and angled forward, using his wide back to block her free arm.

"Stop!" She grabbed his hair and pulled hard. He didn't budge. She pounded his shoulder with her fist. He didn't seem to notice. The man was a solid wall of muscle, preventing her from defending herself, blocking her vision. She couldn't see what he was doing, but she'd seen the hypo.

"Be still, *Rishka*. Neither of us wants the needle to break." He smoothed something soft on her skin above the vein. The red stuff?

The needle pierced her skin. She closed her eyes in resignation when it glided deeper. Her forearm ached as the liquid entered her bloodstream. She rolled onto her back. What was done was done.

He let go of her wrist and turned, leaning over her. The intensity in his eyes captivated her.

"*Rishka, sa' skaiin d'haiila,*" he whispered.

She didn't understand the words, couldn't recognize the language, but the gentle way he spoke made her feel protected, almost cherished. It was an absurd reaction considering what he'd just done to her.

Rhyel sat back, capped the hypo, and returned it to his pocket. He expected a confrontation, but she simply turned her face away. He had little doubt that she would soon regain her spirit and cause herself more trouble. He regretted having to wait for Cintar's return before seeing to her safety. The woman seemed determined to do herself harm.

A glimmer of gold drew his attention to the bedside stand. A round locket on a braided golden chain lay beside the lamp. He picked up the pendant to examine the elaborate A etched in the center. His fingers found a catch, and the top sprang open to reveal two photographs—a man and a woman.

He lifted his gaze to Amber. She and the woman in the picture shared a delicate beauty—the same red-gold hair and ivory skin.

The man's eyes were the exact shade of green as the healer's. She possessed his stubborn jaw too, though her feminine bone structure softened the effect. The images must be those of her parents. He snapped the lid shut and placed the necklace inside his vest.

His attention returned to his captive. Aadrok had warned that she would defy him, but the seer hadn't mentioned her appearance, and Rhyel admitted to himself that he hadn't been interested enough to ask.

That omission had nearly compromised his honor. The lovely woman standing in the moon's beam had mesmerized him. The soft glow filtering through her thin gown had created a misty silhouette of her delectable body. He was no voyeur, but he hadn't been able to turn his eyes away. Even now, under the glare of the lamp, she was beautiful, her skin as smooth as the petal of a rare Centallian orchid.

He was attracted to her—extremely attracted. The realization caught him by surprise. Such was not supposed to occur between....

She groaned. He bent forward and brushed the hair away from her face. She flinched and he straightened, giving her space.

"How do you feel?"

Her eyes shot to his, revealing the anger she'd been harboring. "How am I supposed to feel, light-headed, groggy?" She rubbed the tender spot on her arm. "What did you give me?"

"It was a vaccine, something to protect you."

"I'm a doctor. I know you don't inject a vaccine into the vein."

He didn't argue. She would discover the truth soon enough. A vibration from the pack at his hip alerted him to Cintar's return. He stood and reached for her hand.

"We must go."

She pushed back against the pillow. "I'm not going anywhere with you."

"I am sorry. You have no choice."

There's *always* a choice. Amber ignored his offer of help and managed to stand without aid. Her legs shook, but when he tried to steady her, she stepped away.

"I need to change clothes. The bathroom's down the hall." And it comes with a solid lock on the door and a fair-sized window.

He looked around, spotted the robe she'd draped over a small chair and reached for it. "This will suffice," he said, handing it to her.

She grudgingly slipped it over the gown and secured the belt. Remembering the broken vase, she stepped into her slippers. It was a miracle she hadn't cut her feet trying to get away from him.

"At least let me leave my grandfather a note. If I just disappear, he'll be frantic. He's an old man, and the stress could kill him. He needs to know when I'll be back."

"You won't be coming back."

3

✧

Amber's mouth opened in denial, but she couldn't form the words. She simply looked at him.

"I know you mistrust me," he said after a moment. "Be assured I have no dark motive for taking you. A healer is vital to the survival of my people. But I cannot bring you back. You will make your home with us."

She shook her head. "We both know you don't have to kidnap a doctor. The World Health Organization is available for you to turn to."

"I wish it could be otherwise, but you will go with me."

She had to stall him long enough to figure out how to get away. "At least let me leave Grandpa a note. He needs to know something."

"Will you tell him you've been kidnapped and will not return?"

"No, of course not."

"What will you tell him?"

"I don't know yet. Anything to keep him from worrying."

Rhyel looked toward the screenless window, the shattered remains of the bud vase, and finally, the bloodstained tissues. "He will know you fought me."

"That's why I need to leave him a note. I have to tell him that you didn't hurt me, that you don't intend to." When he hesitated she placed an imploring hand on his arm. "Please."

He looked down at her hand, and she jerked it back. "You will make the note short."

"Thank you. I have a pen and paper on the counter downstairs in the kitchen."

"You have writing utensils here, as you do paper."

"I want him to see the note before he sees this room. We have to go downstairs anyway."

After a moment's consideration, he nodded. She quickly turned toward the door, and swayed. Her entire body trembled with the adrenaline rushing through her system.

He immediately grasped her arm and pulled her back around to face him. His hand came up, and his knuckles gently traced the high line of her cheekbone.

"You are pale," he said. "Perhaps I should carry you."

She jerked away from him. "Of course I'm pale. I'm being kidnapped!" Her knees might be a little wobbly, but she hadn't given up the idea of escape—something she couldn't do trapped in his arms. She straightened to her full five-foot-seven. "I can walk out of here without your help."

He looked skeptical. "You are sure?"

"Absolutely." She started for the door.

He took her arm and walked her out into the hall. When they started down the stairs, she grabbed the banister for balance. The last thing she needed right now was a tumble down the….

She crooked an elbow around the banister, pulled back a step behind him, and kicked out hard. Her foot caught the back of his knee, buckling it. He pitched forward, releasing her arm. She hugged the banister and watched him catapult down the staircase. His descent ended one step from the bottom. She took the stairs two at a time, vaulted over his prone figure, and kept going.

His groan stopped her.

She turned to see what kind of damage she'd caused. The man had made it to his knees but cradled his head in both hands. She doubted he'd regained his senses yet, but he didn't appear to be seriously injured. Fair enough.

She gave the house phone brief consideration as she passed it on her way through the kitchen to the back door. He'd catch her if she stopped to use it.

Releasing the deadbolt, she yanked the door open, and pushed the screen wide in her race for the Jeep.

Amber's phone was in the vehicle. She'd forgotten to take it off the charger. She'd drive out of the valley to safety and call for help when she got a signal. Right now she had to get as far away from him as fast as possible.

She reached the Jeep, swung the door open, and glanced over her shoulder. He hadn't followed—not yet. She slid behind the wheel and reached for the key. It wasn't there! She switched on the interior lights and scanned the dashboard. Not there either. She checked the passenger's seat where her phone lay, then bent and ran her hand along the floorboard under her seat. Where was it?

When she reached for the latch on the glove compartment it came to her—the pocket of her jacket... hanging on the peg by the kitchen door. She'd run right past the keys.

Something crashed in the house. She grabbed the phone and scrambled from the seat. She gave the Jeep a regretful look, and bolted for the woods and higher ground.

The screen door slammed. She darted behind a huge cedar at the far edge of the yard and peeked out through the shaggy branches.

Rhyel staggered into the yard and stopped, massaging the back of his neck. He shook his head as if to clear it, and then looked around. She ducked back, regretting her choice of nightwear. The moonlight made her gown and robe glow white.

She checked her phone. No signal. What had she expected? The woods offered protection for now, but soon the moon's light would yield to the brighter light of the sunrise. She had to make it to the ridge top and call the sheriff while she still had the cover of darkness.

She took off at a run, heedless of the deadfall and rocks littering the forest floor. The pungent odor of decomposing vegetation rose to mark her passing as she climbed higher.

Several times she paused to catch her breath, and listened for pursuit. She checked her phone as often in a vain effort to find a signal. How long had she been climbing? A rosy hue flushed the eastern horizon. She had to find a place to hide—a place where she could call for help before the light gave her away.

Something thrashed about in the underbrush below. She slipped behind a large sycamore, wishing she could blend like a moth against the gray-and-white-mottled bark. The thrashing grew louder then stopped.

A minute passed… two… five. Nothing moved.

He's waiting for me to make a mistake, to break and run. She pressed closer to the tree. Thin, curling bark snagged her robe and scratched her arms.

She wanted to scream in frustration. Why didn't he move? She couldn't hide here indefinitely. Even now, dawn's murky light diminished the shadows, and she needed the darkness to get away.

Brittle leaves crackled. She flinched and tightened a fist against her stomach. In spite of the cool morning, a sheen of moisture dampened her palms.

She barely managed to stifle a cry when the buck stepped into her line of sight. The magnificent animal tested the wind and turned to look at her.

She sagged against the tree and drew a steadying breath.

The deer shook his antlered head and stomped the ground. He raised his nose high and tested the air again, snorting this time.

She straightened, sensing the animal's unease.

A twig snapped. The buck bounded into the undergrowth.

She bolted in the opposite direction—straight into Rhyel's arms.

She attacked her tormentor, her nails seeking his face. He threw his head back to avoid her hands and grabbed her wrists.

"No!" she screamed, aiming a knee at his groin.

He veered out of harm's way and twisted her arms behind her back, securing them with one hand. He pulled her closer.

His fingers caught in her hair, holding her head still. "Give it up, Amber." He didn't shout the words. He didn't have to. Their lips were inches apart. "You've lost."

His hand slipped around to the front of her neck to briefly touch the wound on her throat before moving lower. He loosened the top of her robe and she gasped when his hand blazed a fiery path to the hollow between her breasts. His palm was hot on her skin as it nestled over her pounding heart.

She raised her eyes to his. "Please let me go."

Rhyel denied her with a slow, somber shake of his head, and defiance returned to those deep-green pools. She tried to wrench free of his grasp—and almost succeeded. She had courage. He respected courage. Her racing heart betrayed her heightened emotions, though, and for her own sake he needed her calm. He regretted what he was about to do.

"I will keep you safe, but you must remain absolutely still. Your life depends on it." He saw the burst of fear in her eyes a moment before he closed his own. He concentrated on her heartbeat then applied a sudden jolt of pressure with the heel of his hand. She slumped against him. "Trust me," he whispered, gently lifting her into his arms, holding her tight against his chest.

Standing against the dawn, he raised his eyes to the heavens. "Now," he commanded and held stone still. A silver-blue vapor enfolded them, and they faded like mist in sunlight.

4

✧

The small, dark-haired girl squealed in delight and toddled through the doorway. She stumbled, lost her balance, and fell giggling into Amber's outstretched arms. Amber returned the child's exuberant hug and looked up as her sister, Laanil, and brother-in-law, Saing, entered the room.

"Is that proper behavior for the granddaughter of an Elder?" Laanil admonished little Dzang.

"Don't scold my niece, Laanil. How else will she tell me of her happiness at my return?"

"You think she cannot talk?" Saing put his arm around his wife. "You only need to acquire a trained ear. Stay home longer, and you will not only understand her, you will speak like her."

"Saing is right." Her mother entered the room, leaned forward, and kissed her cheek. "You spend little enough time with your family, and now your father tells me you have an emergency diplomatic mission. How soon must you leave?"

"Within the hour. We'll be gone—"

The house trembled. Saing reached for his daughter and looked around as the vibration changed to a rumble, then a deafening roar. Brilliant white light scorched the sky beyond their window. Little Dzang wailed and grabbed her father's neck.

"Please, no." Amber reached for her mother.

Arms enfolded her, but not the gentle arms of her mother. These arms kept the terror at bay. They pulled her away from the danger....

Awash in the aftermath of the dream, she held tight to the warm body she was pressed against. They were gone. Her mother, Dzang.... She sobbed into the soft shirt that covered a solid chest, her fingers gripping the cloth lifeline to keep from tumbling into despair.

Long moments passed before the dream diminished, and her mind separated nightmare from reality. Her head hurt. It was hard to think. Fragmented memories of pursuit and capture swirled in a confusing fog. Was that part of the dream?

A face materialized, a dark, untamed visage—obsidian eyes, long, black hair. The image expanded to include massive shoulders and arms, and thick-muscled thighs.

She stiffened. "Rhyel."

"So, you remember."

She shoved out of his arms, the action making her head throb with every heartbeat. A wave of nausea hit her stomach and she lurched toward the side of the bed. Rhyel grabbed her shoulders, supporting her as dry heaves wracked her body.

The heaving stopped when her stomach finally realized there was nothing to bring up. He eased her back against the pillows. She closed her eyes and willed the queasiness that still tormented her insides to go away.

She took deep breaths—as much to calm her fear as her stomach. She'd seen enough of the room to know she wasn't home. Where had he taken her? How far?

He slipped an arm under her shoulders.

Her eyes flew open, and she stiffened as he lifted her off the pillows.

"Easy," he cautioned. "Drink this." He brought a glass to her lips.

The thought of putting anything into her weak stomach made her groan. She pushed the glass away.

"It's only water."

"My stomach won't tolerate it."

He set the glass aside. "I know you are afraid," he said, his voice calm, soothing, "but I will never hurt you. A man does not harm his hope for the future of his world."

His cryptic remark had all the earmarks of an unstable mind. She looked up at him. His stoic expression gave nothing away. She caught her lower lip between her teeth. How unpredictable was he? She tried to remember what had happened when he'd kidnapped her, but the pain overrode clear thought.

"Where am I?"

"In my home."

The throbbing in her head intensified as she fought to remember. He'd told her he was taking her to his home. She was sure of that, but she didn't remember the trip.

"Where is home?"

"A great distance from your grandfather's cabin."

"That doesn't tell me anything."

He shrugged.

She pressed her fingertips to her temples, trying to control the ache. "I was running through the woods. I saw a deer—a buck. Something startled him and he... I panicked and ran. You came out from behind the tree and... what did you do to me?"

"We call the technique *Mensolm*. It's an ancient discipline, a method of self-protection."

"And you thought you needed protection from me?" The idea was ludicrous.

He must have thought so too. He chuckled, but quickly sobered. "No, *Rishka*, I was protecting you. It was necessary to subdue you before you killed yourself."

"I didn't endanger my life, you did."

"You attempted to jump out of a window. You nearly cut your jugular with a piece of glass, and you might have broken your neck on the stairs."

"I didn't fall down the stairs. You did."

He leaned in close, his hands on either side of her hips. "You kicked me down the stairs, and you could have gone down with me. Once outside, you thrashed around that woods of yours in the dark without even considering what might happen. Do you know how stupid that was? You could have stepped in a hole, or fallen over a rotting log. Once I'd caught you I couldn't chance your escaping again. You probably would have run off the edge of that small mountain you were climbing."

His eyes mirrored the intensity of his voice as he bent even closer. "You were mine, Amber. From the moment you were chosen, you were mine to protect. I would have saved you the discomfort of *Mensolm*, but not at the risk of your life."

She pushed back against the pillows, trying to place some distance between them, and he straightened, giving her space.

Chosen? How had she been chosen? By whom?

"Why me? There are physicians out there who would have been willing to go with you, adventurous doctors who would welcome the opportunity. Kidnapping me doesn't make any sense. Tell me what's really going on."

"Be patient, *Rishka*. All of your questions will be answered. I promise."

"When?"

"You must recover first."

She rubbed the muscle between her neck and shoulder. She felt awful and probably looked worse. It was useless to argue against the truth. Whatever he'd done had taken the starch out of her.

"Your technique could stand some improvement."

He lifted an eyebrow. "My technique was flawless, *Rishka*. You are suffering the aftereffects. *Mensolm* shocks your system. You lose consciousness, which is the desired effect. Unfortunately, the pain you feel is less than desirable. I can assure you it won't last long."

She hoped he was telling the truth. There wasn't a part of her body that didn't hurt. Even her fingernails ached. She didn't have the patience to wait until she felt better. She needed to know where she was *now*, how far away from home he'd taken her. She had this terrible feeling that she was no longer even in the United States.

"I'm not going to feel better until I have some straightforward answers."

He didn't act as though he'd heard her. He moved from the bed and walked toward a door across from the foot of the bed. She hadn't noticed it before. Did it lead outside? Was it a possible means of escape?

She quickly glanced around the room. Two more doors were set in the wall on her right. She didn't think they led anywhere she was interested in going. The furnishings caught her notice, though. An overstuffed chair beside the bed, the standing-mirror in one corner, a table with two chairs near a draped window, even the quilt on the bed had a familiar feel, could have been purchased at any number of stores near her home. New hope overshadowed her pain. He couldn't have taken her far, not out of the country, anyway.

Was she closer to home than she thought, maybe in a one-room cabin—who puts a dining table in a bedroom? She'd know as soon as he walked through that door.

He paused with his hand on the doorknob.

She leaned forward in anticipation. Open it.

He heaved a sigh. His fingers released the handle and he walked back to her. Dropping into the overstuffed chair, he leaned forward, resting his arms on his thighs.

"My home was destroyed, and nearly all of my people annihilated," he began. "There are ninety-seven known survivors." He shook his head and took a steadying breath. "All ninety-seven were aboard my ship, *Novaria*." He leaned back. "It was *Soial-Anom'du'zolm*, our Holy Week. Centallians were expected to be home for the event. My crew and I were transporting Centallian mediators and their aides home from an emergency diplomatic mission."

"Centallian?"

"I am Centallian."

She'd never heard of them, but there were probably hundreds of small countries she was unaware of. Her hope of still being in the United States evaporated. But there must be a working government in whatever country he'd taken refuge in—a government she could appeal to for sanctuary. If he had a ship, they must live close to a good-sized body of water. There had to be a port close by, and a town or city.

"Who attacked you?" She tried to remember hearing of an attempted genocide. Something that horrendous would have caught the media's attention. Nothing came to mind, and it was a shame to admit, but the atrocity might not have been significant enough for the jaded world news organizations to bother with.

"We can't identify our attackers, but we know what they wanted. That knowledge has dictated every action we've taken since. Our assailants must continue to believe there were no survivors. If they discover our Council still lives, they will know that what they sought still exists. Until we can identify our enemy, we are restricted to a life of secrecy. We dare not draw attention to ourselves."

"You don't believe kidnapping me will draw attention to you?"

He smiled. "No one on Earth will suspect, or find us."

"That might have been true once, but with today's technology it wouldn't surprise me if the authorities weren't outside that door right now."

"You misunderstand, *Rishka*. When I told you my world had been destroyed I wasn't speaking figuratively. Two of your Earth-years ago my home planet, Centallus, was attacked and decimated. We've established a colony here, on a young planet we call New Centallus, your new home."

She was already shaking her head. The poor man was delusional, far more unbalanced than she'd suspected. She shoved back the covers, swung her legs over the edge of the bed, and lunged for the door. Whatever she discovered on the other side couldn't be as threatening as being alone in this room with a madman.

He caught her arm.

She clawed at his hand. "Let me go."

He grabbed her free hand. "When you've calmed down."

"I *am* calm!" Even she didn't believe that lie. Her heart tried to leap into her throat.

He reeled her in like a hooked trout, pulling her up against his body, wrapping his arms around her. "Shh. There isn't anything to be afraid of. You aren't in any danger."

She closed her eyes and raised her face to the ceiling beseeching Heaven's help. She had to regain control. Panic wouldn't get her out of here. She took a couple of deep breaths and tried to relax her tense muscles. "All right. I've calmed down."

His arms tightened briefly in what felt like a hug. "Sometimes, surrendering to the inevitable is the only reasonable option."

She pushed away from him. He allowed the distance. "Have you ever considered surrender?"

He leveled a solemn look on her. "Those who would have me surrender want me dead."

"You do know how unbelievable your story sounds, don't you?"

"The truth is there." He nodded toward the window. Heavy burgundy drapes prevented the light from filtering through—or was it dark outside? "You only have to look." He moved aside, giving her space to walk to the hidden portal. "Are you ready to see your new home?"

She straightened her shoulders and walked to the window on wobbly legs, determined to call his bluff. His story was so impossible even he couldn't believe it. But when she reached out to draw back the curtain, and he still didn't try to stop her, she faltered. His confidence undermined her logic. She suddenly dreaded what was on the other side.

"Do you fear the truth?" he whispered against her ear.

She jumped. She hadn't heard him approach. The man moved like a shadow. He leaned closer. "Do you?"

Yes, her mind screamed. If his claim was true she couldn't go home.

His chest pressed against her back as he reached over her shoulder to grasp the drapes. His hand crushed the heavy fabric as he swept the panel aside.

It wasn't Earth.

5

Beyond the smoky tint of the window pane laid a world of wild imagination, a land shimmering with heat, canopied by a turquoise sky. Wooded giants stood proud and straight, their branches garbed in brick-red leaves. They arched at the crest like great, benevolent mushrooms, shading the lesser trees clustered at their bases. The foliage on the smaller trees ranged from white-lavender broadleaves with pastel pink blossoms to flamboyant orange and yellow conifers. Multicolored fruit hung from several trees. Massive vines in unfamiliar hues tendriled round the stately titans and snaked along the ground. The short blades of grass were as yellow as goldenrod blossoms.

In the distance, jagged rock cliffs framed a half-moon bay and plunged to the pounding surf of an emerald sea. It was an alien world of unparalleled beauty. But it wasn't home.

Amber swung to face Rhyel. "What was in that injection you gave me?"

"The injection?"

"The shot you gave me at home. What was in it?"

He shrugged. "It was an immunization, nothing more."

"Nothing more?" She shoved her fingers through her hair as she glanced over her shoulder at the alien landscape. "I'm hallucinating." She stabbed a finger toward the window. "That doesn't exist." Her arm swept in a half circle to take in the room. "Or this." She crossed her arms, hugging her chest, and tried to control her shivering. "I'm probably wearing a straitjacket, and sitting on the floor of a padded room babbling to myself."

"You can't believe that."

"I can't believe what you want me to. Aliens, flying saucers, little green men—it's crazy."

He grasped her shoulders. "Look at me."

She shook her head.

He gave her a quick shake.

"Look at me."

Relenting, she lifted her eyes to meet his.

"I am neither little nor green. Will you treat reality as an illusion? Will you deny what your eyes see until you can no longer differentiate between fact and fantasy?"

"I am not suffering from self-induced delusions," she gritted out. "You drugged me. It's the only explanation for what's happening."

She turned away from him and stared out the window. "I've never doubted myself," she said more to herself than to him. "Not even when I was a child. But now…. How can I believe what you say when I can't even be sure you exist?"

She swiped at a tear, not wanting him to see how frightened she was. And then the irony struck her. She was attempting to hide her emotions from a figment of her imagination. A giggle, born of hysteria, ended in a stomach-wrenching sob.

He pulled her around and hugged her to his body. He pressed his cheek against the top of her head and whispered, "I did not drug you, *Rishka*. You must believe that."

Figment or not, he was suddenly the only familiar being in a world gone mad. She wrapped her arms around his waist and clung to him as if he alone could anchor her to sanity, as if his powerful embrace kept her from falling into infinite darkness.

✦

Rhyel held her as she cried against his neck until she was too exhausted to shed another tear. His lips touched her brow. "I know this isn't easy for you to accept. You've trained in the sciences. There must have been little room for speculation in your life. But consider how many suns exist in our galaxy and the multitude of planets orbiting those suns. Then consider the galaxies that populate our universe. The number is impossible to imagine—as impossible as it is to imagine that out of the vast universe of planets, Earth alone is blessed with life. My world is real, Amber."

He gently ran his knuckles down her cheek and tilted her face to his. "I am real." His lips brushed hers, the kiss butterfly soft and fleeting. When he lifted his head, there was confusion in her green eyes and he admitted to a like emotion.

His captive had captivated him.

He lifted her into his arms and held her close, silently willing his own strength into her trembling body. She seemed so fragile. He allowed himself a brief smile. That was a misconception. When the effects of *Mensolm* and the shock of finding herself on another world wore off, she would recover her strength and her defiance.

But for now, she didn't protest when he carried her to the large chair, sat down, and settled her on his lap. He reached out to drag the comforter from the bed and enshrouded them both in the soft material to share his body's heat with her.

When she stopped trembling, and her deep breathing told him she finally slept, he lifted her into bed and pulled the cover to her chin.

His sigh, as he sank back in the chair, was heavy and full of frustration. Her wrenching sobs had torn at his insides.

She moaned and turned to her side, facing him. Her hand slipped from beneath the cover and found his hand where it rested on the bed, her fingers curling around his. She needed the connection, he speculated, the warm touch of another person—even if that person had been born on a world light years from her own.

The decision to kidnap Amber may have been made by the Council, but he had brought her to New Centallus. She became his responsibility the moment he'd accepted the Elders' edict. The burden of responsibility lay heavier on his heart than he had anticipated, yet he was loath to relinquish his protection of her to another.

He didn't have to. A word to the Council would give her into his keeping permanently. They wouldn't question his motives. All Guardians were expected to claim a mate, to bond with her and produce children, assuring the continuation of their species. He had never questioned that duty. No Guardian did.

And no Guardian expected more than simple caring in his interspecies relationship. The bond between a Centallian male and an Earth female could never be as strong as the bond between Centallian mates. And few Centallian couples ever achieved *azcure*, the irrevocable bonding of body, mind, and spirit, a connection that could only be broken by death.

His parents had experienced that ultimate connection. He had witnessed firsthand the joy they shared, had hoped that he and Beleece.... But *azcure* was both blessing and curse. Eventually it demanded the ultimate price. His father lived his life in half-measure now. Zitan wrapped the memory of his bond-mate around himself like a shroud. He would never be whole again.

He shifted in the chair, suddenly uncomfortable with his thoughts. He had no time for the past. It was his duty to look forward, to rebuild their lives. He too must eventually take a mate. So why did he hesitate to claim the healer? Because he cared more for Amber than he wanted to.

He didn't need that complication.

She would no doubt find contentment with one of his Guardians, and find her place in this new world. He extracted his hand from her grasp, pulled the quilt over her shoulders, and stood. The Elders were waiting for his report.

The Elders hadn't taken their seats on the dais yet. The colonists wouldn't arrive for the council meeting for another few minutes. Rhyel decided there was enough time to report on their new healer's well-being.

The four men and two women stood in a circle talking. Rhyel's father spotted him and strode forward to embrace his son in greeting. He was nearly as tall and broad across the chest as Rhyel, but his shoulders were beginning to bow and today he looked tired. They all did.

"I'm sorry I wasn't there to welcome your return yesterday," Zitan said. "There was a problem at the mine that required attention."

"Do you bring us news of our healer?" Chief Elder Valdon asked as he and the others joined them. "We understand she is unwell."

"Amber is recovering," Rhyel assured them. "She is awake and knows where she is, but has yet to come to terms with her fate."

"Fate?" Valdon shook his head. "You speak as if we condemn her to servitude. She is an honored and respected member of our community."

"She earned both honor and respect on her own world. She desires nothing more of us than to return home. Aadrok told you she had family and friends she cared for. Our new healer will not thank us for taking her away from her loved ones."

"We debated this issue before you left for Earth," the Chief Elder reminded him. "We had little liking for our decision, but we had no choice. Even you agreed she was the best candidate."

"But not the only candidate."

"No other healer met all of the qualifications."

"Aadrok predicted Amber would be the least likely to accept us."

"If you were so set against us, another could have taken your place. You were not the only Guardian capable of the mission. My son—"

"With respect, Valdon, I am aware of your son's achievements, and aspirations. But we both know that as commander of this colony and captain of the *Novaria*, it was my responsibility alone to bring her here—regardless of the fact that our action bordered on dishonor."

Zitan stepped between the two. "Guardians, you argue a moot point. Amber is with us now. It is our honor-bound duty to see that she adjusts to her new circumstances and finds her place among us."

"Zitan is right." Aadrok moved forward to clasp Rhyel's arm in greeting. "But I fear Amber will find the transition difficult. As our commander noted, she has many ties to her world, as well as responsibilities to those she ministered to as healer. She will not easily relinquish her connection to Earth."

"The sooner she is integrated into our society, the sooner she will adjust," Valdon said. "I suggest she immediately be added to our list of available brides."

"That would be a mistake." Rhyel kept his voice respectful but firm. "Our new healer requires time to make the adjustment. Aadrok's assessment of Amber's reaction is more than a seer's speculation. I have witnessed her determination to remain with her people. If we force a bonding at this time we undermine our efforts to gain her loyalty."

"We need not rush our healer into a bonding that cannot be consummated." Tzarn faced Valdon. "Until the vaccine proves successful, no bonded couple dares intimacy. The resulting pregnancy is unthinkable."

"We are hopeful," Zitan said to Rhyel. "Hiilani assures us Sonya is well and the babe also. But I agree. We should wait. Our healer needs to become familiar with our people."

"The more time we give her, the more willing she will be to cooperate," Aadrok said.

The Elders nodded in agreement.

Rhyel shook his head. "I doubt it will be that easy. Amber is a determined woman. She will pursue one objective—finding a way home. Until she is convinced she belongs with us, she will be opposed to any plan we have for her future, especially bonding her life with a Guardian whose main objective will be to give her children."

"Will she refuse her duties as healer?" Kroyda worried aloud, her dark eyes filled with concern.

"She is a compassionate woman," Aadrok said. "She will care for anyone in need of healing." He turned to Rhyel. "If our healer feels well enough, I suggest you bring her to the council chambers during our session. It will give her an opportunity to witness how our colony functions. Valdon tells me there are numerous petitions to be heard, but we should be able to adjourn before the midday meal. Perhaps she can be persuaded to join us."

"Perhaps." Rhyel bowed his respect to the Elders and took his leave.

6

How long had she been sleeping? Not long if how she felt was any indication. Her head and body ached, but at least she wasn't nauseated. Amber scooted up and leaned against the headboard to glance around. She knew where she was, remembered the room. No frills, only a few pieces of furniture. Spartan.

She remembered the two doors on her right too, but hadn't been interested in them before. Her only concern at the time had been what was beyond the door Rhyel had started to open. She was still interested in that one, but right now she hoped one of the other doors led to a bathroom.

She pushed out of bed and stood. Her legs were a little wobbly, but capable of holding her up. She cautiously padded across the tile floor and studied the entirely different doors. The one on the right looked like any interior door you'd find back home. The door on the left, however, reminded her of the easy access swinging doors at the hospital. She opted for the door on the left, nudged it open, and came to an abrupt stop.

A medical clinic. A very Earth-like medical clinic.

A young, dark-haired woman wearing a white lab coat looked up from a chart she'd been reading and smiled. Amber smiled back and closed the door. There was no way she was ready to talk to anyone at the moment.

She peeked into the room on the right and finally found the bathroom. It even had a lock on the door. Like the clinic she'd just seen, it could have been a bathroom anywhere on Earth—maybe a tad more extravagant than most. It sported a walk-in tub with shower, Jacuzzi, and sliding-glass door. There was a small recessed closet with shelves and a medicine cabinet over the standing sink. She glanced in the medicine cabinet hoping to find some type of analgesic. She found a comb and brush, deodorant, body lotion, new toothbrushes, and even a tube of Crest toothpaste. For a medicine cabinet, it certainly lacked in medicinal items—not even a Band-Aid.

After taking care of her most pressing need, she appeased her curiosity and checked out the closet. A variety of skirts and blouses, many in airy floral patterns, hung above a single pair of ankle-strap tan sandals. Packaged undergarments, some with labels she recognized, were neatly stacked on inset shelves. Every garment, including the shoes, was in her size.

The nightgown she wore wasn't the one she'd put on the night she'd been kidnapped, however long ago that was. She fervently hoped the young woman she'd seen in the clinic was responsible for dressing her. What she had on was clean, but she wanted a shower and a fresh change of clothes, something other than sleepwear.

The shower helped to ease the tension from her sore muscles. She wrapped a soft bath towel around her and walked to the closet. Undergarments directly from the packages would have to do. She chose a flowing, pastel-green skirt, and white pullover blouse and slipped into them before taking care of her hair.

A blow-dryer hung from a hook on the wall beside the sink. There were several electrical outlets in the wall. So this new world of theirs has electricity. She was no longer surprised by the familiarities.

She plugged in the hair dryer and tested it. The familiar whir of the motor preceded a stream of hot air. She grabbed the hairbrush and glanced around. There wasn't a mirror in the room. How strange. She dried and brushed out her hair, then buckled on her sandals. She was as ready as she was ever going to be to face whatever was out there, be it a brave new world or a very earthbound problem. Regardless, it was time to meet the challenge. She unlocked the door and walked into the bedroom.

She eyed the window. Everything she'd seen so far was familiar, except what was on the other side of that window. Rhyel had convinced her she wasn't on Earth, that he wasn't from Earth. Now she wasn't sure what to believe.

Oh, she didn't doubt that she'd been kidnapped, but she might have fantasized the rest. Had she guessed right after all? Was what she'd seen out that window simply an aftereffect of whatever he'd given her? What had he said—that the answer was out there? She walked toward the draped portal. There was only one way to find out. She was going to have to look out that window again. She lifted the edge of the curtain. The view hadn't changed.

She blinked back tears. How far away was home? Was her own sun even visible in this planet's night sky?

Would she ever see Grandpa again? Her grip on the heavy material tightened. He must be out of his mind with worry by now. The note she'd begged to leave would have alleviated some of his anxiety. But she'd lost the chance to reassure him when she'd tried to get away from Rhyel. Grandpa would never know what happened to her.

She turned away from the window and rolled her shoulders to relieve the tension. Did she look as battered as she felt? At least the bedroom had a mirror she could use to check for damage. There were no evident bruises from struggling with Rhyel, or scratches from her race through the woods. She lifted her head and traced the thin line on her throat. The laceration was healing faster than she expected. Maybe there was hope for the red powder.

She pushed her hair behind her ear for a better look. A small square of gold glittered from her left ear. Curious, she skimmed a finger over the flesh-warmed metal and felt—or did she hear—a faint buzz. The thing seemed to be embedded in her earlobe. Funny. She hadn't been aware of it until she'd looked in the mirror.

"It's a translation device."

She jumped at the unexpected voice and jerked around to see Rhyel closing the door across from the bed—the mystery-door. She still didn't know where it led.

He moved to her side and brushed his hair back. An identical gold square glittered from his ear. "Everyone on New Centallus wears one. The translator makes it possible for you to understand the various languages spoken here."

"How do I remove it?"

"You don't."

"Great," she muttered. It's like wearing one earring forever. She sighed, resigned. "I can always take up pirating."

"Pirating?" He looked confused.

"Never mind." She tried to walk away from him.

His hand on her arm prevented her retreat. "The Elders wish to meet you. They've asked me to escort you to the council chamber."

"The Elders?

"The Elders govern this colony. They—"

A knock at the mystery-door interrupted him.

"Captain," a calm voice called from the other side, "Cintar has been injured."

Two years of trauma center experience kicked in and Amber ran toward the door. Rhyel reached it before she did, and took her hand as he opened the door. He pulled her into an immense room filled with trestle tables, and walked toward a circle of people gathered in front of the huge entry doors.

The crowd parted at their approach. A large man lay unconscious on a stretcher on the floor. A long, ragged gash ran from his upper left thigh to an inch or so above his knee.

Rhyel bent to examine the wound. "What happened?"

"He was trimming branches at the new clearing site," one of the men explained. "His ax slipped."

An ax? She looked at Rhyel. What were these people doing with axes?

Rhyel stood. "Liiam, go to the council chambers and inform the Elders of Cintar's accident. Assure them that he is in no danger. I will report to them directly." He nodded at the two men standing beside the litter. "Take him to his chamber."

"No, wait." She skirted around Rhyel and knelt at the man's side. "Don't move him yet." She felt for the pulse at his throat. There was none.

Rhyel leaned across and took her hand, moving it to a point behind the prone man's ear.

She looked up in surprise when she felt the heartbeat where it shouldn't have been.

The man's pulse was strong but alarmingly slow. Why was he unconscious? The wound wasn't life-threatening. His clothes were blood-stained, but not blood-soaked. He couldn't have lost much blood. His heart would have been rapidly pumping what blood he had left if that were the case. Instead, it acted like it would stop any moment.

Until she could get him into the clinic, her best guess would be shock. She gently slapped the man's face to see if she could rouse him.

Several gasps erupted from the crowd. Rhyel grabbed her hand and pulled her to her feet.

"Don't." She struggled against his grip. "I have to wake him."

"I can't allow that."

"I'm not hurting him. I promise." She looked down at the man she considered her patient. "He may die if we don't wake him. You brought me here to help your people. Let me do my job."

"He will not die."

"He will if you don't let me go."

"Cintar is in no danger."

She couldn't believe his arrogance. Did he really think he knew more about medicine than she did?

"Touch him," she insisted. "His skin feels cold. He's unresponsive, and his heartbeat is so slow it scares me. I'm not sure what's wrong. I won't know until I examine him." She placed her free hand on Rhyel's chest. "Let me help him."

The men lifted the litter and started toward a set of stairs she hadn't noticed.

"Wait," she ordered. When they paused she turned to Rhyel. "I saw a clinic earlier. Please take him there."

Rhyel stared at her for a long minute, then nodded to his men. They immediately obeyed.

Rhyel released her hand, but took her arm when she started to follow her patient. "Amber, your concern for Cintar is admirable but unnecessary. Cintar isn't in danger. He placed himself in healing stasis at the time of his accident.

As a result, his body cooled, and his metabolism and heart rate slowed. Even his blood loss was minimized. Cintar will remain in stasis until the wound is sufficiently healed, or we wake him."

He let go of her arm. "You may go to him now, but don't wake him. He won't thank you for it. Hiilani is waiting. She will make sure you have whatever you need. I will return shortly."

She moved toward the clinic door. Hopefully Hiilani could give her some answers. She had a lot of questions.

7

✧

The clinic boasted two examining tables, a sterilizer, cabinets, oxygen tanks and more, everything necessary for the efficient operation of a small medical facility. Amber recognized every piece of equipment, had worked with identical instruments in the hospital at home.

Cintar lay on one of the examining tables. His clothes had been removed and a white sheet draped his midsection and legs. The sheet was folded away from the damaged thigh. A linen cloth lay across the wound.

The young woman she'd seen earlier set an instrument tray on a stand beside the patient. Short, and slightly plump, her skin tone reminded Amber of rich caramel. Straight dark hair was pulled back into a ponytail at the nape of her neck. A golden square decorated her left ear.

Apparently this was Hiilani.

The two women exchanged smiles as Amber lifted the cloth and made a quick assessment of Cintar's condition. She turned as Rhyel entered the clinic. "His wound will require a number of stitches," she told him.

Rhyel nodded and motioned to the young woman. "Hiilani is a nurse-practitioner. She is experienced in treating Guardians in stasis."

"I have everything ready for you, Doctor Donovan. You can scrub over there." Hiilani gestured toward a sink set into a long counter against the back wall.

Amber put on a lab coat, washed up, and returned to the examining table as she slipped on sterile gloves.

The man looked near death. Was this stasis Rhyel put so much faith in more superstition than science? She'd put the question to Hiilani later.

She covertly studied Rhyel as she checked the instruments on the tray. Emergency room experience had taught her that a big, strong man keeled over at the sight of blood as often as anyone. Neither the wound nor the blood had bothered him, but he'd yet to see her apply the needle to his friend's ragged flesh.

"Perhaps you should wait outside," she suggested hopefully. His absence would have the added advantage of preventing his interference.

He shook his head. "I will stay."

She shrugged. Had she expected another answer? She turned to Hiilani. "We'll need a local anesthetic. What's available?"

The young woman glanced at Rhyel, clearly waiting for him to answer.

"Cintar will not need the anesthetic," he said.

"You do know I have to clean the wound and sew it up."

"I expected as much."

"The sting of the antiseptic alone will bring him out of his stupor, and it will take at least thirty stitches to close the wound. If I were your friend, I'd want to decide for myself how much pain to endure."

"Cintar is in full control of his body. Be assured he will feel nothing."

"You're sure?"

"I am."

She still wasn't convinced. "I want you over here beside me," she told him. "If he loses control you'll have to subdue him." She turned to Hiilani. "I want an anesthetic at hand if we need it. I won't have one of my patients suffering needlessly."

This time the nurse nodded without seeking Rhyel's permission. Amber felt like she'd won a small victory.

"We'll also need an antiseptic," she called out to the nurse.

"The red powder—"

"I've experienced the red powder, thank you. I want something I'm familiar with." She looked back at Hiilani. "Do we have anything else?"

Hiilani glanced at Rhyel for his permission before rummaging through the cabinet. So much for small victories.

The nurse returned with a bottle of alcohol and another of iodine.

Amber resigned herself. "The iodine." It might not be her first choice, but it wasn't red powder. "Can we get a blood pressure reading?"

Hiilani shook her head. "The readings mislead you when the patient is in stasis."

"How can you treat them without accurate vitals?"

"There isn't much treating to do. Once Guardians go into stasis, they basically heal themselves. I clean their wounds and monitor them, but I don't think they really need my help." She looked up at Rhyel and grinned. "I believe the Centallians humor me."

Amber glanced from Hiilani to Rhyel and back to the nurse again. "Am I being humored?"

Hiilani's grin widened. "Perhaps a little."

Amber lifted the cloth from Cintar's leg. "Then we may as well take advantage of their indulgence and see what we can do for him."

Hiilani moved to the opposite side of the examining table. "Yes, doctor."

The gash was deep and dirty. Over the next forty-five minutes, she removed the slivers of wood and bits of dirt and vegetation that littered the eight-inch laceration, and flushed the area with sterile water.

She basted the wound with iodine, expecting Cintar to come roaring off the table any second. When he didn't, she stopped long enough to place the stethoscope over his heart.

Nothing.

Rhyel's hand covered hers and guided it to a place more centered and slightly lower than normal. She heard the man's slow but regular heartbeat and looked up in question. Rhyel shrugged. Her patient never moved, never made a sound—and he didn't bleed.

She felt uneasy about that.

Thirty-three stitches later, she daubed iodine over the closed wound and swathed the leg in gauze bandages. "I don't suppose he's had a tetanus shot recently?" The nurse shook her head. "Do we have any here?"

"Yes, but the Guardians refuse it. They appear unaffected by Earth viruses."

It was Amber's turn to shrug. "Normally a patient with this type of wound could hobble out of the ER with a prescription for antibiotics. Since he's still unconscious, we'll set up an IV." She looked at Rhyel. "Do we have antibiotics?"

"They are unnecessary."

"His wound was filthy." She turned to Hiilani. "Do we have antibiotics?" The nurse nodded.

Rhyel regained her attention when he placed his hand on her shoulder. "The Centallian immune system functions more efficiently in stasis. Additional medication is wasted."

"You're taking a chance with his life."

He gave her shoulder a gentle squeeze. "You will trust me on this."

Resigned, she peeled off her gloves. "Do we at least have a bed for him?"

Hiilani carried the surgical instruments to the sink. "We don't have a ward set up yet, but we can put a bed in here for now."

"That's fine. I'll need to watch him tonight. Can you have someone bring the big chair from the other room in here?" She kneaded the stiff muscles at the base of her neck. The headache was back—had never really left.

"Is something wrong?" Rhyel asked.

His question irritated her. "Of course something's wrong. You tell me your people need a healer, but you've countermanded every decision I've made. You obviously don't believe you need a doctor and I'm tired of trying to figure out why I'm here."

"You are here for the women."

Her eyes shot to his. "The women?"

"The Guardians have taken bond-mates from Earth."

She was horrified. "You've kidnapped other women?"

He raised a hand to forestall her. "They came to us willingly, with their families' blessings. They are from what you call Earth's third world nations. The gold we provided will feed and clothe entire villages."

"You bought them?"

"We paid a bride price—what was required by their families," he said, irritation creeping into his voice. "Most of my bonded Guardians honored the customs of their chosen mate's society, exchanging vows before their families. Many of those women would have suffered hardships and possible degradation on your world. Here they are valued, treated with honor and respect."

"Am I the only kidnap victim here?"

"Yours was a special situation." She guessed that was a yes. "A healer is not easy to obtain."

"I'll bet." She glanced at Hiilani. "Is a nurse-practitioner also a special case?"

Rhyel turned his attention to the young woman in question and smiled as he said, "I will let Hiilani tell her own story, but not now. The Elders are waiting."

"I can't now. My patient—"

"—will remain in stasis for the next twelve to twenty hours. Your presence here is not required. Hiilani can send for you if his situation changes."

8

Rhyel pressed his hand to the small of Amber's back and guided her to the door. Hiilani gave her an encouraging smile as they left the clinic and walked into the main room.

"The Elders are hearing petitions in the council chamber." He indicated a large, ornately carved wooden door on the opposite side of the immense hall.

She looked around as they made their way across what was obviously the commons area. She was reminded of the great halls found in feudalistic castles.

The commons was as long as a basketball court, and as wide. Graceful, curved staircases on each side of the hall accessed the upper level, where multiple doorways led to what were probably living quarters. Massive wood columns supported the high ceilings and rooms above.

On the main floor, trestle tables lined each side of a center aisle that ran lengthwise from the huge hearth at the front of the room to the large entryway at the back. Interior doors were set into the walls of the main level as well, though there were fewer and they were spaced farther apart. The council chamber door was the most impressive.

The tantalizing aroma of baking bread wafted on the air. A number of women bustled about the tables. Each table was set for six to ten diners.

"How many people are here?" she asked as they navigated the room.

"We currently number one hundred sixty-four. Ninety-seven are Centallian Guardians and Elders."

She did the math. "Sixty-seven are women from Earth?"

"Yes."

"All married to Guardians?"

"Most of them are bonded—what you call married. Soon the others will bond. Several Guardians have yet to choose an available bond-mate."

He sidestepped and pulled her with him to avoid a woman carrying a large platter of bread and cheese.

She looked up at him. "Are your Elders also buying mates?"

"Not buying, Amber," he said, a note of irritation in his voice, "paying a bride price. We didn't toss money at their relatives and drag them from their homes."

"Like you did me."

He took a deep breath and let it out slowly. "When we left your world," he whispered softly, "you were in my arms, safe and protected."

Suddenly uncomfortable, she quickly rephrased her original question. "Are your Elders searching for brides?"

He shook his head. "The council is comprised of four men and two women. The men have refrained from choosing mates. They believe their energy is best spent in the council chamber rather than a nursery. Kroyda and Zsaor are beyond childbearing age, and have chosen not to seek mates."

He opened the chamber door and they entered the smaller room. The noise of the great hall was shut out when the door closed behind them.

The six Elders, wearing rich-toned robes-of-state, sat on a raised dais listening to a discussion between two men. Rhyel led her to a vacant pew-like bench close to the front, away from the crowd.

"I will introduce you when the council session is finished and the room clears," he whispered.

"Can we come back after they've finished? I have a patient—"

"Who is resting comfortably."

She glowered at him.

"The man is unconscious," she whispered back. "There is a distinct difference between resting comfortably and being out cold." She turned her attention to the Elders, who were more than likely responsible for her being here.

Since no one sat in front of them, she had an unrestricted view of the people who governed what was left of their civilization.

Each face bore the evidence of great suffering. Strain etched their features, marring the laugh lines born of another life and time. She recognized the loneliness in their eyes. She'd seen the same look in her grandfather's eyes after her parents were killed in a plane crash and again, years later, when her grandmother had passed.

"It's hard for them here, isn't it?" she asked Rhyel in a hushed voice.

He nodded. "Unlike the young men of our colony, the Elders do not relish the challenge of building a new world. Their lives were wrenched from their grasp. The past still holds them, yet they strive to help secure our future."

"Though they have no heirs of their own to leave that future to," she said in sympathy.

"We all inherit the benefits of their efforts. The Elders will leave priceless gifts of wisdom and knowledge to all who come after. But two Elders do have descendants living on New Centallus."

"I'm glad for them. You said they were on a diplomatic mission, that it was the reason they were on your ship?"

He placed an arm across the back of her seat and angled around so they were close enough to speak without disturbing the others. "Their mission was the reason we all survived. No one should have been aboard my ship the day of the attack. Centallus was destroyed during Soial-Anom'du'zolm, our Holy Week, a time of pilgrimage, meditation, and renewal. Off-world Centallians were encouraged to return to Centallus during this solemn occasion.

"The *Novaria* had arrived home and part of my crew and I were busy locking down the ship. My father contacted me before we'd finished. The Elders had received an urgent summons to mediate a quarrel between two major factions on the planet Ruiq-Zka, a recent member of our contingent of worlds. Both adversaries possessed the ability to destroy each other, and their world as well."

He nodded toward the Elder on the far right of the dais. "My father,

Zitan, requested our assistance since most of my crew was still on board the *Novaria*. We left as soon as the Elders were aboard." His jaw tightened. "We were returning from Ruiq-Zka when we received a distress call from Centallus. Our home was under attack."

He straightened away from her and faced the dais, but she doubted he saw the men and women seated in front of them. "By the time we reached Centallus there was nothing left to save."

"No one survived?"

"The planet was incinerated, the atmosphere poisoned. We scanned for life-signs. There were no survivors."

"I'm sorry," she whispered, reacting to the pain in his voice.

She looked at his father. He was large-framed like Rhyel, but the eyes that suddenly met hers were gray instead of dark. He smiled before giving his attention back to the proceedings. He reminded her a little of Grandpa.

"Who are the others?" She tilted her head toward the dais.

Rhyel focused his attention on the Elders. "On the far left, in the blue robe, is our Chief Elder, Valdon. His son, Tzorik, is my second-in-command."

She looked up, surprised. "You command the colony? Why do the men call you captain?"

He gazed down at her. "I am captain of the *Novaria*. Cintar is second in command aboard my vessel. The Elders decided my command experience would serve the new colony well."

He drew her attention to the dais. "The man seated next to the Chief Elder is Aadrok, the seer. He is the oldest, and wears the white robe of the priest. The Elder to Aadrok's right is Kroyda, our Story Keeper. She spends most of her time committing our ancient Centallian legends to memory crystals on the *Novaria*'s computers. Storytelling was a precise art on Centallus, performed in exacting detail. My ship's computers didn't contain historical information, thus Kroyda alone possesses the legends that are now our only form of Centallian history. She is gifted with complete memory."

"A photographic memory?"

"Yes. The gift is passed from parent to child. Kroyda's daughter inherited the ability and would have carried the stories into the next generation. She had seen twelve circles of time when our world was incinerated.

"She was twelve years old?"

He shook his head. "She had seen twelve Centallian years. My home planet took longer to circle its sun than yours. By your measure it would have been half again as much time."

"That would have made her around eighteen."

"Yes. She had grown into a lovely young woman."

"How long is a year on this planet?"

"This world's rotation is similar to Earth's." He turned toward the dais. "The woman beside Kroyda is Zsaor. She is gifted in linguistics, and is translating Earth's numerous languages into the *Novaria*'s database.

"Tzarn sits between Zsaor and my father. He is our youngest Elder, having seen only thirty-seven circles of time. He is known as 'The Strong'." The Elder looked like a weightlifter. His robes couldn't conceal the thick shoulder muscles and biceps.

The last petitioner left the podium and the Elders were preparing to adjourn when a voice from the audience interrupted them.

"Elders." A man with long, wheat-blond hair stood and moved to the center aisle. He was close in height and weight to Rhyel.

His cold, pale-blue eyes met hers as he turned toward the Elders. The smile he gave her was filled with dark promise, and possession. She shivered as if someone had draped an icy shawl around her shoulders.

"Amber?" Rhyel said, drawing her attention to him. "Is something wrong?"

She shook her head, but asked, "Who is that man?"

Rhyel watched as the man moved forward to stand before the Elders. "He is Tzorik." The chill in his voice matched what she'd experienced moments before.

"Valdon's son? He's your second in command?"

"Of the colony, yes."

"Elders," Tzorik began, his voice loud in the silent room, "I have come to petition the council for permission to take a bond-mate."

Rhyel stiffened and placed a protective arm around her, pulling her closer. She glanced at him in question. He looked grim.

The Chief Elder smiled. "You have chosen then?"

"I have."

"This is joyful news. Give us her name."

"The woman I claim" —he turned and his eyes locked with Rhyel's— "is our new healer."

She sucked in a breath and started to rise, but Rhyel held her firmly in place. "Remain calm."

She turned on him. "Tell me he isn't saying what I think he is."

Rhyel didn't offer an explanation. "Stay here," he said as he stood. He stepped into the aisle and walked to the front of the room.

Tzorik greeted Rhyel with a contemptuous half-smile. "Have you come to congratulate me, Captain?" That he refused to address Rhyel as commander seemed not to be lost on his audience, and a low murmur ran through the crowd.

Rhyel's smile was deadly. "I've come to deny your petition."

Amber sank back against the bench in relief.

Tzorik laughed. "The Elders alone can deny my petition, and only with an acceptable reason."

"Do not doubt I have the power to deny you," Rhyel said quietly.

The other man bowed—a parody of respect that challenged his commander's abilities. "Then use it if you can."

Rhyel ignored Tzorik's taunt and addressed the council. "According to our ancient laws, 'first choice' is a right of command. As captain of the *Novaria*," he turned to address Tzorik, "and commander of this colony, I claim the right of first choice, and will take Amber to mate."

She couldn't have heard him right. She glanced around to see the crowd's reaction. A few people sat forward as if drawn physically to the tension between the two men.

Tzorik sputtered something she didn't understand, and took a threatening step toward his commander.

Rhyel didn't give ground.

"*I* have the right of first choice," Tzorik shouted, looking from Rhyel to the councilmembers. "My position is greater than yours."

"On Centallus, your claim might have had merit, but Centallus is lost to us." Rhyel's voice was low and controlled. "Here we begin a new life with a new governing body. As commander, my claim takes precedence over—"

"Have you all lost your minds?" Amber found her voice and her feet at the same time. "How can you fly spaceships all over the galaxy and think like cavemen?" She sidestepped into the aisle. "I was brought here to be a doctor. And until I find a way home—and I will find a way home—I'm willing to tend to your sick, but I will not submit to this insanity. And I'm not listening to any more."

She spun around and stalked toward the exit, stopping only when one very large Guardian stepped into her path. She refused to let the man intimidate her.

"Get out of my way."

The semi-human wall looked past her toward the dais. She knew exactly who he sought for help.

"Rhyel," she called over her shoulder, "tell your watchdog to get out of my way or I'll demonstrate a whole new meaning to the word chaos."

9

"Take her to her chamber," Tzorik bellowed. "And keep her there until we've finished this."

Amber stiffened, preparing for battle, but the Guardian didn't move.

"Tiinar, step aside." Rhyel calmly rescinded Tzorik's order.

The Guardian immediately obeyed.

She moved past him and walked out of the chamber feeling a weak-kneed sense of relief. But she was smart enough to know her protest wouldn't stop the debate over her future. Well, they could bicker all they wanted. She didn't intend to be here long enough to have a future with either of them.

✦

Tzorik swung around to confront the Elders, his face florid with rage. "The woman must be punished for her disrespect."

"The woman has a name," Rhyel said quietly. "If you claim a woman to mate, at least discover her name." He leveled a hard look on his second in command. "As for punishment, Amber is our healer, not our prisoner. She is a member of our colony, and possesses the freedom to speak her mind."

"Guardians," Valdon interrupted, "the council must consider your claims."

The Elders stepped down from the dais and walked through the small side door into the conference room.

Everyone in the council chamber remained seated. This was more than a simple challenge for a bond-mate. By refusing to accept his commander's claim, Tzorik not only challenged Rhyel's right of first choice, he challenged his right to command the colony. If the Elders chose to honor Tzorik's petition over his own, the man would use it as a wedge to undermine his authority.

Rhyel watched Tzorik pace in frustration. He had no intention of allowing an insurrection. Nor did he intend to let Tzorik bond with Amber. If the Council ruled against him, he had one more option—a law so old it fell to the realm of legend.

The Elders returned to their respective seats. Side by side, Rhyel and Tzorik approached the dais.

Valdon turned to his son. "Tzorik, the council acknowledges the rank you held on Centallus, and we commend you for your service to our people."

Tzorik bent his head in acceptance of their praise and glanced at Rhyel, with a smirk.

"But Rhyel spoke the truth," Valdon continued, sorrow tingeing his voice. "Centallus is no more. We have a new life here, and a new government. Though I would have gladly welcomed the healer into our family, Rhyel is entitled to first choice."

Tzorik didn't acknowledge the council's decision, or his father's compassion. He turned and left the chamber.

Valdon's attention shifted to Rhyel. "You may set the day and time for the bonding ceremony. May the council be the first to offer our congratulations?"

Rhyel bowed his respect. "Thank you."

Zitan stepped down from the dais as the assembly filed out. He touched Rhyel's arm as he passed, a silent message for his son to follow. When they reached a secluded corner of the room he stopped.

"You are sure of your decision?" Zitan asked without preamble.

"I have vowed to protect her. It is a matter of honor."

Zitan sighed and shook his head. "Honor will not warm your nights or give peace to your days. Life on New Centallus is difficult. As leader you shoulder the greatest burden. You need a mate who is willing to share your life, not complicate it. Perhaps you should reconsider."

"Would you have me forego honor to ensure my future happiness?"

"You ask more of yourself than honor requires. You need only provide our healer with a Guardian who will value her."

"If I relinquish Amber, and the matter goes before the council, Tzorik has the right to claim her. I will not provide him the opportunity to abuse her, as you know he will.

"The night I entered Amber's room, I sensed she would not easily accept our plan for her future. I could have left her room as silently as I entered. She would never have known I was there." He leveled his gaze on his father. "But I chose to bring her to New Centallus. That decision makes me responsible above all others for her well-being.

"I watched over her as she recovered from *Mensolm*. My arms held her when she grieved for the world that I—that I—took from her.

"There is cautious trust in her eyes now when we talk. Ours is a fragile bond, but it is more than she shares with any other man on New Centallus. That truth demands I claim her."

Zitan nodded. "Your argument is sound, yet...." The Elder's eyes suddenly widened. "You want her."

Rhyel could wish his father was not so astute. His nod was quick. "I want her."

The two men turned when Aadrok approached. "I assume your bonding will take place soon?"

Rhyel nodded. "It will. Once we've bonded, Tzorik will be forced to accept the council's decision."

Aadrok nodded. "Will you see to the blood samples for the genetic scan?"

"She will be in the clinic with Cintar. We will draw the samples after I've told her what has been decided."

"Be cautious in your conversation, Commander." Aadrok chuckled. "Our healer may find pleasure in letting your blood. She did not seem especially agreeable to your claim."

"Amber is a strong-willed woman, but intelligent. When she realizes the futility of fighting against her new life, she will find contentment in our bonding."

His father placed a hand on his shoulder as he turned to leave with Aadrok. "May it be soon," he murmured.

Rhyel bowed to both men, left the chamber, and walked through the bustle of the midday meal. Aadrok had been right about Amber's outrage. The next hour might prove a challenge.

He smiled.

10

✧

Amber slammed the clinic door behind her.

Hiilani jumped up from the overstuffed chair that sat beside Cintar's bed. "Doctor—"

"Did you know they planned to marry me off to one of them?"

Hiilani gave her a wary look, but nodded. "I assumed that would be the case. Rhyel didn't tell you?"

"Apparently he decided to leave that job to someone named Tzorro or Terric or—"

"Tzorik?" Hiilani supplied, her expression changing from wary to confused.

"Yes, that one." She took a deep breath. None of this was Hiilani's fault and she shouldn't be taking her frustrations out on the nurse. "The man decided to stake his claim. He and your captain or commander or whatever else you want to call him are haggling over me like two dogs with one bone."

Hiilani's eyes widened. "Tzorik— *claimed* you? Really? Everyone assumed Rhyel would—"

"Oh, he did. Only Tzorro—"

"Tzorik."

"Tzorik beat him to it." She pulled her lab coat off the wall hook and shoved her arms into the sleeves. She washed her hands, and swung back to face Hiilani as she dried them. "It doesn't matter. I made it clear I wasn't about to cooperate."

"What did the Elders say?"

"I didn't wait around long enough to find out."

"You left?"

She leaned back against the counter. "Actually, Tzorik ordered a Guardian to lock me in my room. Can you believe that?"

"Rhyel didn't let that happen, did he?" Hiilani shook her head. "Of course he didn't, you're here."

"Rhyel told the Guardian to let me leave."

"I'll bet Tzorik loved that."

"I wouldn't know. I never looked back." She rolled her head from side to side in an attempt to ease her headache. "Do we have any over-the-counter pain relievers?"

"We have ibuprofen, Tylenol, and aspirin."

"A couple of ibuprofen would be wonderful."

Hiilani retrieved a bottle from a cabinet and filled a glass with water. "Hurts that bad?" she asked as she handed Amber the glass and opened the bottle, shaking a couple of tablets into Amber's palm.

"It's just tension," she said before popping the pills into her mouth and following them with the water. "Please tell me this place has coffee."

The nurse laughed. "When I discovered there was a doctor on the way, I ordered a supply of the best brands and a coffee maker. They arrived before you did. I can make a pot if you'd like."

"Yes, please. If the tablets don't work, I may need two pots."

The women talked about the clinic while the coffee brewed. Amber was curious about the nurse's presence in the colony, but Hiilani didn't bring up the subject and she didn't want to pry.

Rhyel returned to the clinic before she got her coffee. That was unfortunate for him. She didn't waste time with small talk. "I'll make this short and easy for you to understand. I refuse to have either of you forced on me." She cast a quick glance at her patient, and walked to the adjoining room.

He followed, catching the swinging door before it hit him. "You will bond with me."

"So you won the tug of war." The surge of relief surprised her. The victor shouldn't matter. She wasn't participating in their schemes. "I'm not playing house with you. Your people needed a doctor and a doctor you have—for now."

He shortened the distance between them. "Since Tzorik has made a gentler telling impossible, I will also be brief and blunt. You were not brought here solely as a healer. You were also chosen because you are a healthy young woman of childbearing age. Tomorrow you will become my bond mate." His voice softened. "Our children will be the future of this new world."

He couldn't have made his intentions clearer, and she could be as plainspoken. "I won't become your broodmare."

His features tightened. "Do you truly believe that is how it will be with us?"

"You've given me no reason to believe otherwise."

"Have I not? What do you think that confrontation in the council chamber was about?"

"Testosterone!"

He smiled, but it wasn't friendly. "Tzorik claimed you, Amber. I saw your reaction to him. He frightens you. My claim prevented you from being bound to him for life."

"I wouldn't have allowed that to happen."

"You couldn't have stopped it. You will be bonded to a Guardian. You cannot change that. I cannot change that. Claiming you is the only way I can protect you."

She groaned. She'd lost control of her life. It was all happening too fast to comprehend. She pressed her fists against her temples, willing the pressure to ease the ache behind her eyes.

"You're in pain." He sounded concerned. He should be contrite. It was all his fault—her pain, her fear, even her anger. Every emotion she'd experienced since he'd invaded her bedroom could be placed at his feet.

"I'll be fine," she said, then qualified, "once I've had my coffee."

"You have yet to recover from *Mensolm*," he said as she pushed through the door to the clinic. "Perhaps you should rest instead."

"I told you I'm fine. Hiilani, is the coffee ready yet?"

Before Hiilani could answer a man stepped into the clinic. Rhyel met him at the door and they spoke briefly before the man left.

"I am needed on the *Novaria*." He paused at the door. "Rest."

She glanced at Hiilani as the door closed behind him. The nurse looked worried. "What was that about?"

"The Guardians keep intercepting what could possibly be transmissions."

"Transmissions? As in there's someone else out there flying around in space?" She didn't know why she had trouble wrapping her mind around the concept. Maybe it was because of all the mystery surrounding the possibility on Earth.

Well, the mystery had been solved—at least in her mind. The Centallians were capable of interstellar flight, so there were probably hundreds, maybe thousands of other species flying around out there—avoiding Earth like the plague.

"It might only be white noise," Hiilani said, "but Rhyel isn't taking chances. He treats every occurrence as a potential threat."

"Why would the Centallians consider the transmissions a threat?"

The nurse shrugged. "It probably has something to do with whoever attacked their planet. I'm sure this isn't anything to worry about. Rhyel has been summoned to his ship many times in the past few months, but they haven't been able to identify the problem."

Amber nodded. It was something else she was forced to consider. She pulled her stethoscope out of her lab coat pocket and went to Cintar. The big man lay as still as a stone. She placed the stethoscope against his chest, and moved the instrument twice before locating his heartbeat. It was far too slow.

She placed her hand on his forehead and frowned. His body temperature was cooler than before. She pulled the cover up over his shoulders.

"Find some extra blankets," she told the nurse. "We need to warm him."

Hiilani came over and felt his head. "Actually, he's responding normally for a man in stasis. The blankets won't help his condition. Rhyel suggests they might even delay his recovery."

"You agree with him?"

The nurse lifted her shoulders in a non-answer. "I was as skeptical as you are, but every man I've seen in stasis reacts exactly like Cintar. They all recovered within a twenty-hour period, or less."

"How is that possible?"

The nurse shook her head. "I can't explain it."

"How severe were the other wounds?"

"I've only seen a few. Most were taken to their quarters to recover on their own before I could get to them. They let me stitch up a few. Most of the time I simply watched them heal themselves. It's amazing."

"Are Centallians accident-prone?"

The nurse smiled. "There have been a number of mishaps."

"They don't play with swords, do they? It wouldn't surprise me. This place feels like a medieval holding."

Hiilani laughed. The lighthearted sound brought a smile to Amber's lips. "They don't wield swords, but they could use a little practice with axes. They haven't yet figured out how to chop wood without hurting themselves or each other."

"Like Cintar did?"

"Yes."

Amber regarded her patient. "So he needs to be kept on ice?"

Hiilani nodded. "In a manner of speaking, yes. It seems to be part of their healing process. I've learned not to be concerned."

She decided to defer to the nurse's experience. "We'll leave him alone then." She tossed her stethoscope on the table. "But if he so much as sneezes I'm setting up an IV with antibiotics, and we're defrosting him."

Hiilani left the clinic briefly, and returned with a tray containing two bowls of vegetable soup and a small basket of wheat rolls. Amber had missed breakfast, and forgotten about lunch. The aroma of homemade soup drifting up from the tray made her mouth water.

The nurse set the bowls and basket of rolls on the desk and they pulled up a couple of small chairs. The two ate in companionable silence for a time. Amber was familiar with most of the vegetables in the soup.

"Did you grow these here?" She lifted a spoonful up so Hiilani could see the carrot slice.

"Yes. Our women brought seeds with them from their homelands. The rest were brought back from Earth on a supply mission. Yulia, Anja, and Sofia are the most experienced cooks, but everyone helps."

After lunch they poured themselves cups of coffee and spent the remainder of the afternoon taking inventory and making notes on what the clinic still needed. The Centallians had provided a state of the art clinic. Add a few more pieces of equipment and it would be the equivalent of a rural hospital.

How could they afford to buy even a quarter of what was in plain sight? Hiilani had mentioned making supply trips but never talked about the cost. Did they steal what they needed? And what about the gold the Centallians used for the bride price when they chose a mate? There were so many unanswered questions.

The two women worked well together and by early evening they were ready to go over the charts. Amber sank into the big chair, a weary sigh punctuating her descent.

"Are there any problems I need to know about?" she asked, closing her eyes against the persistent headache. "Do we have any coffee left?"

"I made a fresh pot. I'll bring you a cup." She moved to the counter. "There is one major problem involving the—"

"You can go, Hiilani. Your discussion can wait until Amber is... more fully recovered."

Rhyel stood in the doorway, a crystal decanter and two matching, stemmed goblets in hand. "I'll keep watch with our healer tonight. We'll see you tomorrow."

Amber took exception to his high-handedness. "You can stay, Hiilani." She glared in Rhyel's direction. "And you can go. I don't need a keeper."

Hiilani escaped through the open door as Rhyel moved into the room, pulling it closed behind her before Amber could protest her defection.

11

✦

Rhyel crossed the room and set the crystal decanter on the counter. He lifted the coffee carafe from the warming plate and poured the steaming contents into the sink.

Amber jumped to her feet. "Wait. Hiilani just made that."

He waved her back into the chair. "I've brought wine."

She wrinkled her nose. "I don't like wine. My first Saturday night in a hospital's trauma center cured me of any desire for alcohol. I can't stand the smell."

Setting the coffee carafe aside, Rhyel filled both goblets from the decanter and carried them to where she sat. He held one out to her.

She simply looked at him.

"*Baquui* is a sweet wine," he explained, "closer to fruit juice than to the wines of Earth. We value the drink for its restorative qualities."

"I. Don't. Want. The. Wine," she said, articulating each word as if he were not quite bright enough to understand. "I want my coffee."

"Coffee is a stimulant, and you need to rest. Drink the wine and relax."

"What I need is to be left alone with my patient."

Rhyel gave his friend a quick look, and turned a more leisurely gaze on her. His eyes traveled from the hair she'd pinned atop her head to the toes peeking out of her sandals. "Cintar is probably in better condition than you are at the moment."

She bristled at his criticism of her appearance. "It won't hurt me to sit with him tonight, and it may save his life."

"I cannot convince you Cintar will not need your care?" He swirled the wine in one of the glasses.

She folded her arms across her chest. "You brought me here to be a doctor. Let me be one." He squatted in front of her—no easy trick considering he held both glasses. She grabbed the one he thrust toward her before it ended up in her lap.

"I know you're in pain," he said. "I can see it in your eyes, in the way you hold your body. The *Baquui* will ease your discomfort."

"I don't trust you enough to drink this."

He regained his feet and took a swallow from his own goblet as he studied her. If he was trying to reassure her it wasn't working.

"You will find the taste of the wine more pleasing than the pain of *Mensolm*," he said, pulling the desk chair closer. He sat down facing her. They were practically knee to knee. Unless she wanted to climb over the top of him, she had to remain where she was and listen to him tell her how bad she felt.

He was attractive enough, with his dark hair tied back in a queue at the nape of his neck and that gold square in his earlobe. If anyone looked like a pirate, he did. How could someone who looked that good be so irritating?

When had she decided he was good looking? She must be sicker than she thought—definitely not feeling up to a war of wills with him tonight. The minute he'd entered the room her heartbeat and headache had escalated from mild to pounding.

Rhyel was right. She probably did feel worse than his friend. But then, the Guardian was unconscious and as far as she could tell, feeling no pain— an enviable condition.

She eyed the powerful man facing her. He wouldn't force the wine down her throat. She instinctively knew that, but he would sit there for the rest of the night if she remained stubborn.

All she needed was a cup of coffee and for him to go away—neither of which was going to happen unless someone gave ground. She guessed it was going to have to be her. Compromise was definitely in order. A sip or two might satisfy him. She held the goblet up.

"I still want my coffee."

He shrugged.

She took that for a yes and lifted her goblet. The "juice" shimmered, almost iridescent, in the frosted crystal. Its color reminded her of honey. She looked up. "This isn't too sweet is it?"

Rhyel rolled his own glass in his hands. The golden liquid misted the glass's lip. "The flavor is tart but not bitter."

She cautiously sipped the wine, testing it on her tongue. The taste reminded her of lightly sweetened lemonade, with a hint of melon. She couldn't discern any alcohol. Maybe it was as innocuous as he claimed. She relaxed into the chair's soft cushion. Her head lulled back and she closed her eyes.

"If I believe you can travel from one star to another, then I have to believe you have an advanced medical technology as well." She opened her eyes and took in the room. "I recognize every piece of equipment in your clinic. It's all from Earth.

"Where's your technology? When Cintar was hurt, why didn't you use...." She waved her hand in the air as she struggled for the right word. "I don't know... a laser, or the equivalent, to heal him? Why did I have to stitch up your friend?"

Rhyel set his glass aside. "Cintar's wound never required stitching."

"Then Hiilani was right. I was being humored."

"Not humored. Your concern for Cintar was noted, and respected. Your ministrations will, no doubt, speed the healing process." He smiled. "And leave a neater scar."

"You still haven't explained why you're using equipment from Earth."

"It solved a problem." He stood and retrieved the decanter from the counter.

She didn't protest when he topped off her glass. She took a sip while she waited for him to continue.

He returned to his seat, swallowed a portion from his glass, and said, "The *Novaria* is equipped with a medical bay, but we had no healer. Our technicians are capable of using the equipment, but have no medical training. Any healer brought to New Centallus would have medical training but lack the knowledge to use the ship's equipment. The solution was obvious—provide the healer with familiar medical equipment."

"And the medical facility on your ship?"

"It is used for research."

She swirled the liquid in the bottom of her glass. She hadn't remembered drinking so much. Rhyel had been right about the relaxing properties of the wine. The tension in her neck and shoulders had eased, relieving the headache that had plagued her most of the day. Her mind was still clear, though.

"Why are you in hiding?" Her abrupt change in topic surprised them both.

He leaned forward, wary now. "What makes you think we're in hiding?"

She had to think about it for a moment.

"A lot of things," she finally said. "Why did you colonize a remote planet instead of seeking sanctuary on a friendly world—I assume there are friendly worlds out there." She waited for him to nod, then continued. "And you came to Earth for brides, and supplies. Earth is incapable of manned planetary travel and therefore of no threat to you.

"As far as Earth is concerned, you aren't that physically different from us. Your blood is red and you have no qualms about taking Earth mates so we must be genetically connected. You could settle on my home world and accomplish the same goal—continuing your species. No one would be the wiser if you avoided medical scans. Trying to explain why your heart isn't where it should be could be a problem.

"But you didn't settle on Earth, and I think it's because you were protecting us. Everyone is paranoid about the white noise on your communications system. It's obvious you don't want to be found. Why?"

"I don't have all of the answers you're looking for."

"What do you have?"

He took another swallow of his wine and sighed. "A long story."

She looked toward the window, and over to her patient, then back to Rhyel who still hovered close. "I'm not going anywhere."

12

✧

"I don't want to frighten you."

"I can handle fear." Amber had certainly coped with her share recently. "Why would I be frightened?"

"Whoever attacked Centallus will come after us if they discover that we have survived."

All right, so now she was frightened. "Why would they come after you?"

"They didn't get what they wanted."

She waited for Rhyel to elaborate. When he failed to, she prompted, "What did they want?"

"The *Acqeli*." When she tilted her head in question he continued. "It's an interpretation crystal—the key to the translation of a dead world's hieroglyphics."

"How do you know that's what they wanted?"

"The Guardian who contacted us asked what an *Acqeli* was. He said the attackers were demanding the *Acqeli*. That was when the com-link went down."

"Why is it so important?"

He refilled her glass. "*Acqeli* literally means crystal-key. The Ancients who transcribed it etched their secrets on every temple wall on their planet, Aliitzar. We believe the inhabitants knew their planet was dying and left the temple writings as a legacy.

"The hieroglyphics were indecipherable. Scholars from every known civilization attempted to translate the cryptic symbols and failed. But nearly five hundred years ago a Centallian archeologist, Riistren, discovered the *Acqeli* on a moon orbiting Aliitzar. He realized it was a translation stone.

"Suspecting a relationship between the crystal and Aliitzar's hieroglyphics, Riistren spent months secretly decrypting the alpha-numeric code and used the *Acqeli* to translate the temple writings. What he discovered terrified him. He destroyed everything—the codes, the translations—everything but the crystal itself. He couldn't bring himself to destroy the *Acqeli*."

Rhyel paused, leaned across, and set his goblet on the stand. "Riistren entrusted the crystal into the Elders' keeping and told them only that the *Acqeli* was an *Eeschari*—a Pandora's Box containing deadly secrets.

"The *Acqeli* has been safe with the Elders for multiple generations." He rested his elbows on his knees, clasping his hands together. "The *Acqeli* should have been destroyed, but the Elders, like Riistren, felt honor-bound to preserve the knowledge of a dead civilization. Since that time, the *Acqeli* has remained a secret held only by the most trusted Elders."

She set her nearly empty glass on the stand beside his. "But you knew about it—and the attackers found out somehow."

"I was aware of the temple writings, of course, but not the *Acqeli*, not until after the attack, when Valdon entrusted me with their secret."

Suddenly, everything came together for her. "You still have the *Acqeli*," she whispered. "You're protecting it."

He looked as if he wished she hadn't put the pieces together, but nodded.

"It wasn't on Centallus?"

"The *Acqeli* was aboard the *Novaria*. It never leaves the Chief Elder's possession."

"That doesn't seem very secure."

"It's worked for hundreds of years."

"So you and the Elders should be the only ones who know the artifact exists."

"The attackers knew before I did. We still don't understand how they found out about it."

She rubbed her tired eyes as she contemplated what he'd told her. The headache didn't seem as bad now. It was easier for her to think. She glanced at her nearly empty glass. Maybe the wine did have its benefits.

"Don't you have... *friends* from other worlds you could turn to for help?"

"It isn't that simple. We don't know who we can trust. We can't afford for our friends to know we're alive."

She retrieved her goblet and swallowed the last of her wine. She covered a yawn with her hand. "Why don't you destroy the crystal now and be done with it? You wouldn't have to hide if it didn't exist."

He shook his head. "I doubt the attackers would believe it's gone. We can't take the chance."

She tried to hide another yawn.

He carried the goblets and decanter to the counter. "Why don't you go to your room and rest? I'll sit with Cintar and call you if his condition changes."

She shook her head. That made her dizzy. She tried to focus on Rhyel. "I must be more tired than I thought." She stood on unsteady legs.

He slid the desk chair out of his way when she lurched sideways, and slipped an arm around her waist to keep her from falling on her face.

"I'm sorry," she said, grabbing his shirt for support. She pushed away from him. "I think I need to sit down." She reached back to grab the chair arm for support and couldn't find it.

"You need to go to bed," Rhyel told her.

She angled her head to tell him what she thought of his suggestion, and her knees buckled. He caught her before she hit the floor and lifted her into his arms.

She held his neck tight. "What's wrong with me?"

"Nothing, *Rishka*." His lips brushed her ear. "Let the *Baquui* do its work. Close your eyes. I'll keep you safe."

"You drugged me?" Her head fell against his shoulder when she looked up at him.

"We shared the wine, *Rishka*. It wasn't drugged." He carried her to the adjoining room and gently placed her in the center of the bed and loosened her grip on his neck. He pulled a light cover up around her shoulders. His lips touched her forehead.

She mumbled a half-hearted protest, feeling too mellow to take exception to his action.

"You are a temptation, *Rishka*, a complication I don't need, and tomorrow, honor requires me to join my life to yours."

She yawned and snuggled deeper into the covers. "That's nice."

13

✧

Mauve-tinged fingers of morning light penetrated the distant woods to touch bleached stone towers and the high-walled enclosure below. Amber's breath caught as the growing light revealed the radiant white city within. Its unadorned beauty always drew her back home.

Home?

She shook her head. She'd never seen this place before. Yet the feeling of familiarity was real.

A cool, water-scented breeze caressed her skin. She turned to watch soaring birds dive and plunge into a distant lake, then emerge and feed on their catch. The water's surface glittered like fire opals in the early morning sun.

On the far bank, trees, larger even than the California redwoods, dominated the landscape. Other trees, twisted and gnarled, hunched like misshapen beasts at the water's edge. Their leaves, and even the grass, appeared blue in the strange, muted purple sunrise.

Her attention centered on the tower gate as it opened below. Laughter accompanied a small group of people leaving the city. Most of them wore cream colored tunics and matching loose-legged trousers. Multicolored belts and gold jewelry adorned the otherwise plain garments. Several women carried empty woven baskets.

Their leader, a tall, lanky man of around fifty, laughed as he took the hand of a woman who looked only slightly younger than he.

A tiny, black-haired toddler tried to keep pace with a slender, equally dark-haired girl of about twenty. The young woman fondly touched the baby's head, and bent to swing the giggling child to her shoulders. The young blond man beside her placed a protective arm around her waist.

An older woman, crowned with a coronet of silver braids, wore a long, flowing, blue caftan. She looked up, smiled, and waved. Amber returned the greeting, suddenly warm and happy—she'd been gone a long time.

A vague foreboding sharpened. She was suddenly afraid. The rough trail the group followed wound around a hill. Soon they would be out of her sight.

Anxious now, she stumbled down the rock-strewn incline, unmindful of the sharp stones and prickly brush that scraped her feet and snagged her gown.

The tall man stopped to watch her haphazard descent. He turned to say something to the older woman when a brilliant shaft of hot light whited everything out.

The baby screamed. The ground rumbled and shook underfoot. This was *it*. A thunderous explosion rent both ground and air. *This* was the danger.

The next blast slammed her against an outcropping of rock. She pitched forward, rolling down the hill. She clawed at tree sprouts and clumps of grass. Her wrist hit a sapling and she grabbed its spindly trunk. The abrupt halt wrenched her shoulder, shooting pain through her neck and arm. Tree bark tore her skin, embedding splinters in her fingers, but she held fast.

She grasped the stopgap lifeline with both hands and pulled herself to her knees. She closed her eyes and gasped for breath, trying to block the pain. She waited for her world to quit spinning. New explosions cleaved the ground, and a cacophony of anguished cries assailed her ears.

She stared down at the city. Flames leaped so high they dwarfed the four towers. People trapped inside the crumbled city walls ran to escape the tongues of fire. The inferno expanded with each successive blast. Buildings ignited. Acrid, gray smoke roiled through the streets, lifting and swooping back to the ground to separate a mother from her child, a husband from his wife.

Heat radiated from the blazing pillars, sucking the breath from every living creature within range. A man fell writhing to the dirt, dying before the flames reached him.

An errant breeze carried smoke and the stench of burning hair and flesh to her. She held her breath. Her eyes watered and stung. She choked, the wracking spasm ending in stomach-wrenching gags.

The smoke swirled upward and she gulped quick lungsful of cool, clean air. There was a great rend in the ground where her people had stood. Bodies dotted the landscape. The tall man lay still, head tilted at an odd angle.

Rock fall pinned the young woman against an uprooted stump, her body half-buried in dirt and rubble. She moaned, called out, and thrashed her exposed arm against the jagged stones.

Amber couldn't see the baby. She grasped the willow-like branches of the sapling and pulled herself up, then skidded downward, stumbled and fell, climbed to her feet, and stumbled again.

The smoke wafted skyward. Less than twenty feet away, the gray-haired woman crawled perilously close to the edge of the rift, her knees catching on the long folds of her caftan. Twice, she nearly fell into the abyss.

"Don't move," Amber cried out.

The woman ignored her warning and reached out to something hidden by a fallen tree. A small hand appeared above the prone trunk. A tiny head popped up and the baby toddled into the waiting arms.

She was alive. They were *both* alive.

Amber ran toward the woman, her feet scattering rocks, sending them down the slope ahead of her.

The woman looked up. Terror clouded her gold-flecked eyes.

"Don't move. *Please* don't move," Amber begged. "You're too close to the edge. I'm coming. Wait for me. I'll save you both."

Firm hands held her back. She fought the restraint. She needed to go to the people she loved. She struggled against the arms enfolding her.

"It's all right," a familiar voice whispered. "You're safe."

The scene faded into darkness. She whimpered, pressed closer to the comforting warmth, and drifted away from the pain, away from remembering, into the peaceful void.

She lay cradled in Rhyel's arms, her face pressed against his warm chest. His deep, even breathing told her he slept. She didn't move, afraid of waking him.

What was he doing in her bed? More important, what was she doing in his arms? She wouldn't have willingly allowed him access to her bed… or her body.

Had he considered his commitment to their union reason enough to seduce her?

He snuggled closer, a familiar, almost intimate action. She caught her lower lip between her teeth, momentarily uncertain. No. She wouldn't have succumbed. She was old-fashioned enough to believe that commitment came before sex. She was probably the only twenty-seven-year-old virgin in America—at least that was what Chris had told her. He'd always talk about having sex, instead of making love. The omission had made it easier to deny him and finally break off their engagement. She'd never regretted ending their relationship.

She tried to move away and his arms tightened. Why couldn't she remember much from last night? Her memories were like a half-finished jigsaw puzzle, mere fragments of the whole. She had been sitting with Cintar, talking to Hiilani. Rhyel had insisted she have a glass of wine… or was it two?

The wine. Her eyes widened. He'd drugged the wine—and her.

"You lecher!" She slammed her fist into his chest.

Before she could strike again he caught her wrist, twisted it above her head, and rolled on top of her. His fingers closed around her throat.

Stunned, knowing her death might come with the suddenness of a quickly clenched hand, she looked into the blazing, gold eyes of a stranger capable of killing, eyes just beginning to spark with awareness. She stared, spellbound as the harsh angles of his face changed from murderous rage to simmering anger. The volatile gold receded into black until only gold flecks remained in his obsidian eyes.

"Don't you know better than to hit a sleeping man?" The hand that only moments before promised death, now softly stroked her bruised throat.

"Your eyes…."

"Are normal for a Centallian."

He levered himself to the side of the bed. He drew two long shuddering breaths, and ran a hand through his hair. He looked over his shoulder at her.

"Did I hurt you?"

"No." She was still having trouble coming to grips with the fact that his eyes could change their color.

"Did I hurt you during the night?"

That question got her full attention. She shrugged her shoulders, wondering now if he had taken advantage of her drugged condition.

He reached for his boots and put them on before turning back to her.

"Why did you hit me?"

That was when she realized they were both fully clothed.

"Answer me," he demanded. "Why did you hit me?"

Amber scooted off the opposite side of the bed and glared at him. "You drugged me and you… you…."

He raised a questioning eyebrow at her apparent inability to finish the sentence.

She walked around the foot of the bed and stood in front of him. "Why were you in bed with me?"

"You were having a bad dream." He pulled the lacings of his tunic together and knotted them.

"I was—what kind of a lame excuse is that?"

His eyes locked with hers. "I don't make excuses. You asked a question. I answered it."

"Why didn't you wake me?"

"You wouldn't wake up."

"Because of the wine?"

"Probably."

"You had no right to crawl into bed with me and—" She looked away, her face hot with embarrassment. She was acting like a naïve teenager.

"And what?" he insisted.

Did she have to spell it out for him? "I don't want to talk about it."

He stood and gripped her shoulders, turning her to face him. "What do you think I did to you last night?"

"I said I don't want to talk about it."

She knew the minute he understood. She saw it in his eyes, in the softening of his hard features. His grip on her shoulders loosened and he touched her cheek with his fingertips.

She ducked back. "Don't."

His hand fell away. "It would seem even a doctor's knowledge falls short of experience," he whispered.

She glared at him. "What's that supposed to mean?"

"That you wonder if you're still a virgin."

She shook her head and opened her mouth to argue, but his fingers touched her lips.

"You are a beautiful, desirable woman, *Rishka*, but I only held you through the night. Honor forbids more. Your virginity is to be respected." He grinned and his eyes sparkled. "When we come together you will not be sleeping. I promise."

He turned to leave when an unsettling thought occurred to her. She reached out and grabbed his arm. "Wait."

He swung back around to face her.

"How do you know?" she asked.

"How do I know what?"

She swallowed hard to soothe the tightness in her throat. The tension abated, but the words still didn't come easy. "How do you know I'm a virgin?"

His dark expression told her he'd rather she hadn't asked that. "As a healer, Amber, you possess the knowledge of the physical act of love between a man and woman, but you have no memories of an intimate relationship." He leaned in. "No man has left his mark upon your mind." His warm breath brushed feather-light against her cheek as he whispered, "You wonder how it feels to have a man touch you intimately. You climb into your lonely bed at night and dream of a lover's hard body pressed against yours, the feel of his weight as he—"

"Stop!" She slapped both hands over his mouth, her face hot with more than just embarrassment. His dark eyes told her he shared the heat his words evoked in her. She stepped back. "You can't know what I feel. You'd have to be a mind reader to—"

"I do not possess that gift," he was quick to assure. "Aadrok is our seer. He alone knows your thoughts."

She gasped. "He read my mind?"

"There's no reason for concern. What he learned will not become common knowledge."

"Obviously he shared a few secrets with you."

His eyes widened. "You are angry?"

"What did you expect?"

"I expected you to be relieved at the method by which we obtained our information."

"Relieved!" The need to scream her frustration made her throat hurt. "Your friend invaded my mind, and you want me to be relieved?"

He shrugged. "You have nothing to hide."

"You shouldn't know that."

"Aadrok and I have discussed many things concerning you, but never your virginity. That you were chosen by the Elders revealed that truth."

"The Elders discussed my—*virginity*? Okay, let me get this straight. Your mind reader—"

"Our *seer*."

"What*ever*." She waved her hand around to indicate how little his title impressed her. "That man got into my head and found out my deepest, darkest secrets."

"You do not possess any dark secrets."

"That isn't the point, and stop interrupting me. Your... seer read my mind, and told the Elders, and that's why I'm here."

"It is a little more complicated than that, but yes."

"And because I was chosen, this whole colony knows I'm a virgin?" That came out an octave higher than she'd intended.

"It is nothing to be ashamed of."

"I'm not ashamed. I'm furious."

"Why?"

She took a deep breath and calmed her voice. "Do you understand what rape is?"

He stiffened and frowned down at her. "That, you need not fear. I have promised to keep you safe, and I will."

She shook her head. "Every time your seer invades my mind it's mental rape."

"You overreact."

She tapped her temple with her finger. "My thoughts are mine alone. No one has the right to sneak into my head and take them from me."

"Aadrok is our Holy Man. He is the only person on New Centallus who possesses the ability to see into other minds, and he refrains from using his power until it becomes necessary. Every thought he ascertains is held sacred. Your own people have holy men. Confessions are made to them, are they not, and held sacred?"

"In some religions, yes, but I didn't confess anything. Your Aadrok raided my mind like a thief. He took my thoughts and *you* used them against me."

"I needed to know what to anticipate when I came for you. It was necessary for your safety."

She repressed a laugh. "I haven't been safe since you came into my bedroom—and my safety has nothing to do with what we're talking about." She drew a deep calming breath. "I'm almost afraid to ask this, but I'm going to anyway. Why is my virginity necessary to your cause?"

"Strong commitments to your world would interfere with our goals."

"I have strong commitments. I've told you about my grandfather."

"Your ties with your grandfather are strong, yes, but a woman leaves her family when she takes a mate. The bond formed between mates is more powerful."

"Then why didn't your holy man tell you about Chris?"

His eyebrows rose slightly. "Chris?"

"He was my fiancé." She didn't feel the least guilty about leaving the word former out of the statement.

He frowned. "A fiancé is not a mate. It is the intimacy of bonding, or what you call marriage, that brings commitment."

She shook her head. "Fifty or sixty years ago that might have been the norm, but birth control and a more permissive society have changed that, at least where I come from. Most engaged couples are sexually active before they get married."

He skimmed his fingertips across her cheek. His touch felt as light and warm as sunshine. "You have admitted you are a virgin," he said softly. "Do you expect me to believe now that you are not?"

"If Chris and I were lovers, would you take me home?"

"No." His voice was firm.

"But you just said—"

"You are here now, and willing or unwilling, committed to our cause."

"But—"

"Shh." His thumb brushed her lips. "You will stay." His eyes held hers for a long moment before his hand dropped away. "Were we mistaken, Amber?"

"Would it matter to you, personally?"

He cupped the back of her neck, and pulled her into his arms. She started to protest and he took advantage. His open mouth covered hers and softened, his tongue gently tracing her lips before the kiss deepened. He groaned and leaned back to capture her gaze.

His voice was gruff when he said, "Only a little."

A little what? It took a moment to recall their conversation. She traced her lips with her tongue. She could still taste him. His kiss had definitely been personal.

"Were you and your fiancé lovers?"

He was giving her the choice of being honest with him or following through with her deception. As a child she had learned that the truth generally kept her out of trouble.

"No," she whispered, "we were never lovers."

Appeased, he nodded. He released her and walked to the door. He paused to look back. "I will return later and we will discuss what to expect at our bonding ceremony."

14

✧

Amber found Hiilani in the clinic, sitting beside Cintar's bed.

"How long have you been here?" She hoped the young woman hadn't been ordered to sit up all night.

"Only an hour. I'm glad you decided to go to bed. You needed your—"

"Don't say it," she warned. "I'm tired of hearing about how much rest I need. I'm fine." She crossed to the sink. "And I wasn't given the chance to decide." She turned to face Hiilani. "Did you know what was in that decanter Rhyel brought to the clinic last night?"

The girl's eyes turned wary, probably due to the tone of the question, but she didn't hesitate giving her answer. "Yes, *Baquui*. I recognized the color."

"You never thought to warn me?"

Hiilani looked puzzled. "About what?"

"He drugged me. How could you condone that?"

"Rhyel would never drug your wine. It wouldn't be honorable."

"Can you explain why I can't remember getting into bed last night?"

"It probably was the wine, but there were no drugs involved. *Baquui* relaxes your body completely. If you're exhausted, sleep is inevitable. You would never have fallen asleep if you hadn't needed the rest. The commander only provided the catalyst for your body's natural inclination."

"Don't defend what he did to me."

"I'm not defending his actions." Hiilani paused. "Well, maybe I am a little, but I remember how you looked the day Rhyel carried you into this clinic. You were so pale. If you hadn't been breathing, I would have thought you were dead.

"Rhyel was worried about you. He told me he'd never seen such a debilitating reaction to *Mensolm*. He stayed beside your bed until you regained consciousness. I was the only one he allowed into the room."

"I don't remember."

"I'm not surprised. You were pretty much out of it. I was amazed to see you so alert yesterday." Hiilani glanced over at Cintar. "You took good care of him."

"Thank you, and I'm sorry. I always seem to take my frustration out on you."

Hiilani smiled. "It's okay. This has to be traumatic for you."

Amber nodded. "It's that I'm not used to being—I don't know." She shook her head.

Hiilani laughed. "Being watched over?"

"More like being watched, period."

"Rhyel is taking care of you the best way he can. This is frustrating for him, too. You're not fully recovered, yet you refuse to admit it. Last night it was obvious you were in pain. You were nearly as pale as you were the day Rhyel brought you in here. The *Baquui* was his way of solving a problem you refused to acknowledge."

"I needed to take care of my patient."

"Rhyel knew Cintar was fine. You were his main concern. Because he used *Mensolm* to restrain you, he feels responsible for seeing you safely through its effects. One thing does confuse me, though." Hiilani inclined her head toward the adjoining room. "The doorstop was holding the door open when I came in this morning, and a chair sat between the two rooms. I believe Rhyel was keeping an eye on you both. But I can't understand why."

"He promised to stay with his friend if I went to bed."

"That explains it. A Centallian's word is his bond. A promise given is a sacred trust."

"But the door was closed when I woke up this morning."

Hiilani laughed. "I've had years of practice tiptoeing around sleeping patients. I retrieved the chair and closed the door without even waking Rhyel."

Heat rushed to her cheeks. "Then you saw him in my bed?"

The nurse smiled. "You needn't feel uncomfortable about that. I know the commander didn't take advantage of you. And you shouldn't be embarrassed. No one will consider Rhyel's presence in your bed improper."

"How could they not?"

"The Centallians adhere to a high moral standard that few will ignore."

"Then why was he in my bed?"

"He must have had a good reason."

Amber crossed her arms, still outraged by his actions. "Oh, he had an excuse, but it was as thin as mist."

"You didn't believe him?" Hiilani actually sounded surprised.

"He told me I was having a bad dream. Can you believe that?"

"Yes. No one will question his motives."

"No one but me," Amber muttered as she slipped her lab coat on and scrubbed up. She was still muttering to herself when she moved to Cintar's bedside.

Hiilani failed to hide her grin as she lifted the sheet from Cintar's leg. Amber ignored her nurse and began removing the bandage that covered most of the man's left thigh.

"Have his readings changed?" she asked as she pulled the gauze away from the wound.

"No, but they won't until he's awake. The swelling in his leg is down, though."

"I can see that." She glanced at her assistant. "His leg is nearly healed." She examined the pink scar tissue. "We can remove the stitches today."

"The Centallians have a remarkable capacity for healing. It astounds me."

Amber lifted her patient's eyelid and noted the lack of pupil reaction to the overhead light. "He's still unconscious, and that worries me. Are you sure it's normal?"

"If Cintar is like the others, he is in full control. He will return from stasis as soon as he can function proficiently."

She looked up. "Not even a limp?"

Hiilani grinned. "Not even a limp."

"Well, let's remove the stitches while he's still out. I love a patient who doesn't complain."

The nurse moved the tray closer to the bed, and they worked in silence for a while. Amber appreciated her quiet efficiency.

"I can't believe they fly around in spaceships, and he doesn't know how to use an ax. He may resemble Paul Bunyan, but he lacks the big man's skill."

Hiilani smiled. "What do you find so incredible, that they fly starships or mishandle rudimentary tools?"

"Both."

"You have to understand that they've never needed to cut down or trim a tree before. The only tools on their ship that proved useful on New Centallus were laser-torches. They can be used to fell huge trees, but they're too powerful for trimming branches or notching logs. After studying what was available on Earth, the Centallians opted for the lowly ax."

Amber paused. "Why choose something so primitive? They might have at least used chainsaws."

"If you think about it, it makes sense. Chainsaws require gas, which would have to come from Earth. It's too dangerous to transport and store the amount of fuel that engine-powered tools need. An ax, however, requires only muscle, and basic skill. After seeing the Centallians you have to agree they do have an ample supply of muscle."

"And the skill?"

Hiilani's sigh sounded resigned. "They are getting better."

Amber inclined her head toward Cintar's leg. "You're sure?"

The nurse shook her head. "Actually, that's the worst I've seen. The others—"

Amber held up her hand. "Please, spare me the gory details."

"You were instructed to rest." Amber jumped at the unexpected voice and looked up.

Rhyel leaned against the door frame, frowning, arms folded across his chest.

She turned back to remove the last stitch from Cintar's thigh. Only after she discarded the suture thread and placed the tweezers on the tray did she acknowledge him again.

Rhyel pushed away from the door and walked into the room. He'd changed into a tan linen pullover shirt and buff pants. On most men the lightweight garments would give the appearance of leisure. On Rhyel, they failed to mask the inherent power and intensity of a truly remarkable male physique. She sighed, and pulled her thoughts back to what she was doing.

"We'll leave the wound open to the air," she told Hiilani as she took off her gloves and lab coat. "If you need to take a break, I'll keep an eye on him."

The nurse nodded. "I could use one. Can I bring you something to eat? I know you didn't have breakfast."

She shook her head and was pleased the action didn't cause her pain. "I'm fine. My breakfast usually consists of a cup of coffee and a piece of toast. Coffee is enough this morning." She glanced at the coffee maker, saw Hiilani had already made a pot, and waved her new friend on. "Looks like I'm good, thanks though."

After pulling the sheet over Cintar's leg, she walked through the open door to the adjoining room. She expected Rhyel to follow and he didn't disappoint her. She turned to confront him.

"I've been thinking."

"And?" he said cautiously.

"Tzorik forced you to claim me, but you don't have to marry me to protect me. There has to be another way."

Rhyel slowly shook his head as he moved closer. "Tzorik didn't force me to claim you, Amber. He only changed the manner in which you found out. It was my intention to speak with you before presenting my claim to the Elders."

A flutter of awareness tightened her stomach. Under different circumstances she might be attracted to him. Was she crazy? The man kidnapped her—dragged her to another world in who knew what part of the galaxy—and she might be attracted to him? She wasn't just crazy, she was certifiable.

Did he desire her? This morning's kiss seemed to indicate he did. It had obviously affected him. It had affected her, too. Their mutual attraction scared her more than he did.

How could she protect herself from something she didn't understand?

He frowned down at her. "I see apprehension in your eyes," he said softly. "Tell me what you fear."

You. "Who will protect me from you?" she whispered. "What will happen when I refuse you? Will your vows give you the right to force yourself on me?"

"Never." He rested his hands on her shoulders. When she stiffened he began to knead the tense muscles. "You will be my *Zharkra*—my honored mate. When we come together there will be no force, only passion, and joy." His arm slipped down her back and slowly drew her closer until their bodies touched. She should have pushed away, but she didn't. His hands, and voice, and those dark intense eyes held her as fast as the sticky web of a spider. Would he devour her?

"There is an elusive connection between us," he said, "that goes beyond duty or desire. You've felt it too. It allows you the freedom to defy me, because you know I am incapable of harming you." His hands trailed up to cup her face, his fingertips caressed her cheek. "Were you a Centallian woman, I might put a name to this connection."

"What name?"

The smile he gave her was soft, a little wistful, and very sexy. "The name is unimportant, *Rishka*, a part of the past." He bent his head, and brushed her lips with his.

She was shaken by the gentle urgency in that brief kiss. She wanted to pull away, she really did—but a part of her wanted to discover what came next.

"Kiss me," he breathed.

Her mouth opened in denial—or was it anticipation?

Invitation must have been his interpretation. His mouth covered hers, and his tongue swept in to taste her, to let her taste him.

She moaned and tried to convince herself it was fury that made her tremble. She braced her hands against his hard chest, but his heat robbed her of the strength to push him away, robbed her even of the desire to do so.

"Touch me," he breathed against her lips.

She couldn't seem to help herself. Of their own volition her fingers slipped under his shirt seeking the fire. She didn't know if the moan her touch elicited was his or her own.

He slanted his lips across hers to deepen the tentative kiss she offered. Heat pooled in her belly, a delicious, debilitating heat that made her knees weak.

He straightened, lifting her feet from the floor and held her closer still. His arousal nestled intimately against her. She resisted the urge to cuddle him, to revel in feelings she'd never allowed herself to experience.

"I seem to have misplaced my pants."

15

✧

Amber started at the unexpected voice. She pulled her lips free and pushed at Rhyel's chest. He seemed reluctant to let her go, sought to regain the kiss.

"Don't," she insisted, mortified that someone had discovered them.

He stood her on the floor, touched his forehead to hers, and drew a long shuddering breath. He looked over her shoulder. "You could have slept a few minutes longer, or at least knocked."

"The door was open," a man said, his voice gratingly cheerful. "Have you seen my pants?"

She turned and saw Cintar standing in the doorway, holding a sheet around his middle. He looked amused. Rhyel's friend was taller than she'd thought, nearly as tall as his commander. But where Rhyel's physique reminded her of a Greek statue, Cintar was built like a bull, a handsome bull, she qualified. He had a strong, square chin, straight nose, and beautiful brown eyes. His short, chestnut-hued hair tended to curl around his ears, giving him a roguish appearance.

"You shouldn't be out of bed," she scolded, and felt a perverse sense of satisfaction when his smile eroded.

He looked mildly confused. "I should have been out of bed and working hours ago."

Rhyel put his arm around her shoulder. "Amber has been taking care of you since your accident. She was concerned about your condition. I saw no reason to cause her unnecessary distress by waking you before you were fully healed."

Cintar's eyes crinkled and the grin was back to goad Amber's irritation. "I can see how responsive you are to our healer's needs."

She pushed away from Rhyel. "Come into the clinic. I'll take your vital signs—if you have any."

Cintar glanced at his commander. "If I have any?"

Rhyel chuckled. "Amber is troubled by stasis life signs readings."

Cintar sidestepped as she walked through the clinic door. Both men followed. Cintar paused just inside the door. "Will she give me my pants if I let her take the readings?"

"Probably." Rhyel continued into the clinic. "Let her have her way. She has more than your health to consider today. I don't want her needlessly upset."

"Too late," she muttered.

She nodded toward the examining table. "Sit there."

When Cintar complied she took his blood pressure, then lifted the sheet away from the wound. There wasn't much to look at, only a thin, pink scar. The improvement in his condition astounded her. Less than an hour had passed since she had removed the stitches.

She prodded the spot. "Any soreness?"

"No." Cintar pulled the sheet over his leg when she stepped back. "Can I have my pants now?"

"Yes. Hiilani assumed you would wake up today. She asked one of your friends to bring fresh clothes for you. They're in the bathroom." She had to practically shout the last, since Cintar was halfway across the room before she finished speaking.

Five minutes after entering the bathroom, he returned, pants in place. "I hope there's something left to eat in the kitchen," he said as he pulled a tunic over his head. He looked at Rhyel. "Want to join me and fill me in on anything I've missed?"

Rhyel shook his head. "Perhaps later. Amber and I must supply the technicians with blood samples."

She looked up from a chart she'd been updating. "Why?"

"Our blood must be scanned for genetic compatibility."

Cintar pounded his friend's back in enthusiastic congratulations. "Incredible," he said as he walked to the exit. "Apparently I've missed more than a day's work. When is the bonding?"

"Never." She turned back to the chart.

Cintar glanced from her to Rhyel. "Did she say never? After what I saw—"

Rhyel practically pushed Cintar out of the clinic. "We will discuss it when I join you later," he said before closing the door in his friend's face.

She diligently ignored Rhyel after Cintar's departure, until clattering instruments caught her attention. She looked back at him. "What are you doing?"

Rhyel held up two disposable syringes. "Will these do for the blood test?"

"If you plan to spend the next hour waiting for your blood to flow through that tiny needle."

He didn't look as if he appreciated her sarcasm. "Where are the appropriate needles, then?"

She sighed. "You're going to insist on this aren't you?"

"Yes."

She walked to the cabinet, jerked a door open and snatched up two sealed packets and a pair of latex gloves.

"Sit down. I'll take the samples," she said as she snapped the gloves in place and nodded toward a straight-backed chair beside the counter. "This doesn't mean I'm going along with your scheme. I'm just not chancing a staph infection."

He sat without comment and rolled up his sleeve. She tied a rubber tourniquet around his bulging bicep.

"Make a fist."

When he complied, she slapped his forearm with a vengeance. He looked at her with a raised eyebrow. She smiled sweetly and pointed to the vein that had risen on the abused area. She swabbed the spot with alcohol. In spite of what he probably expected, she gently inserted the needle, loosened the tourniquet, and triggered the plunger. Five seconds later she removed the needle, and capped and marked the vial of blood. She swabbed his arm with more alcohol and before he could protest, put a Band-Aid over the spot. She suppressed her giggle at the look on his face when he noticed the protective strip had cute little yellow ducks on it.

"It's your turn," Rhyel said, reaching for the other package.

She hesitated. She'd taken a little of her frustration out on him. Was he about to reciprocate? She handed him a fresh pair of gloves and they exchanged places.

He pulled a chair close and sat with his knees on either side of hers. He put on the gloves and picked up the tourniquet. He studied the counter.

"No red powder?" he teased.

"Not in my clinic," she said, relieved that he was apparently still in a good mood. "Use the alcohol swabs." She held out her hand. "Give me the tourniquet."

"It will be easier if you allow me to help." He positioned her arm on his knee.

"You want me to let you draw my blood?" She jerked her arm back. "I don't think so."

"I've used hypos before," he assured her, repositioning her arm. "This is only slightly different." As he spoke he applied the tourniquet, opened a packet, and swabbed her arm. "You will be here to instruct me should the need arise. Make a fist."

She looked down and saw the needle poised over the vein. The fist she made was reflexive, a reaction to the adrenaline suddenly pumping through her system. Rhyel didn't notice her tension as he found the vein and loosened the tourniquet.

"It is done," he said as he capped the vial.

She jerked her arm back and massaged the place, unmindful of the small spot of blood she smeared.

"Let me clean that." He unwrapped another alcohol swab. When she didn't move her hand he looked up and frowned. "What's wrong?"

"Nothing, I'm all right."

"You look pale enough to faint."

"I said I'm fine." She grabbed the swab and cleaned the blood away. "I was just remembering something, that's all."

He placed the needle and the vial on the counter and took her hand.

"Don't." She tried to pull free of his grasp. "I have work to do."

"The work can be delayed. This cannot. You were remembering the night I kidnapped you."

"Yes." She averted her gaze to the window.

"And you feared me?"

She looked at him. "Of course I feared you."

"Do you fear me now?"

She feared her circumstances, but the man?

No, she didn't fear him, not anymore. It was a realization she wasn't willing to share with him, though.

He took both of her hands in his. "You are in my home and safe. Soon you will become my bond-mate, and I will vow to protect you, to cherish you, to be your life's companion. We may face dangers in the future, but I promise never again will you find reason to fear me, or what I do." He leaned forward. "By my honor," he breathed, sealing his vow with a touch of his lips to hers.

The kiss was infinitely gentle, void of the passionate heat they'd shared earlier. Still, Amber's every sense centered on the taste of him, the soft touch of his lips against hers, and on his vow so fervently given.

An overwhelming sense of despair assailed her. How was she ever going to keep herself distanced from this man if she succumbed to his seduction of her mind and body? His effect on her was potent, nearly impossible to resist.

"Don't," she whispered, pulling away from him. "Please."

He allowed the distance. "I must take the blood samples to the *Novaria*. I will return this evening to share a meal." He kissed her and left before she could muster a protest.

She stared at the closed door. Touching her mouth with her fingertips, she sighed.

How long had she been here? She only remembered yesterday and today. It was hardly enough time to remember his name let alone feel something for him. Yet, she'd never been more aware of a man. He'd believed they shared a connection. She felt it, too.

There hadn't been much time for men in her life. She'd been driven to achieve her dream of becoming a doctor. She hadn't allowed anyone to interfere with that goal. Then she'd been caught up in her profession.

Rhyel had literally taken her away from all that. She felt like an astronaut with a severed umbilical cord, floating aimlessly. Did she need someone solid to cling to? Was that why her connection to him seemed so strong? She sighed and picked up a chart. She didn't have any answers, but she knew one thing for sure.

She had to find a way home—and soon.

16

✧

Amber expected Rhyel's knock on her door. But when she opened it, Tzorik stood waiting. By any woman's standard, the tall, muscular Guardian would be considered handsome. His fawn-colored tunic and buff leather pants went well with his light complexion and hair. But she had never been overly impressed by a man's good looks, preferring to judge him by merit rather than appearance. And she didn't like this man's manner at all.

"Yes?" she said, overcoming the urge to shut the door in his smirking face.

"Yes," he mimicked. "Now that's a word I hadn't thought I'd hear from your lips—yet." He pressed forward, forcing her to retreat into the room. The door closed behind him, and she flinched at the quiet click of the lock.

"What do you want?"

"Only to be the first to give you the good news," he said as she started around him toward the door. He caught her arm. "You aren't going anywhere."

She looked at his hand. Cold anger chilled her voice. "I'm unlocking the door and you're leaving. Let go of my arm. Now."

"I prefer it locked." Tzorik did release her arm, but remained between her and the door. "Once dried, the wood on this planet is as strong as any metal on your world. The alloy used to make the lock is stronger. No one's coming through that door until I'm finished. My news requires privacy." He reached out and touched her hair. She ducked away, but he snagged a curl and wound it around his fingers.

She snatched her hair from his grasp. Several strands hung in his fist. She'd never liked the casual, seemingly innocent touch that some men used to intimidate a woman. But Tzorik hadn't even bothered to mask his tactics with subtlety. Even now he taunted her by slowly winding the few broken strands of her hair into a tiny circlet and placing it in his tunic pocket.

"You said you have a message for me?" Amber reminded him.

"Ah, yes, the news." He seemed to savor the moment of telling. "You will be pleased to know your genetic make-up is incompatible with our honorable commander's." He grimaced as if the mention of his nemesis left a bad taste in his mouth.

"And that means?"

"You will not be forced to bond with Rhyel."

Dread sat like a heavy weight in her heart. Tzorik looked too satisfied, too victorious for her peace of mind.

"Why are you here? Why didn't Rhyel tell me himself?"

Tzorik's predatory leer caught and held her like a gripping talon. "You are no longer his responsibility. You belong to *me* now."

She shook her head and stepped back. "I don't believe you."

He grabbed her arm to stop her retreat. He bent close, his voice deadly. "Believe what you wish. It will change nothing. My blood was also tested with yours. It is gratifying to know we will produce healthy children."

"That's not going to happen."

"My petition remained before the council. The moment Rhyel's scan proved incompatible you became my mate, subject to my dictates… and my desires."

"That's not true. I'll never agree."

"Agree or not," he snarled, tightening his hold on her arm until she winced, "it makes no difference to me. Before the onset of the second season, I will get a child from your body."

"I've heard enough. Let me go and get out of here." She tried to twist free. "I can't stand you touching me." He may have forgotten the door to the clinic, but she hadn't. She regretted not having run for it the minute he locked the other one. If he turned her loose she wouldn't make that mistake again.

His gaze moved over her face, down to her breasts. "Soon I will do more than touch you. Don't look so horrified. I can make it feel good, if you cooperate."

Tzorik pulled her forward. His fingers grasped the back of her head, making it impossible for her to turn away. She could only push against his chest with her free hand.

"You are a beautiful woman, Amber. You may even rival the beauty of our Centallian women. At first I wanted you because Rhyel controlled you. But now… now my body aches to possess you."

His arm came around her hips, lifting her high enough to force his arousal against the juncture of her legs. His mouth muffled her screech of rage, and his tongue plunged so deep she gagged. He moaned his pleasure. Revulsion overwhelmed her. A nauseous bile rose in her throat. His mouth slid to her ear.

"I do not think we will wait for the bonding ceremony." His teeth found the tender lobe, and he bit down.

She cried out in surprised pain—and the pervert *laughed* at her!

She leaned away and slashed her nails across his face. He released her, but as soon as her feet hit the floor he grabbed her hand and shoved her arm behind her. He prevented her free hand from raking the other side of his face, and imprisoned it with the first. He used one hand to keep her arms secured behind her, and covered her mouth with the other when she drew a breath to scream. His smile was cruel and triumphant as he forced her backwards until she was sprawled over the table.

"It will not matter that I take you here, now." The hand over her mouth forced her head against the table. Her arms were pinned beneath her. She couldn't free them, not even when he pulled his hand out from under her. He slid that hand over her body, covered one breast, and squeezed.

She growled and bit the hand that covered her mouth—hard. She tasted blood before he yanked his hand away. She screamed and he smacked her across the mouth, the force of the blow wrenching her head to the side, dazing her. The blood she tasted now was her own.

"Lay still for me and you'll enjoy this," he said wedging his heavy thighs between her legs to force them apart. "Scream again and I'll make it hurt enough to shut you up." He glanced at the door when it rattled. "Fight me and you won't be able to walk to our bonding tomorrow."

His nails sliced the tender skin high on the inside of her leg as he shoved her skirt up and fumbled with the fastenings on his pants.

She clenched her teeth, lifted her foot, and tried to kick him. He grabbed her ankle, twisted it painfully as he leaned forward, and slapped her again.

A rage-filled roar fused with the ringing in her head, and Tzorik was suddenly gone.

She rolled to her side and saw Rhyel slam her attacker high against the wall and hold him by the throat. Tzorik's terror-filled eyes bulged as he dangled in Rhyel's grasp.

The man was close in height and weight to his commander. That Rhyel held him above the floor with one hand attested to his strength and fury. Rhyel's body blocked Tzorik's defenses as his fingers tightened on the man's jugular.

She struggled away from the table and grabbed Rhyel's arm. She couldn't budge him. "Rhyel, stop! Let him go."

"Give me a good reason why I should," he snarled looking down at her, his eyes the color of molten gold.

"He didn't hurt me."

"Don't lie for him, woman. I heard you scream. I saw him strike you."

"But that's all he did. Hitting me isn't enough reason to kill him, and you will kill him if you don't let him go now." She pulled at his arm again, realized the futility of that, and stepped back. "Please."

Rhyel shoved Tzorik toward the door. "Leave now, before I forget the plea in her voice and kill you."

Tzorik stumbled out of Rhyel's reach. "The woman is mine now," he managed to rasp out before a cough stopped him. He stepped closer to the crowd gathering at the clinic entrance. "You have no right to interfere."

"She is mine to protect until you rend the veil," Rhyel warned. "It is best for you to remember that."

Tzorik moved through the opening. "Tomorrow will see it done," he promised in a gravelly whisper. He turned to Amber. "Be prepared to yield what is mine." He pushed through the crowd and a second later the clinic door slammed. Someone urged the crowd out and closed the door to her room, giving them privacy.

She wrapped her arms over her breasts and stared at the closed door. She felt violated, vulnerable.

"He will never touch me again," she vowed. "Never."

A warm blanket fell across her shoulders and she jumped.

"It's all right," Rhyel murmured. He pulled the blanket together under her chin and she grasped the edges to pull it closer.

He carefully lifted her face and brushed back her hair to inspect the damage. She hoped it didn't look as bad as it felt. But the renewed fury in Rhyel's eyes told her it did. He abruptly turned for the door.

"Wait."

He stopped and looked back at her.

"Please don't leave me." She watched the battle in his eyes, his need to avenge her conflicting with his need to stay and comfort her. "Please stay." She began to shake uncontrollably.

He reversed direction, scooped her into his arms, and strode to the overstuffed chair. He sank into the cushion, wrapped his arms around her, and held her close to his warm body. He didn't speak. It was then she realized he was shaking as much as she was. She nestled closer, as if her life depended on their connection. He adjusted the blanket and rested his cheek against the top of her head. It took a long time for the emotional storm to pass.

"Is it true?" she finally asked. "Are Tzorik and I married already?"

His arms tightened at the mention of Tzorik's name. "You are betrothed and nothing more. But the bonding is scheduled for tomorrow morning." His words sounded like they'd soured on his tongue.

She snuggled into the security of his embrace. "They can't force me to cooperate. I won't promise myself to him."

"Tzorik is the only person required to speak the vow of bonding. Your presence is all that is required."

"That's barbaric."

"On Centallus a woman's willingness was never in question. During the ceremony one voice spoke for them both. Unfortunately, tomorrow that voice will be Tzorik's."

"I won't be there to hear him."

"You will not be given that choice."

She looked back up at him. "Then I'll be dragged to the ceremony kicking and screaming?"

"Hopefully you will have more dignity."

"*Dignity?* You've got to be kidding me. You're giving me to that monster and you want me to be *dignified?*"

"I'm not giving you to him." He sounded insulted. "Tzorik uses the same ancient law of first choice I used to stop him before. Since I am no longer eligible to bond with you, he demands the right by second choice. The Elders are bound by honor to allow the bonding."

He sat her up and looked into her eyes. "I'm not concerned with your dignity. I want you to be safe and you won't be if you resist them. I know Tzorik will set guards at your door tonight. And he will make sure you arrive for the ceremony. Don't fight the men Tzorik sends to escort you to the bonding. They will not care how they get you to the hall, only that they get you there. Tzorik will enjoy forcing you to his will. Do not enhance his pleasure by waging a battle you cannot win."

He stood, and settled her in the chair he'd just vacated. The sudden loss of his body's heat made her shiver.

She watched him walk to the window, push the drapes back, and stare out through the tinted glass. He stood unmoving for a very long time and she wondered what was going through his mind. When he finally turned and walked to her, she sensed a new determination in him. He'd settled something in his mind.

He knelt in front of her. Taking her hands in both of his, he said, "I cannot prevent your bonding, *Rishka*. It is one of the reasons you are here." When she started to argue he shook his head. "Nothing you say to me will change what must happen to ensure the survival of our species. But Tzorik is not the only eligible Guardian on New Centallus. I cannot protect you as your bond-mate, but believe me when I promise Tzorik will not have you.

"I will post my own guards at your door, and the clinic's as well. Tzorik will not bother you tonight. I'm sure Hiilani is waiting in the clinic. She also heard your scream." He reached up and touched her lip where the skin was broken. She winced and he pulled his hand back. "I'll send her in to look at that. She will stay with you until morning." When she shook her head, he sighed his exasperation. "No argument. I don't want you alone tonight."

He pulled the blanket closer under her chin. "I'm sorry, *Rishka*. I should never have allowed Tzorik the opportunity to abuse you. But I will not fail in keeping my promise to prevent your bonding with Tzorik. Do not put yourself in harm's way tomorrow. Trust me."

Hiilani didn't wait for an invitation. As soon as Rhyel closed the door behind him, she came into the room, carrying a tray of supplies including a bottle of alcohol and an ice pack. Amber still sat cocooned in the blanket. She looked up at her friend.

The nurse gasped. "Your poor face." She leaned down to examine the bruises Amber assumed were there. Hiilani set the tray on the stand and grabbed the ice pack. "Here, hold this on your lip. It's pretty swollen."

Amber complied, and the nurse tore open a gauze pad.

"I wish we had something that didn't sting," she said as she dampened it with the alcohol. "Tzorik did that didn't he?" Hiilani shook her head. "You don't need to answer that. Of course he did."

Amber set the pack aside and reached for the pad. "Thanks." She touched the gauze to the corner of her mouth and winced. "I need a shower—and to brush my teeth. He...." She didn't want to think about what he'd done, what he'd tried to do.

Hiilani nodded. "We need to check you out first. Your face is pretty swollen. Does it feel like anything's broken?"

She shook her head.

"Any other damage?"

She set the gauze aside, picked up the ice pack, and carefully pressed it against her bruised cheek. "I have some scratches on my thigh. They're not deep. I'll disinfect them after my shower. I feel like I need a tetanus shot, or maybe one for rabies. The man's mad enough to be infected."

Hiilani stared wide-eyed at her. "He didn't…."

"Rape me? No. Rhyel stopped him before he got that far."

"Do you need to talk?"

"About how vulnerable I feel, how violated?" She laughed. "I'm too angry to talk." She jumped up from the chair, tossing the blanket on the bed, and headed toward the bathroom. "Bring me the strongest soap you have in the clinic. I'm going to wash the smell and the feel of that degenerate from my body."

She began peeling her clothes off before she reached the bathroom, not caring that the nurse was there.

"Burn these." She kicked the skirt and underwear out of her way. "*He* touched them. They'll never be clean again. I don't want them tainting my skin."

Hiilani nodded, grabbed up the clothes, and disappeared into the clinic. Moments later she returned with a bottle of antibacterial soap.

Amber stepped into the walk-in tub and slid the frosted glass door closed, shutting out the world. She adjusted the shower temperature to as hot as she could stand and let the steaming spray cascade over her shoulders and back. She scrubbed every inch of her body, rinsed, and scrubbed it again until her skin felt sunburned. She reduced the force and temperature of the spray, and allowed the tepid water to gently cool her overheated body.

The tears started then.

She hated being helpless. Tzorik had been too strong. She hadn't been able to stop his attack. She hadn't been able to stop Rhyel either, when he took her from her home. Tomorrow the Elders intended to give her to her attacker. She'd die before she let him touch her again.

Even if Rhyel managed to stop Tzorik, another Guardian would claim her. He wouldn't touch her either. She didn't know how she'd stop either of them, but she would. She was tired of being a victim.

She raised her head and let the water wash the tears from her cheeks. She had to do something. She couldn't let their plans cascade until she was so caught up in their lives she would never be free.

She stepped out of the shower, dried off, and put on one of the folded cotton nightgowns from the closet shelf. She returned to the bedroom and saw that Hiilani had turned down the covers on the bed. The nurse wasn't there. She climbed into bed and pulled the blanket to her chin.

Rhyel entered Amber's room in the middle of the night. Hiilani slept in the large chair beside the bed. He silently walked to her and placed a gentle hand on her arm. The nurse started, but didn't make a sound. He bent his head close to hers.

"Go find your bed," he whispered. "I'll stay with her."

Hiilani nodded. After a quick look at Amber, she vacated the chair, then the room.

He took the seat and leaned forward, resting his elbows on his thighs. He hadn't been able to sleep. He'd spent most of the night weighing his options for tomorrow. He concluded that there was only one choice available to him. He had to speak to Cintar in the morning. Even if his plan was successful, the final outcome would be decided by the Elders. And if they decided against him? He leaned back against the chair and sighed. He'd find another way.

17

✦

Hiilani knocked twice and peeked around the door. "Good morning," she said cheerfully.

Amber turned over in bed and looked at the nurse. "Good morning? What time is it?"

"Still early," Hiilani said, walking into the room. "I thought you might want to eat in here this morning." She set a tray of food on the table and hung the material she carried across the back of the large chair.

Amber ran her fingers through her hair to get it out of her eyes.

The nurse eyed the side of her face. "Your cheek's still puffy. Rhyel didn't exaggerate when he confronted the Elders this morning."

"Rhyel spoke to the Elders?"

"He demanded Tzorik's right to claim you be revoked."

"What did they say?"

Hiilani looked away. "The Elders are bound by the law. On Centallus the bonding ceremony was no more than a formality. Although the couples were expected to wait until the veil was rent, they were not chastised for prior intimacies.

"Valdon refuses to believe Tzorik would force himself on his future bond-mate. Our Chief Elder is a wise man, and fair, but when it comes to his only son, he's blind to the obvious. He reminded the council that a Centallian first mating can be heated, almost out of control. He used the scratches on Tzorik's face as an example of what can happen when passions are high." She gave Amber a pitying look. "He will explain away the bruises on your face with the same excuse."

"You and I both know that isn't true."

The nurse nodded. "I didn't witness what occurred last night, but when it comes to Tzorik having his own way, especially if he's besting Rhyel, he could be capable of rape."

Loud voices and scraping sounds filtered in from the great hall. "What's going on out there?"

"It's a madhouse. They're moving the tables. I'm surprised it didn't wake you."

"Why are they moving the tables around?"

Hiilani paused a moment before explaining, "The hall is used for all of our ceremonies. Your bonding is still scheduled for this morning. That's also why I'm here. I brought your dress." She picked up the white material she'd draped over the chair and held up the Roman-style garment. "You are to wear this for the bonding. It's lovely, isn't it?" The nurse's voice lacked enthusiasm.

Amber barely glanced at the shimmering material. "Yes, it is. I won't wear it."

A hint of alarm shadowed Hiilani's features and she thrust the dress toward Amber. "Touch it. The fabric is so fluid it almost feels wet."

"Take it away. I'm not playing their games. They may force me to go through that farce of a ritual, but they can't force me to act like the obedient 'little woman.' What he did was criminal and I won't let him get away with it." She got up and walked to her closet. "I'll wear what I normally do."

The closet was empty. Amber swung around. "Where are my clothes?"

Hiilani shrugged, wary of Amber's tone. "I imagine Tzorik had one of the women move them to his quarters while you were sleeping."

"He had no right. I want them back. Now!"

"Tzorik is the only one who can give them back to you and we both know he won't." Hiilani's voice softened. "Be reasonable, Amber. They're only clothes and you need to be careful. It could be dangerous to defy Tzorik. You know that already."

Amber stood and slid her damp palms down the sides of her cotton nightgown. "I won't let him bully me. If I go meekly to that ceremony the Elders will believe Valdon was right. In their minds it will justify everything they've done."

"Tzorik isn't concerned with justification," Hiilani argued. "You are a prize he has taken from Rhyel, a weapon in his power struggle against his commander. He won't allow anything or anyone to prevent this bonding."

Hiilani spread the gown across the bed and moved to the door. "I could try to bring you something of mine, but the guards will never let me in with it. Don't make an issue of the dress. Save your strength for a bigger battle." The young woman opened the door.

"Hiilani, wait." Her friend paused and looked back. "I need to know what to expect at the ceremony."

If there was any part of the proceedings she could use to stop the bonding, she wanted to know about it ahead of time. Hiilani closed the door and Amber patted the bed beside her.

When her friend sat down, Amber said, "Please tell me what you know."

"The Centallians are a peaceful people," Hiilani began, "but their ceremonies are steeped in ancient traditions born of a violent past. You will await Tzorik on the dais. He will come to you as a warrior, complete with battle mask, shield, and long-knife. Two Guardians will extend a translucent wisp of cloth, like a veil between you.

"Tzorik will give his vows. Aadrok will instruct him to rend the veil. Tzorik will use his long-knife to slice the material that separates you. Rending the veil is symbolic of the physical consummation of bonding. The bonding isn't complete until that moment. That single act binds the couple irrevocably. There are no divorces or annulments."

"Basically I'm supposed to stand meekly by and let it happen?"

"Yes."

"The Centallians talk about honor but they don't have much."

Hiilani shook her head. "You're wrong, Amber. They give up much for the sake of honor."

"In what way?"

"You will bond with one man for life, and you will be his only mate. Have you considered how much faster they could reach their goals if each man mated with several women? If the Centallians were less honorable, you might have found yourself in a harem, or worse, you might have, over time, been forced to bear the children of several Guardians, in order to enlarge the gene pool.

"With their technology, the Centallians could bring as many women from Earth as they want, but the Centallians are monogamous. They believe in strong family ties. Each Guardian will bond and remain with one mate."

"Why are you defending them?"

"I'm not defending them, but I do empathize with their plight, and respect their tenacity. They're fighting for the survival of their species."

Hiilani's thick, dark lashes lowered to hide her eyes, but Amber still saw the truth they held. Despite their own burgeoning friendship, Hiilani's loyalty belonged to the Centallians. "I don't agree with what has happened to you. I don't think many here do, but no one will help you.

"The Elders must abide by existing laws. Any exception would weaken their position as a governing body. Ignoring any law invites eventual anarchy, and threatens to destroy any chances for survival.

"The right of first choice is an old law. I hadn't heard of it until Rhyel used it. It would have worked to your advantage too, if your genetic scan had matched his. Unfortunately, the same law now gives Tzorik the advantage over anyone else who might claim you." Hiilani stood and walked to the door. "I wish you happiness, Amber." She didn't look hopeful that her wish would be fulfilled.

After a few minutes of debate, she finally heeded Hiilani's advice and put on the gown. Her right shoulder was bare, the other covered by a wide, pleated sash that slanted up from the bodice and draped over her back. The fabric did feel liquid as Hiilani had suggested, flowing like water over her body, clinging seductively to her every curve. She reluctantly agreed with Hiilani. The gown was lovely. *Too* lovely.

Where was Rhyel? She'd expected him to be here before now, and tell her he'd put an end to this insanity. He'd promised to protect her from Tzorik.

She moved to the window and drew back the drapes. Dark clouds roiled in the distance. Did New Centallus have storms like Earth? She supposed it did. The atmosphere had to be similar to home—she was breathing the air after all. The coming storm seemed appropriate to the moment. Thunder and lightning fit her mood.

She walked back to the bed and sat down. Had Rhyel believed he could talk the Elders into denying Tzorik's claim? Had that been his plan? Did he have another plan in mind or had he given up? Was that why he hadn't shown up yet?

She couldn't fight Tzorik's men. As Hiilani had pointed out, she needed to conserve her strength for the confrontation to come. Tzorik might win this battle and force the bonding, but he'd soon discover the war was yet to be decided.

She caught her lower lip between her teeth. The boast sounded good, courageous even. But Tzorik had overpowered her last night, had proven that she didn't stand a chance against his strength. He would overpower her again if the bonding was completed, with the blessing of the council.

She couldn't wait for Rhyel to rescue her. There had to be a way to stop the monster. Whatever happened, she didn't intend to make anything easy for him.

18

✧

Tzorik's men didn't knock when they came for her. They simply walked into the room uninvited.

"Tzorik awaits you," the shorter of the two announced. "You will accompany us now."

The burly Guardians took their places on either side of her, each grasping an arm. She felt like a prisoner being led to execution.

The Guardians led her to a large, double-tiered dais set up at the front of the hall, opposite the huge entry doors. The structure reminded her of a small stage. The upper tier looked about five feet wide and six feet long. The lower level extended another six or so feet, circling the higher structure.

Five Elders stood in a convex half-circle on the highest level. Aadrok, dressed in a white robe, stood in the center. Their demeanor was solemn as they watched her approach.

There was no ceremony to her entrance. Her guards came close to dragging her. The shorter Guardian propelled her onto the wide lower tier and remained beside her, hand clamped on her arm. The taller man stepped away from the dais, but stayed within easy reach.

Aadrok frowned down in disapproval at the Guardian who held her. Her arm was immediately released and Tzorik's man joined his friend off-podium.

Zitan and Kroyda had positioned themselves to the left of Tzarn and Zsaor to his right. The Chief Elder was absent.

So was Rhyel.

Had she missed him? She looked around. The tables and benches had been pushed to the walls. The colonists stood on either side of a wide, teal-blue carpet runner that extended from the entry doors to the dais. She scanned the crowd. She even looked for Cintar, since the two men might be together. Both seemed to be missing.

Irritation mixed with apprehension. She had come quietly to this ceremony—as meek as the proverbial lamb—because Rhyel had asked her to trust him. How could he leave her to face this mockery alone? It was his fault she was here.

Her throat tightened, her lungs strained to draw air through the constricted passageway. Rhyel had practically delivered her into Tzorik's waiting arms.

Drums drew her attention to the entry doors, a heavy, booming pulse.

"It begins," Aadrok proclaimed, and the assembly turned as the large doors swung open. Thunder rumbled in the distance. An omen?

Her heart beat a path to her throat and lodged there.

What was she going to do?

Two swordsmen dressed in leather body armor over knee-length linen tunics marched forward in slow cadence to the rhythm of the drum. Each held a long, fearsome-looking broadsword in salute position.

Valdon followed, resplendent in silver and black robes. In his outstretched hands he carried a tiny, black-enameled chest adorned with what appeared to be rubies and opals.

Tzorik entered behind his father. As Hiilani had described, he was dressed for battle. Silver arm and shin guards gleamed in the light. His matching breastplate was embellished with the image of a great horned beast. The shield strapped to his left arm bore the same engraved effigy. A helmet-mask rested under his arm, as grotesque as the gargoyles that decorated old castle ramparts. A lethal curved long-knife hung from a braided leather belt at his waist.

He looked powerful, and dangerous, and victorious as he ascended the first tier of the dais and faced her. There was triumph in his eyes as he appraised her with possessive satisfaction. How could she hope to fight him by herself?

Aadrok stepped down between them and off the platform to face the assembled colonists. The swordsmen knelt before him. One man presented a folded cloth in both hands for the priest's inspection. Aadrok placed a hand on the cloth, closed his eyes, and raised his other arm in what looked like a silent blessing.

"The Guardian, Tzorik, has claimed the woman, Amber, to mate," Aadrok decreed in a voice gauged to encompass the hall. "Does the council acknowledge his right?"

"He has the right," the Elders replied in unison.

The priest stepped aside and waited as the Guardians moved onto the lower dais between Amber and Tzorik. Each man grasped a corner of the filmy cloth and stretched it between them, creating a gossamer barrier separating Tzoric and Amber. The broadswords were held at salute arching above the veil. Valdon approached, placed the black chest at Amber's feet, and joined the Elders on the upper level.

Aadrok turned his back to the crowd to address Tzorik. "Your claim has been acknowledged, Guardian. Do you accept the responsibilities of this bonding?"

Tzorik bowed to the Elders. "By my honor I accept all obligations."

"Will you acknowledge the issue of this bonding? Will you provide for, and protect your mate and the children she gives you?"

"By my honor I will."

"Then Tzorik, son of Valdon, rend the veil and gift your chosen mate with the seed of life. Let all present witness the rending of the veil."

Tzorik lifted the long-knife from his belt and raised it above his head to bring it down across the veil.

Thunder vibrated the room, and the entry doors crashed against the inner walls. *"Hold!"*

"No!" Amber cried in the same moment and lunged forward, throwing her arms around the cloth, pulling it from the Guardians' hands. She fell to her knees and hunched forward, clutching the veil protectively against her body.

The clash of metal above her head almost stopped Amber's heart. She looked up. The swordsmen's blades were at cross-point, blocking Tzorik's long-knife.

"Is the veil rent?" a muffled voice shouted.

Amber turned her head and saw two men in the entryway. Like giants, they stood ready for battle, long-knives and shields in hand. Each wore a battle mask, his identity hidden by an effigy as grotesque as the image on Tzorik's mask.

Speculation coursed through the crowd, and the name Cintar was repeated more than once.

The council stood, stunned by the interruption. Aadrok was the first to regain his composure. He looked down at Amber, then raised his eyes to the intruder.

"The veil is intact."

Amber looked at Tzorik. Rage contorted his features as he lowered his knife and watched the two men stride down the center of the hall toward them.

What's going on? Amber hugged the veil to her waist, afraid to give it up while Tzorik still held his knife. In her mind it was all that prevented him from achieving his possession of her. She glanced around.

Everyone looked confused.

"Why do you interrupt these proceedings?" Aadrok demanded when the two men reached the podium.

"To claim the healer," came the muffled reply, "by right of combat."

"The right of combat has not been invoked for a thousand circles of time," Tzorik shouted. "The ceremony is finished." He jerked Amber up from the floor. "The woman is mine." He dragged her with him as he raised his long-knife and charged off the platform. "Who are you?"

The man didn't retreat. Instead, he stepped forward, a growl emanating from behind the mask. "Release her."

Tzorik immediately dropped her arm and slipped his shield down into battle position, grasping the front strap.

"Answer my challenge," the stranger demanded, "or you will relinquish your claim to her."

Tzorik shoved her out of his way and slashed out with his long-knife. The challenger's shield slid under Tzorik's blade as he deflected the unexpected blow. The knife's point clipped his shoulder as he charged forward, turned, and slammed his body into Tzorik's.

Tzorik staggered back but stayed on his feet. He lunged toward the masked Guardian, but the challenger's shield caught his knife square and the man swung his own blade. Tzorik danced out of harm's way.

Shaken, Amber stood between the podium and the battling men. She couldn't take her eyes from the combatants long enough to seek safety. The two warriors were well matched in strength and skill. Neither gave ground as they slashed and thrust, each trying to get past their opponent's shield.

"The healer!" cried a voice in the crowd, and the stranger spared Amber a glance, barely deflecting Tzorik's next thrust. With a roar, he suddenly slammed his shield into Tzorik's, forcing him to back away from the dais.

"Protect the healer!" He held his ground, keeping his body between her and the swinging blades.

Zitan grabbed her arm and pulled her onto the dais and up to the highest level. The Elders closed ranks around her. The second masked Guardian stepped onto the first tier to stand in front of her and the Elders, his shield raised. The two armored Guardians joined him to provide protection for the Elders.

She pushed aside an arm that blocked her view and saw the crowd part as a volley of blows from the challenger forced Tzorik to retreat. "What's happening?"

"You have another suitor." Zitan was forced to raise his voice to be heard over the clang of steel. "One who is willing to risk his life to have you." The Elder never took his eyes from the combatants. The big men moved with startling speed, each knife promising death as it sliced the air. The challenger's wound didn't appear to hamper him.

"Who is he?"

"We will discover that at the end of the battle."

She watched, horrified, as the men tried to kill each other. "Make them stop." She gripped a fistful of Zitan's robe. "*Please* make them stop."

"We cannot, child." Zitan took her hand and patted it. "The challenger has claimed the right of battle. It is an ancient law, but it is valid. If Tzorik intends to keep you he must defeat the stranger."

How long had they been fighting? Five minutes? Ten? Strain intensified the harsh angles of Tzorik's face. He was exhausted. The challenger's mask gave nothing away, but he had to be as tired as Tzorik, probably more so. Blood continued to seep from his shoulder, trickling down his arm, dripping onto the floor.

They slowly circled, stalking one another in a macabre waltz of death, knives pointed to the floor, each seeking the opening that would allow his knife to taste the flesh of his opponent. She willed the challenger—her champion—to victory. The irony of the situation was not lost on her. In this instance it was definitely not better to go with the enemy she knew.

Rushing Tzorik, the stranger sidestepped and dropped to one knee, raising his shield above his head to block Tzorik's knife. With a grunt of satisfaction, he slipped his blade deep into Tzorik's thigh.

The stranger regained his feet in one fluid motion and pivoted, catching his heel behind Tzorik's ankle as he slammed his shield into Tzorik's knife hand, crunching bone, sending him howling to the floor.

The challenger's bloodstained knife hovered above Tzorik's throat. "Yield the healer to me."

Tzorik's pale lips thinned and he shook his head in defiance. But when the tip of the blade pricked the skin near his jugular, Tzorik called out. "I yield."

"Noted," Aadrok announced.

The victor stepped back to allow Tzorik's men to lift him to his feet. He groaned and supported his wrist with his good hand as they assisted him to one of the benches.

Amber stepped off the high platform with Zitan, who still clutched her hand. Four Elders followed. Valdon left the podium and hurried to his son. The Guardians stepped aside as the victor moved to face the Elders.

"Is my claim acknowledged?" His labored breathing made the question sound harsh, angry.

Aadrok answered. "Both the council and the law recognize your claim," he said. "Identify yourself."

Her champion bent forward and removed his helmet-mask.

19

✧

"Rhyel!"

He watched the shock in Amber's eyes turn to confusion. She hugged the veil to her chest, stared down at the long-knife he held, and moved closer to his father. Rhyel looked at his knife. Tzorik's blood streaked the blade. He stepped back and concealed the weapon behind his shield.

He ignored the rising murmur of the crowd. His attention was centered on Amber. The wariness in her eyes, though understandable, irritated him. He'd placed his life in jeopardy to prevent her bonding with Tzorik. She should be thanking him, not behaving as if he'd murdered someone.

Still, he wanted to comfort her. "Amber, I—"

"The challenge is invalid." Tzorik limped toward the podium with the aid of his friends. "The woman is mine. I demand the right to rend the veil and complete the bonding."

Rhyel swung around. "Your right has been overturned by defeat."

Aadrok left the dais and moved between the two men. He turned to face Rhyel. "You challenged Tzorik knowing you cannot have our healer to mate. Why have you compromised your honor?"

"Amber is mine to protect until her bonding is complete and the veil rent. I will not allow Tzorik the opportunity to further abuse her."

"You slur my honor," Tzorik snarled.

Rhyel's eyes narrowed on the man. "Do you challenge me now?"

Tzorik backed off. "You know I can't defend myself. I cannot hold a knife."

"Guardians," Aadrok interrupted, "I will not tolerate your dissension. Rhyel, we've established that you cannot have Amber to mate. What gain you by claiming her?"

"I did not challenge Tzorik to claim the healer for myself." Rhyel caught and held Amber's gaze. "I fought to give our healer the right of choice." Amber's eyes widened and he was gratified to see a glimmer of hope in those beautiful green orbs.

"He cannot do that!" Tzorik roared, his eyes gold with rage. "There is no precedent for it."

The priest shook his head. "This is most unusual. Tzorik is right. No one has ever challenged for the sake of choice."

"Is there a precedent for what we ask of our healer?" Rhyel countered. "For what we did? We took her from her home, by force, and decided she was to have a mate—one not of her choosing. On Centallus, no woman was forced to bond with a man she did not want. It is only reasonable that our healer be given the opportunity to choose the man who will father her children."

Aadrok looked to the Elders before returning his attention to Rhyel. "Your argument is compelling, but the council must confer before making a decision. Our healer risked her life to prevent the rending of the veil and stop the bonding. The council will consider that as well." He looked from one man to the other. "You will await us." He joined the others as they left the podium to file into the council chamber.

Cintar had unmasked when his captain had, and was standing at the side of the dais. Zitan led Amber to the big man before joining the Elders in the chamber. Cintar gently pried the veil from her hands.

"You won't need to protect this now," he said, handing the cloth to a nearby

Guardian. "It will be burned." He placed a protective arm across her shoulders and guided her to where Rhyel stood alone.

"You should have trusted me with your secret," Cintar chided when they reached his captain's side. "I wouldn't have tried to prevent you from challenging Tzorik if I had known your true motive. We were almost too late to prevent the rending."

"You should have trusted my honor," Rhyel returned, his eyes on Amber.

Cintar nodded agreement. "Yes, I should have."

Rhyel dislodged Cintar's arm from Amber's shoulder. He had no right to feel possessive, but he did. She was his until she chose another to mate. He took her hand.

"Perhaps you should sit down," he said, leading her to a bench across the room from Tzorik. "You're trembling."

She didn't argue. The incessant clang of deadly steel still rang in her head. She took the seat he offered and tried to control her ragged breathing.

"You could have been killed," she accused, suddenly angry that he had put himself in such danger. "There's blood all over your shirt. I need to look at your wound."

Rhyel glanced at his shoulder. "The bleeding has stopped."

Cintar nodded toward Tzorik. "Your opponent seems more in need of our healer's ministrations." The man glowered at them while his friends tended the knife wound and wrist. A temporary measure until he could enter stasis.

Rhyel shook his head. "Amber isn't going near him."

She started to argue, and realized she didn't want to be any closer to Tzorik than she was now. Still, she was the only doctor here. "I think I should—"

"—stay right where you are," he finished for her.

"The Elders are returning," Cintar warned.

The room grew silent as Valdon stepped forward to speak for the council. He glanced at his son, concern evident in his features. Tzorik stood expectantly, but his father shook his head before turning to address the colonists.

"The council believes Rhyel has acted honorably," he declared. "Thus, our healer will be given the right to select her bond-mate." He looked at her and his voice softened. "Our unbound Guardians will make themselves known to you, Healer. We will allow you time to make your choice."

She stood. She hadn't really expected any better option and was grateful for this much. But it wasn't enough. She didn't want a mate, or children—not here, on this world. But she needed a protector, and the idea that suddenly came to her made her tremble all the more. Rhyel reached out to steady her.

"I would like to ask a question."

"Of course," Valdon said.

"I believe you are honorable men and would not knowingly deceive me. But I need to be completely clear on what you've decided. Have you agreed that I will not be forced to marry someone not of my choosing?"

Valdon nodded. "We have."

"Will the council promise by their honor that I can marry any unbound man that I name, that no additional restrictions be placed on my choice—and that the man I choose cannot refuse me for any reason?"

Valdon turned and received nods from the other council members before returning his attention to her. "The council agrees. You may choose any Guardian. The only restriction is that he must not be bound or promised to another. We will not deny your choice."

"By your honor?" she pressed.

Valdon sighed. "Yes, child, by our honor. As I have said, you will be given time to select a Guardian."

"That won't be necessary," she said quietly. "I choose Rhyel."

The collective gasp was followed by a cacophony of speculation. The Elders were the only ones who seemed speechless.

Rhyel pulled her around to face him. His dark eyes were flecked with gold. "You know we must not bond."

She raised her chin. "The Elders promised."

"I am not eligible."

"Valdon didn't say you had to be eligible, only without a mate."

Rhyel's fingers tightened on her shoulders and he pulled her aside. "Do not dishonor what I fought to give you."

She looked away, and struggled against a sense of guilt. But she couldn't weaken now, not when the next few minutes might mean eventual freedom.

"Don't you understand?" she whispered. "My life and my body are mine. You can sugarcoat the truth with honor and ceremony, but it doesn't change a thing. Any other man I choose would have one goal, to give me children." She shrugged away from his hands. "I'm not stupid. I know the dangers of allowing that to happen. A child will not only bind me to his father, but to his father's world and his people. I don't want those ties. I want to go home."

"New Centallus is your home," he said. "Her people are your people. Some day you will accept that truth. Then you will want the ties. Choose another."

"No." She turned to the Elders. "Will you take back your promise?"

"We did not believe you would choose a mate who is incompatible or we would have qualified our promise to you," Valdon said.

"But you didn't qualify your promise to me. 'Any unbound Guardian... by your honor.' That's what you promised."

"Child," Zitan said, "consider the consequences."

"I already have. I won't change my mind."

The six Elders moved to the back of the podium and stood in a huddle. Their whispered conversation was punctuated with head shakes, arm swings, and heavy sighs. When they returned, Valdon looked grim.

"You have manipulated us shamefully, child. We will not deny you," he said quietly, "yet we ask you to reconsider."

"Think of your future," Zitan added, a note of pleading in his expression as well as his voice. "Eventually, you will consider New Centallus your home. You will yearn for the fulfillment and joy of children. My son cares for you. Doubtless, he will grow to love you. But he can never allow himself to consummate that love. You will never have fulfillment, never share a child."

She was counting on that.

Rhyel stared at her for a long moment. He was willing her to change her mind. Suppressing the guilt and indecision he made her feel, she shook her head.

"As you wish," Rhyel said, his voice resigned. "We will bond this evening. Pray your stubbornness does not give us an empty life." He turned and walked away.

"You will regret this," Tzorik shouted. Valdon had gone to him, but Tzorik turned his back on his father and limped away.

She was already regretting her actions, but she couldn't back down from her decision to choose Rhyel. There was simply no alternative.

Zitan turned her attention when he gently took her arm to guide her back to her room. "Regardless of the circumstances, I wish to welcome you into our family. Some months ago, I asked Anna, Tinar's bride, to fashion a bonding gown in anticipation of Rhyel's choosing a mate. Anna is a talented seamstress. The garment is reminiscent of Rhyel's mother's bonding gown. You would honor her if you wore it this evening."

She nodded, touched by his overture.

"I'm sure Anna can make any needed adjustments. I will send her to you with the dress and return for you one hour after the evening meal."

She smiled wryly. "Surely you aren't sending guards to assure my presence at the ceremony?"

He didn't return her smile. "The choice was yours, child. It is assumed you are willing." He opened the door to her room and waited for her to walk inside. "Until this evening," he said, closing the door.

The room was blissfully quiet. She sank into the large chair and closed her eyes. She'd complicated a number of lives today, but she refused to feel guilty. She'd taken the only steps available to protect herself.

She felt compassion for the Centallian's cause. But there were people at home who needed her too. She had to get back to her grandfather. When she found a way home, she didn't want ties—no mate she'd been intimate with, no child to take from its father. She refused to consider leaving a child of her own behind. Her choice of bond-mate ensured she wouldn't face that possibility. Once she was gone, the Elders would realize she would never settle in to their plan. They would find another doctor, and annul Rhyel's commitment to her, freeing him to choose another. It was the perfect solution.

Wasn't it?

20

✧

The dress Zitan sent was gold, and as fluid in sight and texture as the dress she'd worn that morning. Anna had arrived a few minutes after the dinner hour with the dress over her arm and her hands clutching spools of thread with needles attached. She introduced herself and asked Amber to put on the gown so she could alter it.

The tall, dark-haired, dark-eyed woman concentrated on her work, giving the occasional order to turn or raise an arm. "I think we are finished," she said, knotting the last stitch and severing the thread with her teeth. Stepping back, she inspected her work and smiled. "The dress is beautiful on you, Healer." She picked up the spools and slipped the needles under the thread as she walked to the door. Looking back, she smiled again. "The women of our colony are relieved that you have joined us. I wish you well."

Amber nodded, but couldn't meet her eyes.

She didn't exactly dread the summons to the hall. The ceremony would be similar to the first, but her emotions were far from the same. The fear was gone, the threat of rape no longer part of the equation. But her heart refused to calm its pounding and she couldn't seem to settle in one place for more than a moment.

Rhyel had saved her from Tzorik and she'd repaid him by stealing his future.

She had betrayed him and he was furious with her. She'd seen it in his eyes, heard it in his low voice.

He had a right to be angry.

Someday, and she prayed it would be soon, his life would return to the path he'd set. She didn't intend to stay on New Centallus any longer than it took to find a way back to Earth. When she was home again, for all purposes dead to her life here and to him, he could have the future he wanted with a mate who could give him the love and children he deserved.

She suppressed the unexpected sense of loss that image engendered. She refused to regret what she'd done—what she'd had to do. There was no future for her here. Not even with Rhyel. Especially not with Rhyel.

Cintar arrived, and led her to the podium. He smiled and patted her hand before moving to the side of the dais. She stood alone on the lower tier of the raised platform. Aadrok and four Elders stood above her, on the top tier of the podium. She turned to face the entry.

Drums heralded the beginning of the ceremony and, as before, two Guardians entered, their swords held high in salute. Zitan followed, a jewel-crusted, red-and-gold-enameled chest held in both palms. His steps were slow and dignified.

Amber drew in a long breath when Rhyel strode into the hall. He held the battle mask under one arm, and carried the shield, scarred from his battle with Tzorik.

She took in every detail, the way his long black hair caught the light from the chandelier, the play of muscle in his arms and thighs as he moved, the strength of his well-honed body. The man was magnificent, powerful, and a little frightening. He mounted the dais and faced her.

He wasn't smiling.

She tore her eyes from him when Aadrok stepped down between them to bless the veil, and moved aside while the Guardians positioned the wisp of translucent cloth between them. Zitan placed the chest on the floor at her feet, and ascended the podium to stand with the Elders.

Rhyel spoke his vow in a strong, somber voice. He promised to cherish and protect her, but when the priest spoke of children, he shook his head. "I will not promise what I dare not fulfill."

The priest nodded his acceptance of Rhyel's vows. "Then Rhyel, son of Zitan, rend the veil and gift your bond-mate."

Rhyel stepped back, and raised his long-knife above the veil. Capturing Amber's gaze, he whispered, "This is forever." His knife sliced downward. The gossamer material parted and the two halves fluttered to the platform. He bent to retrieve the chest.

She didn't move when he offered her the small box. She knew the symbolism of the seed within, and felt it was almost blasphemous to open it.

Rhyel took her hand and turned it palm up to receive his gift. "Open the lid."

She touched the clasp, lifted the lid, and cried out. Her gold locket lay on the deep blue velvet pillow within. Stunned, she lifted her eyes to his in question.

He leaned forward. "I saw the locket on the stand beside your bed the night I came for you. I thought you would want it."

He took the necklace from its resting place and, with great care, fastened the chain around her neck, centering the locket below the pulse point at her throat.

"The Seed of Life should have rested inside the chest," he said, his voice rough, "my promise to give you children. You should have chosen a Guardian who has the right to fulfill that promise. You will want children eventually." He traced the etching on the locket with one finger. "I cannot give you the future. But I can return to you this remembrance of the past. It is my hope that you will be comforted by the images within. I would cherish such an image of those who are lost to me."

The pain in his voice made her vision blur, and she blinked back tears. He had lost so much. If she didn't make it home, her actions would condemn him to a life of celibacy—deny him his heirs, his family's immortality.

She touched the locket to remind herself of what he had taken from her. She shouldn't feel regret for what she had done. But she did.

He suddenly scooped her into his arms, accompanied by the cheers of the crowd.

She grabbed his neck. "What are you doing?"

"Observing tradition," he answered, stepping from the dais. "On my world newly bonded mates sought the seclusion of their chamber once the ceremony was completed. The first hours of bonding are considered sacred, to be shared by the bonded couple alone." He climbed the staircase opposite the clinic with careless speed.

She tightening her hold on his neck. "But this isn't a traditional bonding."

He stopped in front of a door. "Do you believe we are not truly bonded?"

"We aren't really. You know that."

He managed to open the door with her in his arms, and carried her inside, nudging it closed behind them. He lowered her feet to the floor, but didn't let her go.

"Do not mistake our situation. We are mates for life, bound in every sense but one. We will share our meals, our time, our joys, our sorrows—and our bed."

"I can't sleep with you."

"We will share a bed as any bonded couple does. I intend to experience every intimacy allowed us." Taking the chest, he placed it on a small table in the center of the room.

She folded her arms across her chest as if she'd felt a sudden chill. "This is a sham."

His frown matched the chill in his voice. "The veil is rent. You cannot take back what is done."

"I'm not talking about the bonding."

"Then what?" He removed his breastplate and arm and shin guards.

"I'm talking about sharing intimacies, whatever you imagine them to be. You felt honor-bound to protect me, and yet you never wanted me. I could sense your indecision about becoming bond-mates. Why are you forcing the issue now?"

"Don't ever doubt that I wanted you." He turned away to set the armor on a ladder-backed chair beside the door. "I still want you."

"You mustn't."

He faced her. "After the genetic scans prevented me from claiming you, the thought of you with another man burned like acid in my blood. I wanted to kill Tzorik for claiming you—for touching you."

He laughed, but there was no humor in his voice when he said, "The people from your planet have a saying, 'Be careful what you wish for'. Even as I fought to give you a choice of mates, I wanted you—and got you after all."

He closed the distance between them. Lifting his hand, he smoothed her hair away from her eyes and ran his knuckles down her cheek.

She closed her eyes, fighting to keep from leaning into his touch.

"Do the bruises pain you?"

She shook her head. "Not much."

"Good." He stepped back. "The hour grows late. Your sleeping gown is across the chair. Put it on and get into bed. I will join you shortly."

"The genetic scan—"

"Has not been forgotten, *Rishka*. I will not allow my passion to compromise my honor."

"Why would you even take the chance?"

He bent and placed a chaste kiss on her slightly parted lips. "We must achieve what you fear the most, *Rishka*. We must bind our lives with every intimacy we are allowed to share. I must find a way to tie your heart to mine, to my people, and to our cause."

"I can't let that happen."

"We will see." He walked to the bathroom and closed the door behind him.

She paced the room for long minutes before she finally sank into the nearest chair. Every intimacy, he'd said. She remembered another old Earth adage and paraphrased it in her mind. She'd made her bed, and now Rhyel expected her to sleep in it—with him.

"You haven't changed."

She jumped from the chair.

He walked into the room, briskly toweling his damp hair. His powerful shoulders and chest, golden in the glow of the bedside lamp, still glistened with moisture. She watched one fat water droplet follow the dark line of springy hair down his ridged stomach, before disappearing into the waistband of his loose-fitting pants. He draped the towel over his shoulder and finger-combed the dark strands of his hair back before securing them at the nape of his neck with a leather thong.

She swallowed hard.

Standing beside the bed, he presented the image of some glorious desert prince awaiting his bride.

"Why haven't you changed?" He pulled the towel from his shoulder and she noticed the thin, white scar where his wound had been.

Stasis? Possibly.

She watched him wipe the moisture from muscles that defined his shoulders and chest. She licked her lips and tried to speak, but her throat was thick and dry.

His throat must have felt the same. He had to clear it twice to speak again. "Why aren't you in bed?"

"I'm not going to bed. Not here." She looked away. She couldn't think as long as she watched him. "Please take me back to my room. If you're with me no one will ask any questions."

"The room was never yours. It was only a convenient place for you to stay until you were bonded. It is part of the clinic. Your place is here with me." He tossed the towel aside and whisked the white nightgown from the chair. "I'll help you with this." He moved toward her.

She stared at the gown. And shook her head. "I'm not going to bed with you."

"What are you afraid of? Your innocence is safe with me. You chose me for that reason." He threw the gown across his shoulder and reached for the single clasp that held the draped folds of her dress in place.

She clutched the bodice. "Don't."

"We are mates, Amber." He loosened her grip on the garment and kissed her palm. "Eventually you will become accustomed to these small intimacies. For tonight, look into my eyes. As long as our eyes are locked, your modesty is preserved."

For the life of her, she couldn't look away. Couldn't *move* away. His fingers tugged at the clasp and her dress dissolved around her. His hands encouraged its descent, his calloused palms following the curve of her waist and hips.

The trembling began at her knees and worked its way up. She gasped when he pulled her into his arms and her bare breasts touched the heat of his naked chest.

"Every intimacy we are allowed to share." Abruptly, he set her back, slipped the gown over her head, and waited for her to slip her arms into the sleeves. "Get into bed," he whispered, when the gown fell into place.

She didn't argue. It was a big bed, and keeping on his side would be as much a benefit to him as to her. She scooted under the covers, straightened her gown, and stared up at the ceiling.

He reached for the lamp on the stand. The room took on a dusky hue. After a slight rustling sound, the bed dipped with his weight and she held her breath. Had he removed his pants?

He rolled to face her, his hand coming to rest under the covers on her flat stomach. "Breathe," he said after a moment, a touch of amusement in his voice. His fingers curled against her belly and she gasped. When his hand caught her waist and pulled her closer, she pressed her palms against his chest to keep their bodies from touching.

"Relax," he whispered. "You've slept in my arms before."

"Not like this. You had clothes on before."

Rhyel chuckled. "I have clothes on now." He rose up and leaned above her. "Kiss me goodnight."

Her eyes had grown used to the dim room. She looked into the handsome face above her and couldn't resist the urge to touch him. She traced the high line of his cheek, his strong jaw, his lips. His exotic scent quickened her heartbeat— suddenly, she wanted things to be different. His tongue brushed the tip of her finger and he chuckled when she jerked her hand back.

His fingers threaded through her hair as he bent closer. "Kiss me, *Rishka*." His teeth teased her lower lip just before his mouth covered hers. The kiss was gentle, undemanding, and nice. But when her lips softened in welcome, he pulled away, and dropped back against his pillow.

She was bereft—for about a minute and a half, then she got mad. Not at Rhyel—well, maybe a little—but mainly at herself. What was she thinking? The answer was obvious. She wasn't thinking. Stupid. Stupid. Stupid. Every intimacy allowed, he'd said. She couldn't make it any easier for him. So far his plan was working. She'd been his bond-mate for less than an hour and she'd let him kiss her—no, she'd invited him to kiss her.

"Not anymore," she muttered, scooting to her side of the bed.

He didn't object to the distance she'd put between them. He simply stacked his hands behind his head, and it was his turn to stare at the ceiling.

"Rhyel," she said when she couldn't stand the silence any longer, "what does *Rishka* mean?"

He was quiet for so long she thought he didn't intend to answer. "It means beloved of the heart."

"But I'm not your beloved."

He rolled to his side and pulled her back into his arms. "It is only a word," he whispered against her hair. "Go to sleep."

But it was a long time before she slept.

And longer still before she woke, and watched him leave their chamber.

21

✧

Amber woke to a persistent pounding at the door. She leaned up on an elbow and pushed the hair from her eyes. Murky light brightened a window that should have been on the other side of the room. She sat up and reached for her robe. It wasn't where she expected it to be.

Then she remembered. She swung around, to look at the place beside her, but Rhyel's side of the bed was empty.

"Healer," a shaky voice called, "Healer, please wake up."

"Yes, I'm awake," she called out, responding to the urgency in the man's tone. A large robe lay across the foot of the bed. It was too big, but it would suffice.

The pounding began again. She slipped the robe over her nightgown, secured the belt, and hurried to open the door.

She froze. One of Tzorik's men, the tall one who'd escorted her to the ceremony, stood in the entry.

She took a step back. "What do you want?"

"My name is Siikzo," he rushed out. "My mate needs you."

She didn't trust the man. "What's wrong with her?"

"She carries my child. Something is happening."

"Where is she?"

"In our chamber."

"Can she be moved?" She wasn't about to go to that man's room alone.

"I don't know. She bleeds, and she trembles as if cold. Please, Healer, I fear for her life."

No one could question the anxiety in his voice. "Wrap your wife in a blanket, and carry her to the clinic. Don't let her walk. I'll meet you there."

The Guardian nodded. She closed the door, removed her robe, and found the closet. Thankfully, someone had left undergarments and a blouse and skirt for her. She was still buttoning the front of her blouse when she left the chamber.

She reached the main floor, and shouted to one of the few women in the hall so early in the morning. "Find Hiilani," she ordered as she ran. "Tell her we have an emergency at the clinic."

The woman nodded and raced for the stairs.

Siikzo met her at the clinic door and followed her inside. She smiled at the young woman in Siikzo's arms. Blood stained the lower half of the blanket that enshrouded her. Amber nodded toward an examining table in a curtained corner.

"Put her in there. Hiilani will make her more comfortable."

As soon as the young woman was settled, Amber took her hand and smiled reassuringly. "Try to relax and we'll see what we can do. Are you in pain now?"

The girl shook her head. "The pain comes, and then it stops, and in a few minutes it starts again. Am I losing my baby?"

Amber never lied to her patients, but she tried to ease the girl's mind. "We'll do everything possible to see that you don't." She patted the girls arm. "I'm Amber."

"Everyone knows who you are, Healer. My name is Sonya."

"Well, Sonya, I wish we could have met somewhere besides the clinic, but I'm glad to meet you."

Hiilani rushed through the door and saw Sonya. "Oh, no."

Amber gave the nurse a sharp look before turning back to her patient. "I'm going to wash up now. Hiilani will get you changed and make you more comfortable. Let us know if the pain begins again, okay?"

Sonya nodded.

"We have a possible miscarriage," Amber told her nurse. "Set up an IV, take her vitals, and prep her."

A few minutes later, the girl was in a hospital gown, lying on the exam table. A clean sheet covered her stomach and legs. Hiilani was taking a blood pressure reading. Siikzo hovered close enough to be in her way.

Amber closed the privacy curtains and turned to the Guardian. "You'll need to wait outside while I examine your wife."

The young woman grabbed her husband's hand and shook her head. The big Guardian looked up at Amber and shook his head too. Given the girl's agitation, Amber didn't insist.

"Do we know her blood type, or will you need to check the records?"

The nurse sighed. "There are no complete records yet, but I know her blood type. And there are two women who have the same type."

Amber nodded. "What's her blood pressure?"

"One-fifteen over seventy-eight."

"It's a little low, given her agitation, but not life-threatening. Let's see what we can do to keep it that way."

The young woman groaned and squeezed Siikzo's hand.

Amber pressed her palm to the girl's slightly distended abdomen and felt the tightening that indicated a contraction. She waited until the pain had passed before listening for a fetal heartbeat. She couldn't find one, but the baby was half Centallian. She spent several minutes searching before she finally gave up. She looked at the nurse and gave a slight shake of her head.

In the end, she couldn't stop the miscarriage, but she managed to stem the bleeding and save the young woman's life. Siikzo carried his wife back to their chamber where she would be more comfortable. Amber ordered him not to leave Sonya alone. Hiilani would look in on her hourly and they would see her at the clinic in the morning.

After the couple was gone, Hiilani eased into the desk chair. Amber disposed of her gloves and washed her hands.

"I had hoped the miscarriages were over." Hiilani's voice sounded reedy, as if she were speaking in rarified air.

Amber grabbed a towel and turned to look at the nurse as she dried her hands. "There were others? How many?"

Hiilani's cream and honey complexion looked nearly as pale as Sonya's had. "Twenty- seven. Twenty-eight now."

"Do you know the cause? Is it genetic? Is that why Rhyel and I can't—"

Hiilani shook her head. "This isn't related to genetic compatibility."

Amber removed her lab coat and dropped into the chair opposite her nurse. "You're sure?"

Hiilani nodded.

"Have you identified the problem?"

"We know it's a virus that affects the undeveloped organs of a fetus—lungs, heart, kidneys—and apparently it's indigenous to this planet. We have nothing like it on Earth and the Elders tell me it was the same on their world.

"The Centallian technicians tested everyone on the planet. Each woman carries an inert form of the virus, even Kroyda and Zsaor. All of the men tested negative. Apparently, the virus is gender-specific, at least in adults. As soon as a woman becomes pregnant the virus becomes active and passes on to her unborn child."

"Gender-specific?"

The nurse nodded. "We also believe it's mammalian-related. You haven't been outside yet, but when you do go out, you'll eventually notice the only indigenous life on this planet is avian, aquatic, or reptilian. No mammals, large or small."

"Interspecies?"

"It would seem so."

"If this virus wiped out everything it depended on for survival, why isn't it extinct?

"That's another mystery we've yet to solve. The technicians speculate that it can remain in a dormant state indefinitely, waiting for another mammal to come along and wake it up." Hiilani shrugged her shoulders. "It's as good a guess as any."

"Let me get this straight. The virus only infects women, and only attacks the organs of a fetus."

"That's right."

"Rhyel should have kidnapped a researcher instead of a doctor."

"The Elders told me you minored in research."

"That isn't exactly right. I only studied research during my first year of med school. When I decided to major in trauma surgery, I changed my minor to obstetrics."

Hiilani's eyes widened. "No wonder the Elders chose you."

"Yes, well, this explains a lot. Were any of the other women here harmed by the virus?"

"Not by the virus, but one of our brides died of complications."

"What kind of complications?

"She hemorrhaged, like Sonya. I tried to stop the bleeding, but...."

"You can't blame yourself. You don't have enough training to handle a situation like that and I doubt you had the equipment."

"Thank God you were here this morning. If Sonya had continued to hemorrhage, I couldn't have...."

"Why didn't anyone warn me about the miscarriages?" Amber asked, changing the subject to a little less emotional one.

"It's only been four days, three since you woke, and you were recovering from *Mensolm*. Then there was Cintar's accident, and Tzorik, and the bonding ceremonies. There wasn't any time."

Four days. In four days she'd been kidnapped, taken to another planet, nearly raped, forced into marriage, and now dropped into the middle of a major medical situation.

"Tell me everything you know about the virus."

"We isolated the virus and developed a vaccine two months ago. Every woman on the planet was inoculated."

Amber remembered the injection Rhyel had given her. "You introduced the vaccine directly into the bloodstream?"

"The technicians believed it would be more effective since a woman's blood circulated through the baby's body too."

"How many women should I be concerned about?"

"Fortunately, the Elders were cautious. Only one couple from a list of volunteers was chosen to conceive."

"Siikzo and Sonya?"

"Yes. The Elders had forbidden any physical relationship between the Centallians and their Earth mates until the vaccine proved effective. They decided to wait six weeks from the time of Sonya's baby's conception before giving a second couple permission to try for a child."

"Sonya was only six weeks into her pregnancy? The fetus seemed more developed."

"Actually, it's only been about five weeks."

"You're sure the Elders haven't given any additional couples permission?"

"I don't think so. We can check with them to make sure."

"If they have I want to see the women today. Warn the Elders to keep their Guardians away from the rest of the women." She suddenly grasped the arms of her chair. "Hiilani, the Centallians could have carried the virus home to Earth."

The nurse shook her head. "The techs onboard the *Novaria* have kept a close eye on our planet. They've monitored the villages the Guardians visited. So far nothing unexplainable has happened. But remember, the men aren't infected." Hiilani gave her a wary look. "I'm not sure what would happen if one of the women went back."

She didn't miss the implication. She couldn't return home now. At least not until she found a cure.

Hiilani heaved a long dejected sigh. "We need to report Sonya's miscarriage to the Elders."

Amber agreed. "Gather all of the data the technicians have on the virus."

"Do you think you can stop the miscarriages?"

"I'll know more when I've seen the reports. Why are the Elders allowing the bonding ceremonies to continue? Can they trust so many of their Guardians to refrain from consummating their bondings?"

"Honor is as important as breathing to the Centallians. Each Guardian has promised by his honor to remain celibate until the problem is solved."

"That's taking a big risk."

"The Elders don't think so."

"And if we don't find a cure?"

Hiilani looked away. "If we can't find the cure, the Centallian species won't survive to the next generation. The men won't leave their mates to find another world and other women. It wouldn't be honorable." She walked to the door before turning back. "The Centallians are good people. They've suffered so much. The women as well." She closed the door behind her.

Amber sank into her chair and blinked back tears. Dead babies. The women must have been terrified and grief-stricken by what had happened to them. And they'd gone through it without a doctor. She refused to think of what she might be facing right now if the Elders hadn't intervened and placed a temporary moratorium on reproduction.

Tzorik had boasted that he'd get a child from her. He hadn't intended to wait for the Elders' permission to consummate their bonding. Any child he might have forced on her would have been put at risk, and she as well.

He hadn't cared.

22

"You slept here?" Cintar stood just inside the captain's open doorway. "Did she make you leave your chamber?" He strolled into the room and made himself at home in the only comfortable chair in the room.

Rhyel glanced up from his view pad. "You don't have the watch this afternoon. Why are you onboard?"

"Liiam asked for time away from the ship today. I had no pressing duties so I took his place. I think he's courting one of the women."

"What about the mine? Aren't you needed there?"

"The gold is crated and ready to load."

"Good. Start moving the ore to the *Novaria*." Rhyel set the pad aside. "How many trips will it take?"

"Five, if we use both shuttles."

"That's the largest shipment yet, isn't it?"

Cintar nodded. "The men struck a rich vein this week, almost pure digging. Keeso will be hard pressed to sell it without drawing attention to our Colorado mine. We might consider salting a second mine, maybe in Alaska."

Rhyel found his first smile of the day. "Salting?"

"Keeso says that's what miners call sprinkling a few small pieces—they're called nuggets—of gold in a mine to make it seem more valuable to buyers."

"Not an honorable endeavor."

"Agreed, but that isn't what we're trying to accomplish. Keeso even pays taxes on what we produce, using the false identification he purchased from another not-so-honorable person."

Rhyel was aware of what it took to turn New Centallian gold into Earth currency. "Would you care to speculate on who might be willing to operate a mine in Alaska?"

Cintar grinned. "I doubt you can depend on volunteers to live in that region of Earth. Colorado is cold enough in the winter. We may need to research a more hospitable destination. Did she really make you leave?"

Rhyel sighed. If his friend had one trait he could depend on, it was tenacity. Only occasionally did it prove irritating. This was one of the occasions.

"Do you honestly believe she could make me leave my own chamber, or that she'd even try? Amber is fine with our situation. The choice of mate was hers, if you'll remember. She was sleeping when I left. Aren't you due on the bridge?"

Still grinning, Cintar got to his feet and started for the door.

Rhyel stopped him. "Have the Elders given you the list of items we need ordered for the next supply run?"

"Not yet. They're waiting to hear what is needed for the clinic. Hiilani told me she and the healer are still going over the clinic inventory."

"We'll need their list this afternoon. I don't want to delay the *Novaria*'s departure."

"I'll make sure she knows."

"I'll speak with Amber as well."

The bridge com hummed to life. "Captain?"

Rhyel recognized Tinar's voice.

"Here."

A voice-activated full-body holographic image of his communications officer materialized in front of him.

"Captain, you have an urgent message from New Centallus. Elder Zitan wishes to speak with you."

"Transfer the communication to my private com."

"Yes, sir."

Cintar started to leave, but Rhyel shook his head. "Stay."

"It might be personal."

"My father will tell us if it is. You may as well listen to anything else. It will save me the telling later."

Cintar moved to stand beside his captain's chair as the image of Zitan took form. The older man looked grim.

Rhyel's throat tightened. "Amber?"

"She is well. But I have solemn news. Sonya has lost her child. Hiilani has only now notified the council."

"Is Sonya all right?"

"She is expected to recover. Siikzo is with her. He has been given leave of his duties to be with her."

Rhyel sighed. "I had hoped the vaccine…."

His father nodded.

"Have you spoken with Amber?"

"She is in the clinic. She saved Sonya's life. The girl was hemorrhaging as Danica did before we lost her. We can be thankful our healer was here."

"I will transfer to the surface shortly and join you in the clinic. Amber will have questions."

"We must resume our search for the cure. Our healer's training will be invaluable, I'm sure. I will meet you in the clinic." Zitan's image disappeared.

"This last vaccine seemed so promising." Rhyel stood.

Cintar walked with him to the door. "Do we tell the crew now?"

"Yes. Give the bonded Guardians leave to be with their mates. There are enough unbound crewmen on board to staff the ship. I will contact you after I've spoken with Amber."

Cintar nodded and headed for the bridge.

Rhyel turned in the opposite direction toward the transfer unit.

✧

"But I'm not a researcher." Amber fought down a sense of panic. They couldn't possibly expect her to find a way to destroy the virus. "I studied research, but I'm barely qualified to pass someone a test tube."

Zitan patted her shoulder. "We know you feel out of your depth, child, but the little training you've received is more than anyone here has. All that we ask is that you work with our technicians as they try to find a cure."

Rhyel entered the clinic, took one look at her, and immediately went to her side. He slipped his arm over her shoulder and pulled her against him. She sighed as the knot in her stomach loosened a little.

"Hiilani tells us she spoke with you about our situation," Valdon told her.

Five of the six Elders had assembled at the clinic a few minutes ago. Kroyda had elected to sit with Sonya and Siikzo. Hiilani had returned earlier to help prepare tissue samples to be sent to the *Novaria's* lab. They had placed the baby's remains in a tiny handcrafted wooden casket. The nurse explained that even though Sonya had only been a few weeks pregnant, the child would be given an honorable burial.

"Hiilani told me the technicians have been trying to find a cure for nearly a year." Amber took a deep breath. "Please don't expect me to work miracles."

Aadrok came forward and took her hand. "No one is asking you for a miracle, Healer. But perhaps you can give the technicians new insight into the problem."

She nodded, though still not convinced. The priest patted her hand as he looked up at Rhyel. "Our commander will make you acquainted with our Guardians in charge of the research. They will welcome your help, I'm sure."

"What about the clinic? It's important that we get it organized. We don't have any records…." She suddenly felt overwhelmed.

"Hiilani will be here and if you are needed, she can send for you. You will be able to spend a few hours at the clinic each day, but solving the problem of the virus will be your primary concern."

After what Sonya had gone through this morning, she had to agree. "I understand. When do we start?"

Rhyel squeezed her shoulder. "Now. There's a shuttle waiting."

"Wouldn't it be quicker to transfer to the ship?" Valdon asked.

"A shuttle will transport the samples to the *Novaria*. I thought Amber might like to view my ship before she begins working in it."

Zitan smiled. "It will give her a splendid view of New Centallus, as well."

She wasn't sure she wanted to experience their "splendid view." They were talking about going into space!

"We can set up a lab here in the clinic. That way I can be here if an emergency occurs."

"We already have a working lab on the *Novaria*," Rhyel said. "You won't be that far away. You can transfer directly to the clinic from the ship." He gave her an assessing look. "Do you fear going aboard my ship again?"

"It isn't the ship. It's the thought of being… you know, in space."

He smiled. "You've been there before. This is no different."

"Yes, it is. I was unconscious then."

"I promise you will be safe, *Rishka*." His hand slipped to her waist as he turned to the Elders. "Should you need either of us, contact Cintar. He will know where to find us."

Every science fiction movie she'd ever seen came to mind as Rhyel urged her toward the door. She felt like she was being shoved out an air lock.

23

"I'm not sure about this." She hadn't been outside the walls yet, and he expected her to fly off with him to his spaceship. Her mind had trouble wrapping itself around the whole concept.

She moved through the door he held open for her and stared in wonder as he took her hand and started walking. The view from her bedroom window hadn't prepared her for the world she saw now. The wooded area to her right was familiar. So were the cliffs, though she could see that the large horseshoe-shaped bay started somewhere beyond those familiar woods and extended to a second forest on the far side. The cliffs dropped straight down into the water.

It was beautiful and unspoiled—as her own world had once been. Had the Centallians built a modern monstrosity of metal and who-knew-what to house their colony? She tugged on Rhyel's hand to get him to stop and turned around to see the fortress.

She almost sighed in relief as she took in the two-story rectangular structure. Huge logs, thirty to forty inches in diameter, and at least fifteen feet long, comprised most of the architecture. The ends had been notched to allow the next log in line to slide into place like a three-dimensional jigsaw puzzle. The Centallians were big men, but there was no way they could have lifted even the bottom logs into place. "How did you move the logs?"

He followed her gaze and smiled, a hint of pride in his eyes. "We used cargo loaders from the *Novaria* for the lower logs, and large beams and pulleys for the high walls."

Tinted windows interspersed both top and bottom levels. Rows of what appeared to be solar panels lined the flat roof. That explained their electrical system. The structure wasn't as massive as the castles she'd visited in England and Scotland, but it was impressive.

Rhyel did a little tugging of his own, and they started walking toward a clearing in the distance. A long tarmac stretched before them, and several strangely shaped vehicles sat on the blacktop-like surface. They were too far away for her to see much detail.

"What's that?"

"The shuttle pad. We could have taken a ground vehicle to the site, but I thought you might enjoy the walk after being confined to the fortress for so long."

He was right. She welcomed the exercise, though she had some trouble catching her breath. The air was fresh, but a little rarified. It would take a while for her to adjust to it.

He must have noticed. He slowed their pace and angled his head to their left, directing her attention to the wide plots of cleared land that extended to the foothills of a magnificent mountain range. Guardians used picks and shovels to dig long trenches.

"Those aquifers will carry water from snow-fed basins at the foot of the mountains to our crops. The canals need to be finished before the onset of the long dry season."

"Hiilani told me the vegetables we eat are grown here."

"We grow enough vegetables to sustain us in plots, closer to the stronghold. But until the large fields are productive we are forced to buy grain from Earth." When the canals and fields are finished, the men will begin building homes for future families. The Elders are adamant about providing housing, especially the men." He chuckled. "I suspect they want to ensure their own domestic tranquility. Eventually, the hall will resound with children's laughter—and crying."

She pictured the four solemn older men surrounded by weeping toddlers, and smiled. His assessment was probably spot-on.

"Why didn't you build the smaller homes first? Wouldn't it have been easier?"

"Easier, yes, but not as secure."

"I don't understand. You told me there are no mammals here. No predators—wait. Are there reptiles large enough to be dangerous?" Jurassic Park on a world scale?

He pressed his hand to her back to get her moving again. "Calm yourself, *Rishka*. The danger we anticipate comes not from this world. Have you forgotten that we hide from those who destroyed our home? The *Novaria* can only protect us from a ship's attack. If the attackers came to ground, we would be facing far greater numbers. The fortress would offer protection, and give us enough time to transfer to the ship if necessary."

As they approached the tarmac, she got her first good look at the shuttles. There were vast differences in the four machines resting on the landing pad.

He inclined his head toward the largest vehicle. "That's our cargo shuttle. We use it to transport large shipments to and from the *Novaria*. We have a smaller vessel on my ship for lighter shipments."

The shuttle was half again as high and close to the length of a semi-truck. The machine was nearly as wide as it was long. Its size should have made it look bulky, but the seamless platinum-like exterior curved rather than squared, giving it a graceful line, though by no stretch of the imagination did it look aerodynamic. The cockpit was also rounded, making it look like a huge, silver ladybug—with no legs.

She laughed.

He raised an eyebrow in question and she suppressed the urge to laugh harder. "I assume that since it has no wheels, it flies."

"Have you forgotten already that this shuttle travels from the planet to my ship and back?"

"No, but I'm having a hard time picturing it."

"How so?"

"For one thing, it looks too bulky to fly."

"Cargo shuttles are bulky, but they can hover and fly as well as a transport shuttle." He nodded toward a much smaller ship, with three half-moon-shaped windows running along its side. This vehicle looked more like her mental image of a shuttle, sleek and arrow-shaped with swept-back wings that ended near the tail of the craft.

He left her for a moment to have a word with several Guardians straining under the weight of large crates being transferred from a ground vehicle onto a metal conveyer belt. The belt carried the crates into the larger vehicle. The smaller machine looked like a cross between an armored tank and a pickup. There wasn't a graceful line on it.

"We'll take the small shuttle," he said as he rejoined her. "The samples from the clinic are already aboard."

She hesitated when he reached for her hand, not sure she wanted to make the trip. No, that wasn't true. She was absolutely sure she didn't want to go for a joyride in a space shuttle.

"Still frightened?"

"It's not that I'm frightened—"

He tilted his head, one eyebrow raised in question.

"Okay, I'm frightened. It's outer space."

"You've been out there already." He tugged her along behind him as he moved toward the small transport.

"True, but I told you I don't remember a minute of it." They'd made it to the open panel leading into the shuttle. "Your people may go up in one of these without a qualm, but only a handful of men and women from my world have ever gone beyond our atmosphere. Most of us have never considered the possibility. It's daunting."

"I'll be with you."

Well, that was arrogant. And comforting. She followed him into the shuttle. There was a cockpit with two seats and an instrument board below a half-circle panel of windows. The main body of the ship contained a row of double seats on each side of a center aisle. The vehicle could provide seating for at least twenty people.

She looked around. They were the only two in the shuttle. "Where's the pilot?"

"I'm taking her up." He slid into the pilot's seat and nodded toward the one beside him. When she sat down, he reached over and triggered a switch that activated the seatbelt. Straps slid over her shoulders and across her middle, securing her.

He activated his own belt and turned his attention to the controls, hands flying over the panel so fast she couldn't tell if he touched the glass or not. The shuttle hummed, and the machine rose. She gripped the straps of her seatbelt and watched as New Centallus shrank below them. She glanced at Rhyel.

That was when she realized there was no steering wheel, or joystick, or whatever. Her eyes shot to his and she realized he'd been watching her.

"How are you driving this thing?"

He smiled. It didn't reassure her.

"I'm not. The computer is. Once the coordinates are set, the ship flies itself."

She didn't like hearing that. "And if there's a problem?"

"I can pilot the shuttle at any point in the flight."

"How can you do that without a—"

"Stop worrying and try to enjoy the ride." He pointed toward the front window. "We're leaving the planet's atmosphere."

Already? She looked out, astonished, as the turquoise sky faded into black. Mere minutes had passed since they'd taken off. She hadn't felt any pressure as the shuttle pulled against the planet's gravity.

"How did we get here so fast without being crushed? That kind of speed should have pulverized our bones."

"Our ship projects a barrier that encapsulates it like a bubble, creating a counter-gravitational field. The same barrier protects the ship when it enters a planet's atmosphere."

She barely noted his explanation as she stared through the front window at an incredible, crystal clear view of the night sky. She searched the vast blanket of stars for recognizable constellations, but none of the familiar star-clusters were visible.

"Where's Earth?"

"It is far beyond what you see here."

A wave of homesickness nearly choked her. "Tell me where it is."

He turned his attention to the console. He made a couple of swipes across the board and the ship stopped moving, seemed to hang in space. He bent toward her. "Amber, you need to let—"

"Just point out the direction. Is that too much to ask?"

He sat back and sighed, then ran his hand over the panel. The small ship rotated. When it stopped, he pointed straight ahead. "Earth is beyond those three stars."

She stared hard at the triangular pattern of stars, straining to find the tiny pinpoint of light that was her sun, willing the impossible, willing herself to see one more glimpse of her beautiful, blue home. Her grandfather was out there, her friends, her life—impossibly far away. Hot tears slid down her cheeks. She could never go back. She tried to suppress a moan. She couldn't suppress the sob.

Rhyel released the latch on his seatbelt, then released Amber's. He swiveled his seat and pulled her into his lap. She threw her arms around his neck and buried her face against his throat. Her tears scorched his soul. Her agony filled every pore of his body. He hurt with it. He held her tight against his chest and rocked her as he would a child. He let her cry, let her release the sorrow and the anger tearing them both up inside.

He didn't understand this connection he shared with his bond-mate. He couldn't shield himself from her emotions, didn't even try. If they were truly mated he might believe they shared the azcure, the mind-bond. But that didn't happen between Centallians and their Earth mates. It definitely didn't occur when the mates were genetically incompatible. What he shared with her was more compassion than connection. Yet, as he would have with a Centallian mate, he willed his own strength into her body, his calm into her mind.

Secure in Rhyel's arms, Amber stared at the great expanse, focusing on the three stars. She took a deep, shaky breath. How far beyond that cluster was Earth? Did it matter? The cluster itself was too far. How could she ever hope to find her way home without help? And the time factor—Einstein's Theory of Relativity was more than a theory. The scientific world embraced it as fact. "Are they still there?"

Rhyel turned her to face him. "Who?"

"Grandpa, my friends, everyone I know, are they still alive?"

"Why would you ask that?"

"How much time has passed on Earth?"

His lips touched her forehead and lingered a moment. "They are as you left them, *Rishka*. Nothing of significance has changed."

"But time's different out here, isn't it?"

He leaned around her and his hand glided over the control board. The shuttle began to move. "Your species is only now learning the variables of time and space. In the future, your scientists will discover how to manipulate what you currently consider steadfast laws of physics, enabling your people to travel from one solar system to another as freely as we do."

"How?"

"Travel from one sun to another?"

"Yes."

"Are you familiar with Higgs boson?"

"The final elementary particle in the standard model of particle physics?"

He looked at her as if she'd sprouted another head. "You've studied physics?"

"Not really, but I did follow the news when the theory was proven. It caught my interest and I read everything available on the project. There was even scientific speculation about creating a black hole that would swallow the Earth. Are you going to tell me that you travel through black holes? It's impossible."

"No, I'm not. And you're right, it is impossible. You have to remember that your world is young and your people younger still. Your scientists are on the precipice of discovery. But Peter Higgs's theory-turned-reality is only—how do your people put it—the tip of the iceberg. They're already beginning to suspect their 'standard model' is far from complete."

"You seem to know an awful lot about our scientists." She couldn't help sounding suspicious.

"Don't you study a little of the culture of a country you visit on Earth? We do the same with planets." He turned his attention to the control panel and the ship stopped moving. "You can fold space by manipulating mass. But your theoretical physicists will eventually decide the wormhole is an unlikely answer to the problem of interstellar travel. It isn't necessary to use a wormhole. Our ships are capable of creating mass-fields that condense space. The field snugs one solar system against another, and a ship melds from one system to the other. Time is moot. We lose minutes, not centuries." He touched her cheek. "The distance between Earth and New Centallus is irrelevant, *Rishka*. By my honor, I promise you will see Earth again, and find your loved ones as you remember them."

He lifted her into the chair and activated their seatbelts. Smiling, he nodded toward the window on her right. "The *Novaria*."

24

✧

The starship was sleek and beautiful. Even from a distance it looked massive.

"I'll give you a better look at her."

Amber glanced at Rhyel, surprised by the near-reverence in his voice. Grandpa had taken her to an antique car rally once. They'd stopped in front of a 1957 Chevrolet in mint condition. He'd told her about owning a car just like it. His voice had held the same reverence. What was there about men and their machines?

"It's beautiful," she was compelled to say.

He smiled as he guided the shuttle to the front of the stellar ship. The *Novaria*'s nose reminded her of one of Earth's shuttles—on a much larger scale. From their position she was able to see through the large windows that wrapped around most of the nose. There were two levels on what she assumed was the bridge, a lower deck with seating stations that followed the perimeter of the ship's nose, and a half-circle upper deck accessible from the lower level by two sets of short stairs, one on each side of the room. A Guardian sat at the center of the upper level deck. He leaned forward, reaching for something she couldn't see.

The air crackled and Cintar's voice filled the shuttle. "Good afternoon, Captain. I see you've brought a guest."

"Our healer will be spending a considerable amount of time aboard the ship with the research team," Rhyel responded. "I thought she might like to familiarize herself with the *Novaria*. We'll meet you on the bridge later."

"Acknowledged."

The connection ended and Rhyel guided the shuttle above the *Novaria* toward the bow of the starship. The metallic body fanned out from the bridge's window array like a trillion-cut gem. Grandpa would have laughed and told her to just say it looked like a guitar pick.

That would have been a travesty though. The *Novaria* was a glistening, platinum gem against a background of stars.

"The entire hull of the ship is a solar conductor. Our propulsion system uses solar energy stored in massive cells to produce the field I told you about."

Windows ran the length of the ship's port side, and she assumed there were a like number on the starboard. Five domed turrets formed a row across the top of the bow.

"You have weapons?"

"We do, and forward weapons as well."

He positioned the shuttle behind the *Novaria* and a huge panel opened like a garage door—a very large garage door. Orange lights flashed as the shuttle swooped in to land on one of the yellow circles in the bay.

He shut down the engines, and the panel closed. When the lights stopped flashing, he released their seatbelts.

"Are you ready to see my ship?" He reminded her of a child eager to show off a favorite toy. He pulled her to her feet and she followed him to the door. He deactivated the lock and took her hand.

"The *Novaria's* bay houses this passenger shuttle, a larger personnel carrier, two cargo shuttles, and two ground shuttles small enough to be transported from ship to planet in our largest cargo shuttle." He put his arm around her shoulders and walked her toward the two doors set into the interior wall. "The smaller portal is used by the crew and passengers to enter the ship from the docking bay. The high, wide door is for cargo."

The door opened into an immense hangar-type room with metal walls and stacks of crates like the ones she'd seen on the planet. Several Guardians worked in various locations in the hangar.

"*Novaria* was a merchant ship," he told her as they walked toward a door at the side of the room. "My father encouraged me to study interplanetary diplomacy. He wanted me to assist him, as Tzorik assisted Valdon, but I chose a different vocation."

"The *Novaria* is yours?"

"Yes, and now she serves our colony."

He motioned to the nearest Guardian and the man hurried to them. "Samples from the clinic are in the shuttle. See that they are delivered to the lab immediately."

The Guardian bowed and sprinted toward the shuttle bay door.

"We'll take the freight lift," Rhyel said, drawing her attention back to him. He activated another hand panel. The doors swung open and they stepped inside. "This lift is used for supplies, for maintenance, the kitchen, and lab. Most of the time you'll use a smaller lift closer to the bridge and lab." The trip from one level to the next was brief. The door opened into a wide corridor that looked far different from the level they'd just left.

"How lovely," she breathed as they stepped out of the lift. The seafoam-green walls were luminescent, giving off a soft, white light that brightened the entire length of the hall. She looked up at him. "Are the walls as warm as they look?"

He smiled, obviously pleased by her reaction. He turned her to face the wall and pulled her back against him. "Touch it." His arms came around her waist and his lips touched her ear. "It's safe, I promise."

Safe? Her train of thought had been completely derailed by his heat. Goosebumps raced across her body, yet she was going up in flames because of his touch.

Every intimacy allowed.

"Amber?" He leaned back and turned her slightly so he could look into her face. "What's wrong?"

"I'm okay. It's all so new. I guess I'm a little overwhelmed." She mentally cringed. That was lame.

"Are you going to touch it?"

"Oh. Touch it, yes." She reached out with one finger and tentatively tested the wall. It was cool. She carefully brushed her fingertips across the surface and looked up at him again. "It isn't warm, but it feels… organic, like a flower petal."

He nodded. "An appropriate description. The corridor walls are covered with microscopic organisms called Saarciili. The *Novaria* isn't alive, but it does share what you might call a pseudo-symbiotic relationship with the Saarciili. The microorganisms feed on the small amount of solar energy diverted through the walls of the corridors, halls, and a few common rooms. The Saarciili also produce oxygen and we, in turn, provide the Saarciili with carbon dioxide." He stepped back. "Are you ready to see the rest of my ship?"

When she nodded, he pointed to their left. "The *Novaria's* bow houses maintenance, and one of our transfer units, as well as the cargo lift. The hall at the end of the corridor accesses the turrets."

They moved in the opposite direction. "The VIP quarters and dining area are ahead on the left. Most of the doors you see on the right are bridge crew quarters. The intersecting halls lead to additional passenger and crew quarters."

As they passed the dining area she noticed only a few Guardians sitting at the tables. "How many of your men are on board?"

"When we're in orbit a crew of twenty can maintain the ship. When we visit Earth we need a crew of at least sixty." He stopped at the next door on their left. "These are my quarters." He opened the door. "Your quarters, too, when you're aboard."

As she would expect, the room was small, with only a desk, two chairs—one large, one small—and a bed. An open door at the side of the room led to a tiny bathroom.

"When you work late at the lab, you can sleep here. We will be notified should an emergency occur on the planet."

"We? You'd sleep here too—when I do?"

He turned her into his arms and lifted her face with a fingertip under her chin. "We are mates, *Rishka*. Where you sleep, there will I sleep."

He pulled her closer, and his lips touched hers. Tentatively, they softened over hers and his tongue teased her mouth open, thrusting in to taste her. And she tasted him. She melted into him, her arms circling his neck as his mouth robbed her body of strength and her mind of sanity, aware only of the deep, burning need he awakened in her.

He set her back suddenly. His eyes, golden with passion, were beginning to darken to their normal obsidian.

"Were we free to do so, *Rishka,*" he whispered, his voice rough, "I would demonstrate how satisfying my bed can be." Then he kissed her again, his tongue tracing her lower lip as if he needed one last taste before walking away.

And he did walk away, putting the distance she needed between them. Had he meant to make her weak with desire for him? If he had, the plan had backfired. She wasn't so innocent that she hadn't been aware of his arousal when he molded her body against his. And his eyes... obviously, anger wasn't the only extreme emotion that triggered the change. He hadn't been able to hide his own passion.

She looked at the bed before following him. She'd never be able to sleep in it without remembering his parting words.

25

✧

"You'll use this transfer pod to travel from ship to planet. We'll teach you the controls." Rhyel's voice had taken on a husky quality.

Amber understood the cause. The tension between them tightened her throat too.

They stood in front of a door about twenty-five feet from his quarters. He activated the sliding door to a small room of perhaps ten by fifteen feet in size. A raised octagonal platform, large enough to accommodate several people, sat to their right.

A glass panel imprinted with lighted circles, squares, rectangles, and triangles was set into the opposite wall. Letters, or numbers—she wasn't sure which since none were familiar—flashed in random patterns within the geometrical shapes.

She was relieved when he closed the door and they were still on the outside. He took her hand and they continued down the corridor.

A minute or two later he nodded toward another door on the left. "This leads to the lab," he said, but kept walking. "We'll visit it after we've toured the bridge."

The corridor ended at a set of double doors. He placed his palm on the small access panel and the doors slid apart to reveal the upper deck of the bridge. It looked like a scene straight out of a science fiction movie. From the entry, the deck widened like a cone, ending at the quarter-moon-shaped command center that overlooked the lower deck. Three command stations were positioned in front of control panels, each with a holographic window hovering in front.

Cintar sat in the center chair. He swiveled around and stood, formally bowing to his captain. "Welcome aboard, Sir. Your command awaits."

Rhyel acknowledged his greeting with a formal nod, then smiled at his friend. "The command is still yours. I thought Amber might like to view the *Novaria*'s bridge."

Cintar turned to her. "Welcome, Healer."

She spared him a glance and a smile, but her attention was caught by the *Novaria*'s grandeur. The lights on the bridge were subdued. Looking out at the panoramic view through the large windows, she felt as if she were standing in space. The old adage was appropriate. She could almost reach out and touch the stars.

She caught Rhyel watching her and laughed, easing the tension between them. "I'm impressed."

He grinned back. "I thought you might be. Would you like to look around?"

She nodded. He took her arm and directed her attention to one of the doors set into the left side of the upper deck.

"This leads to our war room." He chuckled. "Since *Novaria* has yet to see battle, a more appropriate description would be conference chamber. The door on the opposite side opens to our map room. The computer that establishes the coordinates for our field destinations is housed there. Every star system we've visited is logged into the star charts."

The lower level had nine stations. Each appeared to be somewhat different. The symbols that flashed were as unrecognizable as the ones she'd seen in the transfer pod. She leaned over one of the consoles of an empty station.

"Are these numbers or letters?"

"A little of both. This station monitors the ship's trajectory." A Guardian had approached and stood to one side, obviously waiting for his captain's attention. Rhyel acknowledged him with a nod and took her arm, leading her away from the station. The man bowed to them both before taking his seat at the console.

"The Guardians are preparing the ship for departure," he told her, "and we still have to visit the lab." He looked up the stairs to where Cintar waited. "I'll introduce Amber to the lab technicians, then return to go over the final arrangements for the flight."

His second in command bowed his respect, then nodded to her as she and Rhyel returned to the corridor.

The lab door opened into a very modern, very familiar research facility, the only difference being the exam table sitting in the middle of the room—a reminder that this was once *Novaria*'s medical clinic.

Three men looked up. She stopped abruptly. "What's he doing here?"

Rhyel's arm came around her waist and pulled her aside. "Who?"

"The man by the sink."

He glanced at the Guardian she'd pointed out. "Kaarz? He's our chief technician."

"He works for you? I thought he was one of Tzorik's men. He and Siikzo practically dragged me to Tzorik's ceremony."

His arm tightened. "Were you hurt?" There was a decided chill in his voice.

"No."

His tension eased, but only a little. "Not all of our Guardians were assigned to *Novaria*. A few were diplomatic assistants or clerics for the Elders. Kaarz was a cleric under Valdon."

"So he doesn't work for you?"

He urged her into the lab and the door closed behind them. "Save for the Elders, every Guardian on New Centallus—including Tzorik—is under my command." He made sure his voice carried to the others. "Discovering a cure for the virus is the single most important challenge our new world faces."

She nodded. "I know. It's important to me too." She couldn't go home until a cure was found. "I'll work with him." She eyed the Guardian who stood glaring at her. "But will he work with me?"

Rhyel leveled a hard look at the man in question. "Will that be a problem?" Kaarz directed a sullen glance her way, but shook his head.

A tall, thin man who looked to be in his mid-forties approached them, smiling. He bowed to Rhyel, then turned his attention to her. "Healer, I am Loraan, and this is Malur." He stepped aside to indicate the younger, shorter man behind him. "We were informed of your arrival. Welcome. Would you like to look around the lab?"

His smile was infectious and she returned it, relaxing a little. "Yes, please."

"I'm due on the bridge," Rhyel said, releasing her. "I shouldn't be gone long." With a warning glance at Kaarz, he activated the door and left.

There were six work stations, though she assumed only she and the three technicians would be researching the cure. The facility was fairly standard—floor to ceiling stainless steel cabinets, a scrub sink, microscopes, beakers and flasks, test tubes, a couple of Bunsen burners. She wasn't surprised to see two DNA sequencers. They were necessary to the genetic comparisons.

An ELISA was in a separate corner of the lab. The immunosorbant assay was invaluable for detecting fluids, like proteins, that were produced by viruses.

She looked up at Loraan. "Have any of you had medical research training?"

He shook his head. "We are flight technicians only, but Kaarz trained in biological research for a short time—before he decided to become a cleric. Hiilani ordered a few medical research books from Earth. She also helped with the research, but as we discovered this morning, it was not enough. We are relieved that you are here now."

"I don't know how much help I can be. My research experience is limited."

"But your knowledge of the human body is far greater than our own. Together, we have a better chance of defeating the virus."

They were surprised when Rhyel entered the lab. He hadn't been gone long. "We need to return to the planet," he told her. "The *Novaria* is preparing to leave orbit."

"Now?" she said in concern. "We need to start working as soon as possible. I need to familiarize myself with the research."

"The samples are on board. Kaarz, Loraan, and Malur can begin the preliminary tests. You will join them when *Novaria* returns in a day, maybe two."

Malur handed her a glass rod about the size of a soda straw. "All of our files on the virus are here. If you haven't had an opportunity to familiarize yourself with a Centallian computer, Hiilani can direct you in its use. She can also answer any questions you may have. She worked closely with us."

She accepted the cylinder and smiled as she and Rhyel left the lab.

"We'll transfer to the planet." He guided her down the hall.

"I thought we were taking the shuttle back."

"This is faster."

"I don't mind slow."

He tilted his head. "I thought you didn't like traveling in the shuttle."

"I do now." She tried to sound convincing. "It just took a little time to get used to."

He took her arm and urged her forward. She had no choice but to go with him. "You'll get used to this too," he said, accessing the transfer unit. "Think of it as an adventure, another new experience."

"I have a rule. I only allow myself one new experience a day and I'm over my quota now. Let's take the shuttle."

"Let's not." He lifted her onto the transfer platform. "Don't move," he warned as he walked to the wall display. His hand skimmed over the panel. Lights blinked and she half expected to hear bells and whistles. Instead, there was a hum and a glass panel began to slide around her from behind.

She was about to jump off when he joined her. He pulled her into his arms and leaned down. His exotic scent enfolded her.

"It's okay," he whispered.

"No it isn't," she squeaked.

"Yes, it is." His mouth closed over hers in a kiss that demanded her full attention. His tongue traced her lips, tempting her to open for him. She did and he deepened the kiss. He tasted wonderful. Her heart picked up its rhythm. Her whole body tingled. Caught up in the magic he wove, her mind and body expanded, exploding into stardust before his arms gathered her to him once more.

The humming stopped. The glass panel began to slide back. He didn't let go. His mouth slid to her ear, his teeth tugging at the lobe. His lips leisurely trailed down to the sensitive spot where her neck and shoulder joined. Goosebumps chilled her hot body. She moaned.

The embarrassed cough was like a bucket of ice water. She jumped back so quickly Rhyel had to grab her to keep her from falling off the transfer platform. A young, red-faced Guardian appeared to be over-interested in the flashing lights on the far wall.

"Guardian?" Rhyel's voice was calm, controlled. He wasn't even breathing hard. How did he do that? She was so disoriented she doubted she could stand without support.

The young man gave Rhyel a bow of respect. "Sir, Cintar reports *Novaria* is prepared to disembark. He wishes to speak with you before he leaves."

"I will be with him momentarily."

"Yes, sir." The Guardian couldn't leave the room fast enough. The door slid shut behind him.

Rhyel grinned at her. "I assume you made the trip without difficulty." He helped her step off the platform.

"The trip?" She looked around suspiciously. "Where are we?"

"In the fortress. The transfer pod to be precise."

"You're certain?"

He chuckled. "Yes, I'm certain."

She glanced at the transfer unit. "Was it safe to... you know... *kiss* in there? Wouldn't there be a chance that our bodies might—Rhyel stop laughing. I'm serious."

"I know you are, and I'm not laughing at you."

She folded her arms across her chest. "Well, you're not laughing with me because I'm not laughing."

"This I can see, *Rishka*." He pulled her into his arms, leaned over to activate the door and the noise and bustle of the great hall assailed them. Funny, she hadn't noticed the noise when the Guardian left.

His head bent, and his lips touched hers in a gentle, quick kiss. "I couldn't resist one more taste. Come, I'll walk you to the clinic."

26

✧

"It's been over a month since you began working with the research team." Hiilani looked up from the file she held. "Is Kaarz still avoiding you?"

Amber pushed away from the microscope. "If you're asking if he walks away every time I approach him, that would be a yes."

"Maybe Rhyel should have a talk with him."

"If it starts to interfere with our research, I'll confront him myself. So far it's no more than an irritation, but I am getting tired of having to go through Loraan or Malur every time Kaarz and I need to exchange information."

"You really should talk to Rhyel about it."

She sighed and stretched her arms over her head. "I'll think about it." She swiveled her chair around. "There is something I'd like to ask, though."

"About what?"

"The virus. I've studied the computer files Malur gave me. They saved samples from several of the miscarriages. The vaccine killed the virus in every laboratory experiment, yet Sonya's baby contracted the virus even though Sonya received the vaccine."

"That's true."

"Were the women tested after they were given the vaccine? I can't find any record of test results after the vaccine was administered."

"I assume so. Kaarz was in charge of the follow-up tests. He assured the Elders the virus had been destroyed." Hiilani leaned back. "We can be grateful the Elders were cautious and insisted only one couple conceive."

"Is it possible the post-vaccine records were filed separately?"

"I'll check the files here. The *Novaria* has returned from its supply run. I can contact the lab and have them check too."

"Don't bother. I'll talk to Kaarz. It'll be quicker."

"Have you found something?"

She shook her head. "I won't know for sure until I talk to Kaarz."

"Will he talk to you?"

"He'd better."

"You've returned early," Rhyel said, descending the stairs to the bridge's lower level. "Did you run into a problem?"

Cintar looked up from one of the consoles and shook his head. "Keeso is well, and we have a full cargo hold. I had a Guardian put your order in your cabin."

Rhyel nodded. "Why did you send for me?"

"We've intercepted another possible transmission." Cintar stepped aside, giving Rhyel a better view of the vid-screen he monitored. "This was recorded about twenty minutes ago. We had just returned to this system when it was intercepted. We may have taken someone by surprise."

"How so?"

"If this is a transmission, it appears to be coming from the planet."

Rhyel straightened. "You're sure?"

"Whatever this is, it's definitely coming from New Centallus."

"Can you locate it?"

"We believe the transmission originated from the same continent our colony is on, but we can't get an exact fix." Cintar moved to another screen. "As usual, we get mostly white noise, but there's an occasional wave pattern that indicates a potential signal. Each wave lasts no more than a few seconds at a time. It could be a speech pattern. As always, the transmission ends before our computer can pinpoint the channel we're picking up."

"We may be chasing ghost-signals, something transmitted long before either of us was born. A rogue signal could have bounced off the planet and been tracked by our receivers. Still, we need to be cautious." He looked through the panoramic windows toward the stars and sighed. "Have you detected anything suspicious out there?"

"We've adjusted the transceiver to scan for a full range of harmonics. If there is a ship out there, it's a stealth craft. We can't detect it."

"I'll return to the fortress to brief the Elders. Contact me immediately if you find something."

"Yes, you do have to share the information with me." Amber kept her voice calm but firm. She was so close to screaming at Kaarz her throat hurt. The man wouldn't let her see the records. "I'm not the enemy. We're supposed to be working together."

"Is there a problem?"

She swung around to see Tzorik standing in the lab's doorway. "What are you doing here?"

"The Elders wanted an update on your progress with the research."

"And they sent you?"

He ambled into the room. "You forget I am second in command of the fortress. I wanted to see for myself what you've accomplished. Apparently, from what I've just heard, not much. Care to tell me what's going on?"

She looked at Kaarz, refusing to even talk to Tzorik.

Kaarz shrugged. "She wants additional records on the tests we performed."

Tzorik moved to her side. "Is there a reason you won't give them to her?"

"We gave her all the records we had. There were no tests after we administered the vaccine."

She sidestepped away from Tzorik, but Kaarz had her full attention. "You could have told me that ten minutes ago." She folded her arms across her chest. "I can understand why you didn't want me to know the truth. You should have tested the women after they were inoculated. Why didn't you? Were you so anxious to be the hero that you couldn't take time to run a few more tests? You could have at least tested Sonya. Instead, you led everyone to believe the vaccine worked. Your carelessness nearly killed Sonya. It did kill her baby. You should be—"

Tzorik grabbed her shoulders and pulled her away from Kaarz, who stood red-faced, and fists clenched. "I think you've said enough, my dear." He slipped his arm around her waist and jerked her against his side.

"Let go of me," she ground out, trying to wrench free.

"I suggest you do as she says."

Tzorik shoved her away so fast she nearly lost her balance.

Rhyel was beside her in two strides. "Are you all right?"

"I'm fine."

He turned to Tzorik. "Why are you on my ship?"

The man shrugged. "I'm here at the Elders' request. They suggested I get an update on the research."

"And which Elder suggested you manhandle my mate?"

Tzorik raised his hands, as if placating an aggressor. "I was merely protecting her from harm. It seems our healer has trouble getting along with our chief technician. It's obvious little is being accomplished here." His attention fell on her. "I will report the problem to the Elders, along with my recommendation that the healer remain in the clinic and allow our experienced research technicians to do their jobs."

She bristled. "You do that. I have the information I came for. And when I'm ready to continue the research, I'll pay the Elders a little visit of my own."

Rhyel simply smiled and followed her out of the room.

Amber was sleeping when Rhyel entered their chamber in the middle of the night. He set the box he carried on the table and removed the sketchbooks, charcoal pencils, erasers, and something called acrylic sealer. He'd seen items like these in her room the night he'd taken her.

His people considered artistic endeavors therapeutic. Perhaps they were as beneficial to her people as they were to his. Hopefully, she would find a measure of peace with his gift.

She moved restlessly, and he watched her snuggle deeper into the covers. Only her head and one hand, curled at her chin, were visible, but he remembered the form hidden beneath the blanket. She was exquisitely made, everything he desired in a woman.

She was his—and yet not his.

Before the genetic scan, he'd anticipated their life together as bond-mates— the intimacy, and eventually the love they would share. He'd imagined what a child of their making might look like—a daughter with Amber's delicate features, or a son with eyes as deep green as an emerald sea.

If he and Amber had been genetically compatible, if the virus had been cured, allowing him to lose himself in her lush body, if he'd given her his child... he shook off the thought. Better to focus on their future. Every intimacy allowed....

She turned and whimpered. She was dreaming again. He moved to the bed. When she cried out and thrashed her arms, he stretched out beside her, pulling her into his side.

"Amber?" He didn't want to frighten her. "*Rishka*, wake up for me."

She didn't wake but the tension left her body, and she scooted closer, her soft breasts pressing against his chest. One hand came to rest on his lower belly. He sucked in his breath. Her gentle little hand scorched him. He fought the urge to push it lower. Sweat prickled his forehead. His peacefully sleeping bond-mate was trying to kill him.

When she moaned, and lifted her leg over his thigh, he rolled out of the bed. Comforting her tonight was out of the question. Her soft body was too much of a temptation, and he regretted the moratorium the Elders had placed on contraceptives.

He understood their reasoning, and conceded the wisdom in their decision.

No form of birth control known to Centallus or Earth was totally effective, the margin for error too great—the cost too dear.

She rolled to her side and grasped his pillow. She wrapped her arm around it, pulled it close to her face, and inhaled. His scent was on that pillow. She smiled. He smiled in response. It was a good sign.

He left without waking her, resigned to spending another night aboard the *Novaria*. Perhaps someday, when they were both too ancient to care, he would not find her so tempting. He shook his head. He couldn't imagine a time when she wouldn't fire his blood.

The sound of the door closing woke Amber.

"Rhyel?" She tossed the covers back and sat on the side of the bed.

Sleep no longer enticed her, not when agonizing dreams waited to claim what remained of the night. She turned on the lamp and that was when she noticed the sketchbooks. She moved to the table and found four large books and two smaller ones. An opened box of charcoal pencils rested on top of the sketchbooks.

Her name was scrawled in bold letters across the front cover of the top one. She'd never seen Rhyel's handwriting before, but knew the gift was from him.

With an emotion akin to reverence, she tested the texture of the paper with her fingertips. It was like touching home. A childlike excitement gripped her. She opened the cover of the top pad and experimented with the feel and response of the materials. Tentative lines and sweeps took form and became flowers, trees, and birds. Her grandfather's face materialized, and she sealed the drawing using the can of acrylic spray.

Then, she drew Rhyel.

Rhyel trimming branches with his men, biceps flexing as he wielded the axe, Rhyel at rest, his head bent in conversation with Zitan.

She flipped the page. In minutes the face of the woman in her dreams stared up at her. Like one possessed, she incarnated her dream family on paper. She drew the faces of the dead and dying, the scenes of horror, the destruction.

Tears blurred her vision and still she drew—her agony, her heartbreak, all there for the world to see. And she wept for people who didn't exist.

Dawn flushed the horizon before her pencil dropped to the table top. Her body ached. Her limbs shook with fatigue. Frightened that someone would discover the terrible secrets of her dreams, she concealed the sketchbook beneath her mattress, hidden, but close at hand.

27

✧

"Are you responsible for Kaarz's humiliation?"

Amber pivoted and watched Tzorik storm into the lab. He halted directly in front of her—too close for her comfort. She took a step back.

"Answer me!" he demanded.

"I might if I knew what you were talking about." She turned away, intent on putting some distance between them.

He grabbed her arm, squeezing it painfully. "Don't pretend innocence with me." He gave her a vicious shake. "I know you went to the Elders with your complaints against Kaarz."

Malur put a hand on Tzorik's shoulder. "It is best for you to release the healer." The two men were of the same height and weight, and the warning in the technician's voice wasn't subtle.

"I'm your commander," Tzorik blustered. "Stay out of this or you'll find yourself working the mines with Kaarz."

"You have no jurisdiction aboard *Novaria*, and Rhyel was commander of the fortress last I understood. Perhaps we should bring the matter to him."

Tzorik pushed her away. "You should never have denied my claim, woman. You will find me a formidable enemy." He pushed past Malur and left the room.

"Did he hurt you, Healer?" Malur pulled one of the desk chairs out. "Sit down. You're trembling."

"I'm fine," she assured the Guardian hovering over her. Concern and perhaps a little anger added golden flecks to his eyes. She did sit down, but the emotion that shook her body and weakened her knees was rage, not fear. She couldn't believe Tzorik's nerve. Had he forgotten Rhyel's warning?

Not that she was going to run complaining to her bond-mate. His interference wasn't necessary as long as she was cautious, and made sure Tzorik never caught her alone.

"Thank you, Malur."

"It is my duty to protect you, Healer."

"Even so, you have my gratitude." She inclined her head toward the door Tzorik had exited. "Do you know what that was about?"

"Kaarz has been reassigned to the mines."

"Because of me?"

"No, Healer, because he failed in his duties as chief technician." He looked away. "Perhaps we all failed. No one thought to question Kaarz's assurances that the virus had been eradicated."

She sighed. "You don't have anything to feel guilty about. You trusted Kaarz to do his job. Even the Elders were convinced. So the Elders have punished Kaarz?"

Malur shook his head. "Being assigned to the mines is not a punishment, though Kaarz will see it as such. And he won't be in the mines long. There are scheduled rotations from the mine to the fields, or any area needing work. Only the *Novaria*'s bridge crew and essential technicians are exempt from the rotation."

"So we're down to three in the lab. Do you know of anyone who is qualified for the research?"

"Qualified, yes, but we're so close to the cure I'm not sure another technician is needed."

She stood and moved to her workstation. "I'm inclined to agree. A few more tests and we'll be ready for human testing. We already have a Guinea pig."

"A what?"

"A test subject."

"Who?"

"Me."

"You cannot, Healer. You are too important to the colony. What if something went wrong?"

"Every woman here is equally important, and the risk is minimal. It makes sense for me to try the vaccine. The virus is in my bloodstream. We won't have to second-guess a test subject's response to the new vaccine. I'll know what's happening in my body."

Laanor entered the lab, saw Malur's expression, and asked, "What's happened?"

Malur didn't give her a chance to answer. "Our healer has decided to test the inhibitor on herself."

"You cannot be serious."

She took a deep breath. "It makes sense." Why did she have the feeling she'd spend the rest of the day explaining herself?

Amber walked into the map room and saw Rhyel, arms braced against an oval table, staring at the holographic vid-screen hovering in front of him.

A Guardian stood beside his captain, pointing to a blinking dot on the screen. "This morning's transmission came from this region of space. We've scanned the area with no results. It's as if we're chasing echoes."

Rhyel brought up another grid and pointed to a green dot on the holo-screen. "Last week we intercepted a phantom transmission from this region." He moved his hand to another dot on the map. "And last month, here." He straightened. "Find any correlation between the locations, and the white noise fluctuations. Check any changes in radiation levels—anything unique to those three points."

"Yes, sir." The Guardian jogged to the door, pausing to bow his respect as he passed her.

"Amber?" Rhyel rounded the table and met her halfway into the room. "Do you need something?"

"No. If you have a problem, I can come back."

"It's more of an irritation than a problem."

"I have good news." She smiled up at him. "I wanted you to be the first to know. We have a cure."

"Already? How?"

"We discovered the viral cells mutated before the vaccine completely destroys them. We've come up with a combination of inhibitors to stop the mutations and allow the vaccine to kill them."

She frowned. "But we don't know if the inhibitors in the serum remain effective over an extended period of time. We'll do regular blood tests, of course. And ideally, the mother should have a booster injection as soon after conception as possible. Knowing when to inoculate will be a best guess."

"Keep a record of each woman's fertile cycle. Vaccinate each woman at the beginning of her cycle."

She shook her head. "A woman's cycle isn't always regular. And your hypothesis is based on the assumption that every woman will conceive within the first month of exposure. That isn't normally the case."

He pulled her into his arms for a long hug, and his lips brushed her forehead. "Do you doubt the virility of the Centallian male?" he teased.

She closed her eyes for a moment, savoring his touch. She had no doubt at all about this particular Centallian's virility.

Too soon he pulled away and set her at arm's length. "I'm proud of what you've done."

"Not me. Malur and Laanor worked as hard as I. It was a team effort."

"You are all to be commended. Are you returning to the planet?"

She nodded. "I need to coordinate the test cases. With the Elders' approval, I should be able to begin working with the first volunteer couple tomorrow."

He slipped his arm around her waist. "We'll go down together. Share the evening meal with me."

She leaned into his half-embrace, welcoming the momentary companionship. In spite of her determination to separate herself from him, they had become friends. The realization troubled her.

Good news did indeed travel fast. She had sent Malur and Laanor to give the Elders the results of the final tests. By the time she and Rhyel transferred to the fortress, the evening meal had become a celebration.

Rhyel led her through a maze of tables and people, stopping occasionally so that she could answer a question or acknowledge someone's gratitude. She felt humbled by the warmth extended to her.

They stopped at Zitan's table. Rhyel's father stood and embraced her. "Thank you, child," he whispered before releasing her. He turned to Rhyel. "Join us."

Cintar and Hiilani sat on either side of the Elder. She slid into the empty place next to Hiilani. Rhyel saw her settled, then took his own seat beside her.

Platters filled with hot bread and a variety of vegetables were passed to them as Zitan offered further congratulations. "Our very existence relied on finding a cure for the virus."

Cintar glanced toward Hiilani, and quickly looked toward the Elder. "How long will you wait before lifting the moratorium on conception? Many of our Guardians are anxious to begin families." His eyes strayed to Hiilani once more.

Amber paid little attention to Zitan's response. Cintar's distraction fascinated her. He took advantage of every opportunity to look the nurse's way. And Hiilani was trying to ignore the man's obvious interest. The young woman watched her plate as if she expected someone to snatch it out from under her nose.

Conversations about work, crops, and future dreams floated in and out of her hearing, favorite topics in any rural community back home.

In essence, the colonists were an extended family who worked together toward a mutual goal and supported each other during difficult times. Tonight, they celebrated their future and the children who would fulfill their lives. She read anticipation on the faces of the young couples, and cautious satisfaction in the Elders' eyes.

Her gaze came to rest on Rhyel. As long as they were together he would never have the sons and daughters he deserved. Had she doomed him to eternal regret?

She looked away. She'd made the only decision she could at the time—a decision she had been forced to make. Second-guessing that decision was useless and unproductive.

The virus was cured. The Centallians had their future, and she wouldn't carry the deadly disease back to Earth. Now she needed to concentrate on getting home. Her life—her real life—was out there with her grandfather and her career.

Hiilani's hand on her arm pulled her from her thoughts. She turned to her friend, but Hiilani was watching Rhyel. Malur had taken the seat next to his captain and was speaking to him in low tones. The conversation was serious by the solemn look on the Guardian's face.

Rhyel didn't like what he was hearing. The muscles in his shoulders bunched as if he prepared for battle.

She leaned toward her friend. "Has something happened?"

"I don't know." The nurse looked around the room. "Malur seems to be the only one who's upset as far as I can tell—if you don't count Rhyel."

Malur caught Amber's eye and gave her an apologetic look before retreating. And retreat he did, leaving the hall before she could ask any questions. She looked to Rhyel for an explanation.

The gold flecks in his eyes were her only warning before he turned his frown on her. "Explain to me why it is only now that I've been informed of Tzorik's second visit to the lab last week."

She lifted her shoulders. "I... Well, I didn't think it was important enough to bother you."

"You should have come to me immediately. And you shouldn't have asked Malur to keep your secret."

"I didn't ask him to keep anything from you. I asked him to let me tell you. He agreed to my request. He shouldn't get into trouble because he agreed."

"He isn't in trouble."

"And I am? Rhyel, I'm not a child. I can fight my own battles."

"You are my mate. Mates share their battles. Don't deny me the right to protect you."

"I don't need your protection."

He drew her closer. "Malur told me he had to warn Tzorik off when the man dared to touch you. Don't shut me out, *Rishka*. You cannot fight Tzorik alone."

He was right. She pulled back. "I'm sorry. I—"

He wasn't listening. He wasn't even looking at her. His full attention centered on the entry doors, his eyes full-gold.

She swung around and saw Tzorik and Kaarz. "Rhyel, don't—"

"Keep her here." He was on his feet and on his way around the table. She wasn't sure who he was talking to, but she didn't like the implication, or the tone.

"Cintar," she cried, "stop him!"

He shook his head, but countered the action by standing and following his captain. She glanced at Rhyel's father. The Elder was on his feet, but didn't move from his place at the table. "Zitan, please do something."

"I cannot. It is my son's right, and as our commander, his obligation to confront Tzorik."

She watched Rhyel stride toward his quarry, Cintar close behind. "His obligation?"

"Tzorik has overstepped his authority several times, mostly insignificant matters. Rhyel chose to ignore them. From what I heard of your conversation with my son, I assume Tzorik is no longer being ignored."

28

Rhyel came to an abrupt halt directly in front of his adversary. "You were warned never to touch my mate again." Tzorik attempted to walk past him. Rhyel sidestepped to block his retreat. "How long did you think you could bite at my heels and go unchallenged?"

"You speak in riddles, Rhyel." He tried to walk away.

Rhyel grabbed his arm. His grip wasn't gentle. "Then I will explain my meaning—outside."

"Is that an order from the commander?"

"It can be made so."

Tzorik glanced around.

Rhyel understood his dilemma. If he denied a direct order from his commander, he might face reprimand from the council. There were too many witnesses this time.

Tzorik gave Rhyel a mocking bow and swept his arm toward the door. "As you wish."

Amber wondered why they bothered to leave the fortress. The furnishings were strong enough to withstand what she knew was about to happen—and most of the Guardians, including the male Elders, filed out behind them.

The brides remained. This was a guy-thing, even if the guys were Centallian. Testosterone was testosterone, regardless the planet of its origin. She turned to Hiilani, who couldn't hide her concern.

"At least they aren't wearing knives." She pushed up from the table. "It's been a long day. I'm going to bed."

The door opened and closed quietly, but Amber heard it all the same. She watched Rhyel move toward the bed, his gait stiff. He stopped at the foot of the bed and stood unmoving.

She got up, turned on the light, and looked at him. She was tempted to turn it back off. "How's Tzorik?"

"In stasis."

From the looks of Rhyel, he should be seeking that state himself.

"Come sit down." She didn't wait for his compliance, but headed to the bathroom and retrieved a basin of warm water and a cloth.

The lamplight fell on his face and upper body. His right eye was beginning to swell shut. There was an abrasion above the eye, and another on his left jaw. He must have washed before coming to bed. The cuts were only seeping now, and his face and hands were clean.

She nodded toward his shirt. "Is that blood yours or his?"

"Both."

"Let's get your shirt off."

She helped him out of the ruined garment and tossed it into the trash can without taking her eyes off his broad shoulders. She'd yet to get used to seeing his bare chest, which, at the moment, was smeared with blood.

She wrung out the cloth and sat beside him to sponge the blood and sweat from his upper body. But when she moved the cloth lower, he stopped her, his hand pressed tight against hers. She glanced up into his eyes and saw gold.

✧

The bloodlust was upon him. He'd fought for her, shed his blood—and Tzorik's—for her. And her sweet little hand was driving him crazy. He saw surprise in her eye—and wariness. He wrapped his hand in her silken hair and pulled her head back. His lips took quick and thorough possession, slanting over hers. He felt her sag against him and knew he hadn't frightened her.

"Open for me. Let me taste you."

She did and his tongue swept inside, touching, caressing, teasing her into joining his play—to taste him as he tasted her.

He moaned, and rolled back, taking her with him to the center of the bed. He covered her with his body, parting her legs with his knee, and buried his face in her neck. She smelled of exotic blossoms and woman.

"I need you," he groaned as he pushed her gown high, and caressed her soft inner thigh. She stiffened and he claimed her mouth in a drugging, tongue-thrusting kiss meant to quell any protest she made. He touched the lacey edge of her panties, his hand slipping under the silken fabric, two fingers sinking into her liquid heat. She stilled beneath him and moaned. Her response fired his blood. He wanted more. He wanted it all. He withdrew his hand, tearing her panties in his rush to remove his clothes.

She pulled her mouth away from his, and shoved against his chest.

"Rhyel, stop. We can't."

He tried to capture her mouth again, to drive her as crazy as she was driving him, but she turned her head.

"Rhyel! Stop! Now!"

He couldn't stop, not when she wanted him as much as he wanted her. Her body had been ready for him.

"Please don't do this." The whispered plea acted like mountain snow on his hot body. He rolled off her and lay staring at the ceiling, gasping for breath.

✧

Amber couldn't stand the silence. "Rhyel?"

"Not now, *Rishka*." The order was abrupt, harsh.

He was angry—obviously with her. How dare he be angry with her! She wasn't the one who started this. He was. She hadn't tried to stop him.

And she *hated* that interfering voice of reason.

"Rhyel, I'm sorry."

"For what?" he growled. "That you stopped me? That you didn't stop me? That you forced this bonding that nearly cost me my honor?"

She sat up and hugged her knees, adjusting her gown so every inch of her legs were covered, even her toes.

"Everything's my fault? Do I need to remind you that I shouldn't even be here? You didn't give me any choices."

"I gave you one choice, *Rishka*. I risked my life to give it to you."

"And I made the only decision I could have."

He levered himself to the side of the bed. Resting his elbows on his knees, he cradled his head in his hands and sighed.

"This can't happen again." He didn't sound angry now.

"I know."

"I'll make sure it doesn't."

"How?"

"I have no idea."

29

✧

Amber tossed the chart on the desk and looked at her friend. "How many expectant mothers do we have now?"

Hiilani was a natural organizer. Her only quirk was insisting they use hardcopy files. She asserted it was faster to pick up a file at the foot of a bed than it was to go to the computer and look up a patient. It worked for her. Amber had come to depend on her ability to keep the clinic running as smoothly as any she'd been associated with at home.

So she wasn't surprised when Hiilani—without even checking the records— announced, "Forty-seven."

"That many?" She might not have been surprised by Hiilani's ability to keep track of numbers, but the numbers themselves did surprise her. "How many women are there on New Centallus—not counting the Elders?"

"Eighty-four, including the new arrivals."

She shot out of her chair. "Eighty-four! Almost half the women here are pregnant? Are the Elders *crazy?*"

Hiilani laughed. "I don't think the Elders had much to do with it. The Guardians are taking their primary goal of procreation seriously."

"A little too seriously. Haven't they considered what we'll be up against in a few months? We're bound to be swamped."

"I know. but what can we do?"

"A few vasectomies wouldn't hurt."

Hiilani shook her head. "I doubt you'd convince the men of that. What do you think about midwives?"

"Midwives?" She briefly considered the suggestion, then nodded. "If we train the right women, they could be invaluable. Can you suggest two or three who are suitable for the training?"

"I know of several, but they're all pregnant."

Amber sighed. "From the sound of things, I have a feeling our only option is going to be expectant mothers. Speak with the two women in our volunteer group. They'll both deliver about six weeks before we get swamped. If we begin their training now, they should be able to help as soon as they've recovered from their own deliveries."

"I'll talk to them this afternoon," Hiilani promised.

"Good." She watched her friend for a moment before deciding to approach a subject that had puzzled her for a while—more so after witnessing the byplay between her friend and Cintar. "Hiilani, how long have you been here?"

"I was the first woman brought to New Centallus. Why do you ask?"

"Just curious. How long ago was that?"

"It's difficult to say. Time here seems so different. The days are a little longer, the seasons, too. It was around six months ago, I think. The others began arriving two months after that."

"Did the bondings take place immediately?"

"Most of the women were bonded before their arrival."

"May I ask you a personal question?" She took a seat at the desk. "You don't have to answer it if you don't want to."

"What question?"

"Every woman here is bonded or soon will be. You're the only exception. Why is that?"

Hiilani didn't speak at first, and Amber thought she didn't intend to answer. Then she sighed. "It's complicated. It all began with the gold the Centallians use to trade for goods."

"The Centallians use gold to trade? That would explain the heavy crates I watched the men load into the shuttle the first day I visited the lab."

"Rhyel never told you about the mining operation?"

"No, but I remember the subject of mines came up when Kaarz was transferred out of the lab. I was too caught up in finding the cure to give it much thought."

"New Centallus is rich in natural resources, including precious metals. The Centallians mine gold here, take it to Earth, and exchange it for the currency they need to buy supplies."

"How can they exchange that much gold without arousing suspicion?"

"The Centallians set up a mock mining operation in Colorado."

"There are Guardians living on Earth?"

"Keeso, one of Rhyel's most trusted friends, acts as owner-operator of the mine. Several Guardians alternate as mine workers."

"Aren't people suspicious?"

"The Centallians studied us before implementing their plan. They learned what we value, and how we go about acquiring it. They studied our attitudes, religions, and relationships, everything right down to our genetic makeup—especially our genetic makeup." Hiilani leaned back and shrugged. "By the time the Centallians purchased a worthless mine and began salting it with Centallian gold, they knew exactly what it took to succeed. So far no one has questioned their operation."

"So what does this have to do with you? You're a trained nurse."

Hiilani shifted her gaze to the clinic's window. "I was a nurse in a small clinic in Connor, Colorado, where the mine is located. Keeso and I met in a convenience store."

She laughed. "You met an alien in a convenience store?"

Hiilani grinned. "Well, he didn't look like an alien. I thought he was Native American. And if you think about it, a convenience store is a likely place to meet anyone. There are certainly enough of them in the United States.

"We were both a long way from home, and lonesome. I had left Hawaii two years before to finish college in Denver, and joined the clinic staff after graduation. I was immediately intrigued by Keeso. He must have felt the same attraction. We kept running into each other. He finally asked me out. He literally courted me—brought me flowers, even took me to a local dance, small town things like that.

"By the time he told me about New Centallus, I was so much in love with the man I would have followed him anywhere. And I did. He made me feel like a heroine in a fairy tale. When he asked me to share his life, I agreed. Since the mine was established before the Centallians actively sought mates, Keeso and I were the first couple to bond.

"I became pregnant the first week of our bonding. Everyone on New Centallus was excited about the baby. He was the first child conceived on New Centallus. Keeso was so proud.

"But soon, I realized something was wrong. I lost the baby." Hiilani stood up and reached for her empty coffee cup. "He was amazingly well-developed for such an early stage of gestation." She walked to the counter and picked up the pot before turning back. "There were appalling deformities in my baby's limbs and spine." She carried the pot to Amber's desk and filled the cup sitting there before pouring her own. Hiilani's eyes shimmered with unshed tears.

"The Elders prohibited any bondings until they knew what was wrong. They ordered intensive tests. It didn't take long for the technicians to discover that Keeso and I were genetically incompatible. Everyone feared the problem was species-related. It would have been catastrophic. The Centallians would have had to find another Earthlike world and the women and I would have returned to Earth infected with the virus.

"The cause was species-related, but it was a rare form of genetic incompatibility. The Centallians devised a scan to screen potential mates. You and Rhyel are the only other couple who are incompatible."

"So you are married."

"No. Keeso and I couldn't stay together. It was too painful. The Elders allowed our bond to be dissolved. It was a shocking concept for the Centallians—unheard of."

"Why didn't you go home?"

"I had no ties at home, and I was needed here. We didn't know about the virus at the time, but I was already infected." The nurse hugged her arms to her chest. "I still get cold chills thinking about what might have happened if I'd gone back. Since Keeso has chosen to remain on Earth and run the mine, my staying wasn't a problem. We haven't seen each other since he returned to Earth. I'm sure he will eventually find another mate. It is expected."

"What about you?"

"The Elders won't require me to bond until I'm ready."

"Good," Amber said quietly. "I'm sorry to make you relive such a heartbreaking time in your life."

Hiilani's eyes widened. "You were engaged. You've experienced a loss too. You must miss him terribly."

To be honest, she hadn't missed Chris at all. "I'd broken our engagement long before I came here." She shrugged. "I only mentioned it to Rhyel because I thought he might reconsider and take me home."

"What about Rhyel? It can't be easy."

She thought about her bond-mate. He ate his meals with her. They spent companionable evenings in their chamber, talking about the day's events. By all outward appearances, they were as content as circumstances allowed. But sometimes, if she woke late in the night, he was gone. Those nights were the most difficult, full of self-recrimination and a little self-pity. The sense of loss she'd never experienced with Chris was a part of her life now. After last night....

Hiilani cleared her throat, regaining her attention.

"I'm sorry, what did you say?"

"I asked how you felt about Rhyel."

Her throat constricted with emotion. "Does it matter?"

Hiilani came around the desk, and squeezed her shoulder. "I think it's my turn to say I'm sorry."

30

✧

Amber leafed through the drawings that filled the sketchpad once again, rapidly passing the first two—Hiilani's smiling face, then Zitan and Valdon, both laughing.

She paused at the third page. Rhyel. For a long time, she had ignored him—at least on paper. But when she'd finally given in to the inevitable and committed his likeness to paper, she couldn't stop the artistic flow of emotions.

She'd drawn him as he'd looked the night he kidnapped her, at work in the fields with sweat staining his tunic, making it cling to the bulging muscles of his shoulders and arms. She'd pictured him talking with Cintar, and with Zitan, his body relaxed, his eyes alight with laughter. She'd even drawn his battle with Tzorik, a scene so exact her mind saw the tinge of red that stained Rhyel's shirt and trickled down his arm from beneath his leather armor.

She turned the page and saw Rhyel half-naked in their chamber, moisture beading his skin.

She closed her eyes and savored every detail of that memory. The muscles in his chest and arms had rippled with strength as he toweled his hair. He had paused when he realized she watched him. *That* was the moment she had captured, the moment she knew he wanted her—the moment she'd discovered she wanted him.

She craved to be free of the restrictions of their bonding. She wanted to touch him without fear, and feel his hands on her body, his lips....

Determined to purge him from her mind, she flipped the page. Wide eyes full of wonder stared up at her. Dzang, the toddler she felt such a connection to. She had drawn the little girl last night, after another dream. She turned the page again. The woman she called mother sat with Dzang's father, Saing. They were smiling.

She closed the cover and hugged the book to her chest. This sketchpad contained the smiles and laughter so seldom experienced in her dreams. She glanced toward her bed, reflecting on what lay beneath the mattress. Her nightmares. She didn't need to see the sketches hidden there. All she had to do was fall asleep. The drawings that acted as a solace by day hadn't denied her demons the power to haunt her dreams. She leaned back and closed her eyes. Would she ever know peace again?

Rhyel watched his sleeping mate for long minutes. He'd been detained on the *Novaria*. She must have dozed off waiting for him. He liked to watch her sleep. When she slept he was free to savor her beauty.

She stirred, and a sketchpad fell to the floor. He bent to retrieve it and saw Hiilani's likeness. He had never seen Amber's drawings. Viewing her work without an invitation seemed like an invasion of her privacy. But the open sketchbook was too much of a temptation, and he studied the page.

Her artistic talent surprised him. She had captured her friend's image and personality as well. She'd even caught that illusive hint of sadness in the girl's smile. Intrigued, he casually leafed through the pages. He suddenly stopped when he saw his own likeness.

She had drawn him with bold, almost aggressive strokes. The first three sketches seemed frenzied. But the fourth drawing was different. He couldn't mistake the desire she had drawn in his eyes. She'd captured the emotion perfectly. The drawing was sensual, as if the hand that drew the lines on paper longed to touch the body—his body. He looked at her in wonder. She'd wanted him that night as much as he'd wanted her. He turned the page, eager to see the next drawing.

Dzang.

He stumbled to the bed and sat down hard. The baby's face blurred and he was forced to blink away the moisture to clear his sight.

Dzang was dead.

She had died long before the first woman was brought from Earth to New Centallus. How could Amber portray his niece with such perfection? She'd never seen her. This sketch was the only tangible image of the baby in existence—and it had been drawn with love. He carefully turned the page.

His mother.

Much later, he gently closed the sketchbook. He knelt in front of his mate. His hand trembled as he touched her cheek. "Amber?"

She groaned and turned her face into his palm.

"Amber—*Rishka*."

Her eyes opened and closed again. "Rhyel?"

"Yes. Wake up for me. I need to talk to you."

The urgency in his voice got her attention. She blinked. "What is it? Is something wrong?"

He held up the sketchbook. "How?"

She shook her head. "How what?"

He held up the book to show her Dzang's likeness, and the others. "How do you know these people?"

She still didn't answer. There was confusion in her eyes.

"Do you know who they are?"

She nodded. "The little girl is Dzang. The man on the other page is Saing, her father. I don't know the woman's name, but in my dreams I call her Mother."

He teetered back as if he'd received a physical blow. He righted himself, and took her hand. "Are there more drawings?"

"Why? I don't understand."

"Are there more?"

"Yes. Under the mattress on my side of the bed."

He moved to the bed, shoved the mattress aside, and retrieved the larger sketchbooks. He leafed through the pages.

"Rhyel, I'd rather you didn't look at those." When he ignored her, she got to her feet. "The sketches can't possibly mean anything to you, and they... they're from my nightmares. I don't want to share them with anyone."

Bending, he touched his lips to hers. "You have already."

Zitan answered the door before Rhyel could knock a second time. "I was told you were detained on your ship." He stepped back to allow his son into the room. "Come sit and tell me why you were so late."

He took the offered seat and placed the sketchbooks carefully on a small side table. He didn't waste words. "We intercepted another garbled signal on the com-link."

Zitan nodded solemnly. "Is there a possibility we've been discovered?"

"There is always that chance, but I don't think we have to worry yet. One ship might be able to evade our detection systems for a while, but not an attacking force."

"We still have no way of protecting ourselves or the *Acqeli*."

Rhyel leaned forward and rested his arms on his knees. "I promise by my honor that the crystal will never be taken. If I cannot protect it, I will see to its destruction." He leaned back against the chair and leveled a hard gaze on his father. "The *Acqeli* should have been destroyed the moment our people discovered what it was capable of."

Zitan nodded. "Perhaps. But remember, it has as much potential for good as it does for evil."

"If the Elders of the period had decided it was too dangerous to keep, our home world would exist today, our people living safe, happy lives."

"I have thought the same often enough, and abhorred the decision made so long ago. But we cannot change the past regardless of our desire to do so."

He nodded. "It is a subject best not spoken of. But the signal isn't the reason I've disturbed you so late. I have a request to make of the Elders. A personal request." He retrieved the sketchbooks from the table. "I want Amber's blood scanned with mine again."

"Another scan? Why?"

He passed the sketchbooks to his father. "She drew these. You will understand when you see them."

Zitan opened the smaller book and gazed down at the first drawing. After a few seconds he smiled at Rhyel. "Amber is quite talented isn't she?" He closed the book and handed it back. "But what has this to do with your request?"

He refused to take the book. "Keep looking."

His father did as he requested. A few pages later, Zitan came across the drawing of Rhyel after his bath. He cleared his throat uncomfortably. "I can understand why you want a second scan, but—"

He shook his head. "You don't yet, but you will. Turn the page."

Zitan flipped the page, saw the baby's face, and paled.

He regretted not having warned his father of what was coming. He reached for the book.

"No. I have to see." With trembling fingers, he turned the page. "Solaange," he whispered, reverently tracing the image of his dead bond-mate. "I thought never to see her likeness again." He looked up in confusion and his voice broke when he asked, "How?"

Rhyel was as shaken as his father. "Amber talks as if she knows them. But we both know that is impossible."

Zitan reached for the larger sketchbook. Rhyel stayed his hand. "These are drawn from her nightmares. They're graphic. They won't be easy for you to see."

Zitan nodded his understanding, but didn't hesitate to open the book and slowly turn the pages.

He read the anguish in his father's eyes.

Finally, Zitan closed the book. He stared at the front cover for a long time, and Rhyel knew his mind still held the images.

"Can you explain this?" Zitan asked at last.

"I think so, but I need that second scan to be sure."

"What do you suspect?"

"That Amber is experiencing my nightmares."

Zitan looked stunned. "You believe you've mind-bonded with Amber? That's impossible."

"You wouldn't say that if she were Centallian born."

"But she is not Centallian, and no Centallian man and Earth woman have ever mind-bonded."

"Until now."

"Rhyel, be reasonable. A couple must be physically compatible to mind-bond and your genetic scans—"

"Are false."

"You know the test is infallible. The computer never makes a mistake."

"Can you look at Amber's drawings and tell me we are not connected?"

"It seems the obvious conclusion, but have you felt the link?"

"There is a connection between us that has plagued me until tonight."

"Have you considered that Amber may have mind-bonded with a Guardian who is compatible? Cintar knew our family well."

"I don't think so. Every Centallian has a mental picture of what happened to our people, but no one knows for certain. In my dreams I have experienced every scene Amber put in that book. No one else would have imagined my mother's death. Another Guardian would imagine what happened to his own family." He studied his father. "Unless you—"

Zitan shook his head in vigorous denial. "I am fond of Amber, but I have not felt the link."

"The only way I can know the truth is to run the tests again." He stood. "This time I will personally witness the process."

Zitan walked to the door with him. "You may initiate the scans. The council will not deny your request." He handed Rhyel the largest sketchbook, but held on to the small one. "Do you think Amber would mind if I kept this for a time?"

"I'm sure she wouldn't."

"Good." He glanced down at the book as if he still saw the drawings. "They seem so real. Her dreams must be quite vivid for her to capture my Solaange so well."

Rhyel nodded. "In her dreams, Amber calls her Mother."

Zitan's eyes widened. "Then it truly is possible that you…."

"Yes."

"I will contact the technicians at first light," Zitan couldn't hide his excitement.

"Tell them to prepare for two sets of scans," Rhyel said at the door.

"Two? Why two?"

"It will save time."

31

✧

Amber withdrew the needle from Hiilani's arm, and handed her a small Band-Aid. She turned to Rhyel. "Appease my curiosity. Why do you need our blood samples?"

He chose his words carefully. He would not lie to his mate. "The technicians will be updating some of their records." He was sure that after the tests were run, the records would of necessity be updated.

She looked a little panic-stricken. "Am I to have every person on this planet lined up for blood tests?"

He smiled. "I can promise that will not happen. Cintar will report here as soon as his watch aboard *Novaria* is finished. His will be the last sample you will take today."

He watched her write Hiilani's name on the vial of blood. He had watched as carefully when she identified his vial and her own. "If these samples are ready, I will take them with me."

She placed the vials in a transport cooler and handed it to him. "Are you a delivery boy as well as the commander?"

"Only when it suits my purpose." He smiled at both women as he left.

✧

Amber stared after the closed door.

Hiilani came to stand beside her. "What was that all about?"

She glanced at her friend. "Beats me. He was acting strange, though. That was the smuggest smile I've ever seen on a man. He acted strange last night, too. Why would the technicians only update four records?"

Hiilani thought for a moment. "Maybe our records were lost."

"That seems doubtful. Our names aren't even close in spelling. And I don't think they would have the Centallian men categorized with the Earth women."

"Do you know anything about the Centallian alphabet?" Hiilani said.

"Not a thing. Why?"

"In Centalese our names might run in sequence."

"Now you're reaching."

"Maybe, but do you have a better explanation?"

She shrugged. "Not at the moment."

Rhyel had taken her sketchbooks last night without a word of explanation. When he arrived at the clinic today, he never mentioned them. She walked to the counter and pulled two cups from the cabinet.

"Coffee?" she called out to Hiilani.

"Yes, please."

She carried both cups to the work table where Hiilani had been sorting supplies. "Well, we don't have time to worry about Rhyel's motives right now. How many appointments do we have left today?"

Hiilani sat down at the work table and picked up her cup. "Eight."

She groaned. "I should have specialized in obstetrics instead of trauma."

Hiilani laughed. "If they all show up to deliver at the same time you'll need your trauma training for my heart attack."

She sank into a chair beside her friend. "Four out of the six women I examined this morning are pregnant. The husbands of the two women I didn't diagnose as pregnant insist I'm wrong."

Hiilani grinned. "You probably are."

She rolled her eyes. "I know. They've been right every time. I'd like to credit it to luck and a healthy dose of male ego, but I can't." She took a sip from her cup. "What I want to know is how they can be so positive their bond-mates are pregnant when my tests can't even confirm it. The last Guardian was extremely upset when I refused to give his mate the vaccine today."

Hiilani finished a chart notation and tossed the pen on the table. "Most likely the answer is so simple we've overlooked it."

"Probably."

"In the meantime, would you like to take odds on how many more women we can add to our expectant mother list today?"

"Too many, I'm sure. What are the probabilities of that many women becoming pregnant within the first month of exposure?"

"I've never seen it happen before." Hiilani's brow furrowed. "Maybe the Guardians are more hot-blooded than the men from home."

"I doubt that."

"I don't know. Keeso felt warm to the touch all of the time."

"Are you speaking from a romantic point of view?"

"Well, that too, but physically he always felt a degree or two warmer than I was." She shrugged. "I thought it was just me."

"I've noticed the same thing with Rhyel, but never thought about it— wait a minute." She jumped out of her chair so quickly she nearly spilled her coffee. "Do we have files on any of the men?"

"Only the few who were in stasis."

"Their body temperatures would be altered during stasis. You didn't give the Centallians physicals?"

"I suggested it, but even the Elders thought it was unnecessary. They acted as if I'd insulted them."

"No one let you take their temperature?"

"Not a one."

"We need normal readings." She was already moving to the door.

"Wait. What are you doing?"

"Research," she said as she walked into the great hall.

Several off-duty Guardians lounged at the tables.

"I need three volunteers. You." She pointed to the closest man. Her finger swung in turn to the two men at his table. "You and you, come into the clinic please."

The men looked at each other in question, but rose to obey.

Once inside the clinic, they lined up like rookie marines waiting for orders. She went down the line popping old fashioned thermometers—the kind that didn't use batteries—under their tongues.

"Close your mouths. This won't take long." She checked her watch. Three minutes later the men filed out looking more confused than ever.

"Would you like to tell me what we're doing?" Hiilani asked, looking a little confused herself.

"Checking a theory." She swabbed the thermometers with a dry cloth and read them.

"So what did we find out?" Hiilani prompted.

She handed the glass tubes to Hiilani. "Read 'em and weep."

After glancing at the readings, Hiilani looked up in amazement. "They're all over a hundred degrees."

"One hundred point five, to be exact."

"They really are hot-blooded," Hiilani said in wonder.

Amber laughed, then sobered immediately. "Our ninety-eight point six womb temperature is a perfect environment for a Centallian male's sperm. Most of their little guys could survive until a woman ovulated. Any woman who engages in sexual activity with a Centallian man may as well consider herself pregnant." The last was said in a near shout as she headed for the door again.

"What are we going to do?" Hiilani called after her.

"We have a few issues to discuss with the Elders. There'll be a ten-year supply of contraceptives returning on the next supply run, or I'll know why not."

32

✧

Amber sank into the hot, scented water and sighed with pleasure as the day's tension melted away. She blessed the Centallian's good sense in utilizing Earth's small amenities. She looked forward to her nightly soak. It gave her time to reflect on the day, to order everything in her mind, then to set it aside for the night.

She soaped the sponge and skimmed the rose-scented suds over her shoulders. Seven of the eight women she'd examined that afternoon were pregnant.

Rhyel had been detained on the *Novaria*. That happened a lot lately. She suspected he did it on purpose. Since their near-disaster the night of his fight with Tzorik, he avoided her as much as possible—only checking on her at night and never staying longer than necessary. He slept on the ship now.

Zitan had invited her to share the evening meal with him. She might as well have been eating alone. Rhyel's father proved as preoccupied during dinner as his son had been this morning at the clinic. Several times she'd caught him staring at her, lost in thought. He seemed vulnerable, and slightly sad. When she asked if anything was wrong, he shook his head and told her that sometimes the past felt very close.

Zitan reminded her of Grandpa. Rhyel's father felt responsible for the colonists on New Centallus, just as her grandfather felt a moral obligation to his patients at home. Grandpa... she'd been too busy the last few days to think about him or her home. Her throat tightened and she blinked back tears. How had that happened?

She recalled a recent conversation with Hiilani. The Centallian's plans for the clinic were long-term. She'd inadvertently projected herself into that future. She tossed the sponge into the water and stood. She still wanted to go home.

She stepped from the tub and grabbed a towel, briskly rubbing her skin dry. The problem was, she cared about these people too. Maybe she cared too much. She opened the closet and reached for her nightgown. The fresh cotton gown she'd placed in it this morning was gone. In its place hung a rather revealing, silken one. How odd.

She ran a hand across the shimmering, silver material, appreciating the fluid texture. She lifted the gown above her head and let it glide like mercury down her body. The fabric melded with every curve. One glance in the mirror told her she looked... *sexy*. For a moment, only a moment, she wished Rhyel could see her. She shook her head over the stray thought.

"Not gonna happen."

She entered the bedchamber and came to an abrupt halt. Someone had redecorated her bedroom while she was in the tub. The table and chairs had been moved to the far side of the room to accommodate a huge, circular, fur rug. The pristine white floor covering was framed by a circle of burning candles. Flickering light danced against the walls of the shadow-dark room.

Rhyel stepped from the shadows into the circle of light, one hand held behind his back as if he held a secret. He wore a breechcloth—and nothing more. In the soft candlelight, his body looked as if it had been oiled with pure gold.

"What are you doing?" She barely got the words out.

"Waiting for you." His voice was low, seductive. He smiled. "Why are you backing away from me?"

"I'm not." She bumped the wall behind her. "You're naked."

He smiled. "No, I'm not."

He may as well have been. That small piece of cloth covering his loins left very little to her imagination—which, at the moment, ran rampant.

"Why are you dressed like that?"

"Tradition."

She waved her hand toward the rug. "Is this part of your tradition?"

"It is. Do you like your gown?"

She folded her arms over her breasts. "It's a little sheer." She looked at him suspiciously. "Why am I wearing it?"

His smile broadened. "I was wondering the same thing. Come here." His grin was so devilish she'd have backed up again, if she hadn't already been plastered to the wall.

"Come to me," he said again.

She moved forward, stopping at the edge of the rug.

"Give me your hand."

She hesitated.

He tilted his head, raising an eyebrow in question.

"I'm sorry," she whispered, "You—this, makes me a little nervous."

"I know." He extended his arm, hand palm up and beckoned her closer. She reached out and his fingers closed around hers, drawing her past the candles.

"Aren't you afraid of a fire?" She kept her gown away from the flames.

"They will extinguish themselves in a few minutes." He pulled her with him to the center of the rug. "Until then we will be cautious."

He still held her hand, and turned her palm up to receive the small, ornate chest he had hidden behind his back. The same chest he'd given her at their bonding. Since that day the jeweled box had occupied the table in their room, a constant reminder of what she had denied them both.

She looked up at him in question.

"Open it."

She lifted the lid. Inside, a tiny seed rested on the velvety interior. Like a small oval jewel, its pearlescent hull gleamed in the refracted candlelight.

"I don't understand."

"I think you do. At our bonding, I refused to promise you what I could not in honor give." He tossed the box to the bed and caught her hand again, tugging her closer. "But now...."

He reached behind her head and released the pins that confined her hair, allowing the mass of curls to cascade around her shoulders. His fingers slipped through the strands.

"Your hair reminds me of fire and sunshine. It is beautiful." He pulled her into his arms. His gaze traveled leisurely over her features. "You are lovely." He snuggled her against him, his heat radiating through the thin fabric of her gown.

Warning bells went off in her head. What was he thinking? This couldn't happen again. She pushed against his chest.

"We can't. The scan—"

"Was wrong."

She stilled. "How can that be?"

"I don't know, *Rishka*, but I intend to find out." He kissed the tip of her nose. "Tomorrow."

He bent to kiss her lips, but she tilted her head to one side and his lips grazed her cheek. His breath warmed her neck. She shivered.

"Rhyel, we can't do this—we weren't supposed to be able to do this."

"I will be gentle." His teeth caught her earlobe, tugging playfully before he whispered, "I've seen your drawings, *Rishka*. You want me as much as I want you. Even now you tremble in my arms, and I know you don't fear me. Can you deny the need we share?"

She opened her mouth to voice her denial, but hesitated, knowing it was a lie.

He took advantage of the moment. His mouth closed over hers, capturing her breath, taking it into his lungs like a drowning man inhales life-sustaining air. His tongue filled the void, tasting her, teasing her, tempting her to play the game.

It was a dangerous game. She struggled for control of her chaotic emotions.

His lips glided to her ear. "Tell me you don't feel our connection and I will stop." His mouth continued a trail down her throat to the delicate hollow where her neck and shoulder joined. "Tell me you can't stand my touch." He licked and kissed her sensitized skin.

She closed her eyes, caught her lower lip between her teeth, and choked back the urge to moan his name.

"Tell me you don't like it when I taste you. Tell me only the truth, *Rishka*."

Honesty. He wanted her honesty.

"I don't know how I feel," she whispered, and the moan she'd tried to quell made the words sound throaty.

"Don't think about how you feel, only what you feel when I touch you." His hand glided over her collarbone to her shoulder. The weight of his hooked fingers dragged the gown's strap down her arm. His fingers strayed to the low-cut bodice. They slipped inside the silken material, just enough to make her aware of their presence, aware of his intent.

He paused and she could have denied him at that moment. But he wanted her honesty. And she wanted him. That admission gave her freedom.

The denial never came.

His tongue traced her shoulder, and he nipped her. When she straightened in surprise, he tugged on her gown. One breast sprang free.

She held her breath. His knuckles brushed the exposed, taut peak, and she whimpered.

His hand stilled. He nuzzled her neck and whispered, "It's okay, sweet. I promise everything will be all right."

His teeth grazed her lower lip, coaxed her to open for him. His tongue teased her mouth, seeking entry.

She didn't deny him. His tongue swept in to tantalize her. His kiss became a gentle persuasion of touch and taste.

And he did taste good.

He cupped her exposed breast. His thumb whispered over the hard nub, sending needle-fine shock waves of desire to other equally sensitive places.

He sank to his knees, his hands sliding her nightgown to the rug as he descended. His arms circled her bared hips, and he drew her down to avail himself of her newly-freed breast. She grabbed his shoulders for support. His tongue flicked her nipple once, twice, a third time.

His gaze rose to hers and he waited.

And she waited, and watched, as ever so slowly, he took her into his hot, moist mouth. Her entire body spasmed with intense, almost painful pleasure. She cradled his head in her arms, pulled him closer as he suckled.

His hands spanned her waist and he trailed kisses to her other breast. She cried his name as his mouth took possession of that orb. He slid his powerful arms under her hips and legs to support her.

"Put your arms around my neck, *Rishka*." His voice was harsh with passion.

Instead, she ran her fingers through the lush, dark hair she'd dreamed of touching. She closed her eyes and brailled his skin, memorizing every inch of his face. When she did embrace his neck, it was to pull her body closer, to nuzzle him, to breathe his intoxicating scent, to run her lips and tongue over his skin as he had hers. She smiled when he growled his pleasure at her bold play.

He pulled her knees to each side of his hips, taking a great amount of time caressing her thighs as he did so. He lowered her body to his.

She felt his arousal at the juncture of her legs, his breechcloth the only barrier separating their bodies. She tightened her hold on his neck.

"It's all right." He stroked her back and hips. His hand slid between them to pull the cloth away. He was hot and hard and immediately drawn to her heat. She tensed and started to lift her body away from his.

He caught her hips and held her in place. "Kiss me, Amber. Let me taste you again."

She hesitated, suddenly unsure.

"Now, *Rishka*, kiss me now."

It was more plea than demand. His eyes were gold with passion, every muscle in his body taut. He didn't just want her, he needed her.

Her death-grip on his neck eased as she accepted the unequivocal truth. Her lips parted in anticipation when she leaned forward to press her mouth to his. The kiss was infinitely tender and he moaned his pleasure when her tongue dueled with his.

Rhyel eased her body down his, leaned back to position himself and pressed into her. She was more than ready for him—hot, wet, and so incredibly tight. He glided deeper—until her maidenhead barred his way.

She stiffened, but he gently pressed forward, stretching the barrier.

And then he saw her tears.

He stilled, and lifted her enough to temper the discomfort, but he didn't withdraw. He couldn't. Not when she was so ready for him. His path was slick. He yearned to sheath himself completely, lose himself in the euphoria.

But first he had to hurt her, and the prospect of causing her pain while he experienced the ultimate pleasure appalled him.

He wanted to share the bliss with her.

"Bring your knees up, *Rishka*. Open for me." His lips found hers again in a devouring kiss that demanded her full attention. "I love you," he breathed against her lips. "I will always love you."

She leaned back and stared into his eyes.

"Forgive me." He surged upward, piercing the barrier, embedding himself fully. She cried out and tried to pull away. He groaned his pleasure and wrapped both arms around her, keeping her from breaking the fusion of their bodies. He gritted his teeth and fought for control, determined not to find his satisfaction until she was ready to share it with him.

"The worst is over, *Rishka*. Be still and let your body adjust to mine."

Amber felt impaled. Her body rebelled against each swelling throb of his manhood. Without separating their bodies, he leaned forward and settled her back against the thick, soft rug. He took advantage of their new position and gently glided deeper. She expected more pain, and there was some, but there was also a flutter of pleasure.

He brushed the hair from her eyes, and cupped her face with his hands. "Our hearts and minds are joined, as our bodies are joined. We are two halves of a whole, *Rishka*, forever."

He slowly withdrew until only the tip remained. His hand slid between their bodies to touch and tease that most sensitive part of her, and a delicious pressure built deep inside.

She moved restlessly beneath him, taking a little more of him into her.

Air hissed in through his teeth as his body throbbed. "The pain has eased?"

She nodded.

"You will tell me if I hurt you again?"

She couldn't speak. He was already sliding into her, so slow and deliberate he made her want to scream.

Her very existence centered on the exquisite pressure building as he filled her, receded, and filled her again. He chanted her name, his voice seductive.

She rolled her hips upward to meet his next thrust and was rewarded with a burst of pleasure so intense it frightened her.

"Rhyel?"

"I'm here, *Rishka*. I'm here." His voice was strained, his breathing labored. "Hold me."

She threw her arms around his neck and touched his ear with her lips. "I love you," she whispered. "I don't want to, but I love you."

He stilled, then suddenly rose up on his knees, taking her with him. He wrapped his arms around her hips, pulling her against his heaving body.

"Forever," he vowed as he surged up into her once, twice, and yet again.

She fragmented. Pleasure curled and undulated through every pore in her body. She tightened around him and cried his name.

He roared hers as he drove into her one last time. He gave her his seed, his love, his life.

Amber sank against Rhyel, too weak to support herself. They fell together into the fleece-like softness of the rug.

He moved to her side and pulled her into his arms. He held her close until they were both breathing normally. His skin was wonderfully warm and she was tempted to give in to sleep.

He lifted her into his arms and rose to his feet. He gently placed her in bed, set the small chest on the floor, and slipped in beside her.

"Try to sleep." He said lifted the cover over them and snuggling her against his hard body.

But she was still awake long after his breathing deepened and his arms relaxed their hold on her. She pressed her palm over her flat stomach, calculated the days of her monthly cycle, and sighed. His timing had been perfect. Their baby's conception was eminent, if not already accomplished.

33

✦

Rhyel was so incredibly beautiful, with his midnight hair falling across his high cheekbones, and those sensual lips slightly parted in sleep—Amber's mate, her lover.

He had been so tender, so incredibly gentle with her. He'd made her want him. No. That wasn't true. She had wanted him, almost from the beginning. She hadn't wanted to admit the attraction, though—especially not to herself.

She'd told him she loved him. She wasn't sure how she felt about that. Her senses were still in overload. Did this new relationship change anything? Did she still want to go home? Of course she did. But now she had their baby to consider... *his* baby....

He sighed in his sleep and the urge to touch him proved too strong to resist. She smoothed her hand across his chest and down his abdomen, reveling in the feel of hard muscle and warm—very warm skin. She smiled as she pressed her face into his neck and inhaled his rousing male scent.

Her hand rested above the light blanket that shielded his loins, but when she glanced lower she discovered the thin cover failed to conceal his arousal. She looked up.

He was watching her.

"I didn't mean to wake you. I'm sorry."

He pressed his hand over hers. "I'm not." He leaned down to nibble her lips, allowing his play to blossom into a tentative kiss.

Her lips softened, inviting more, and he obliged, deepening the kiss, his tongue teasing, tasting her. She sighed and returned the favor, eliciting his growl as he rolled on top of her.

She would have been crushed by his weight if he hadn't braced himself on his arms. But the lower half of his body rested, skin to skin, against her. His arousal nestled at the junction of her legs. White-hot bolts of pleasure shot to every sensitive part of her body.

His teeth grazed her lips, his mouth devouring her. "Let me in, *Rishka*." His words were breathy and seductive.

She didn't deny him. She raised her knees and gasped when he took immediate advantage, pressing into her, but stopping at the threshold.

"There is pain?"

She shook her head, unable at the moment to utter more than a moan. The feel of him poised to plunge deeper robbed her of the ability to speak, or breathe. All she wanted him to do was finish what he'd started and fill her completely.

But he didn't give her what she wanted, was instead slowly pulling away. The worry in his eyes told her he intended to put an end to their love-play.

"No," she cried and lifted her hips to fully imbed him. She threw her arms around his neck and wrapped her legs around his waist. "Don't leave me. Don't leave me."

He groaned and a shudder coursed his body. "I don't want to hurt you." He sounded as if he were being crushed by a tremendous weight.

"You aren't."

"You're sure?"

She pounded his back in frustration.

He chuckled. "I can see that you are, *Rishka*." There was no more time for talk as he pressed into her, and began a slow, thrusting rhythm that promised to drive her over the edge.

She clung to him, lost to everything but his soft, sexy voice, and the burgeoning pleasure that coiled in her like a tightly wound spring.

Suddenly, an implosion of raw sensation centered where he plunged. Tremors radiated outward, building in intensity. Euphoria. She dug her nails into his shoulders. Elation. Tears rolled into the hair at her temple.

Exhilaration....

She throbbed around him and moaned her pleasure when he claimed her mouth, his tongue plunging deep. He thrust, and thrust again, following her into the bliss.

He stayed inside her, couldn't bear to sever his connection with this woman who completed him. He lifted his head from her neck to look into her shimmering green eyes.

Her tears no longer bothered him. He knew the emotion that created them. She was his bond-mate in every sense. His *soul mate*, as her people referred to it.

His body stirred, and her eyes widened. He shook his head, and withdrew, rolling to her side. He laughed at the disappointment he saw on her face.

"You will kill me within the month with your demands," he teased, pulling her into his arms to nuzzle her neck. "Be patient, *Rishka*. We have a lifetime to enjoy each other." He settled her against him, closed his eyes, and sighed.

Amber didn't give him time to fall asleep. "Rhyel?"

"Mmmm."

"How did you know our genetic scans were wrong?"

"Your drawings."

"My drawings? What do my drawings have to do with anything?"

"You drew my mother, *Rishka*."

She leaned up on an elbow. "But I never knew your mother."

"Which is the reason I ordered a second set of tests."

"My drawings probably resemble your mother, nothing more."

"Dzang was my sister's daughter." He pulled her back into his arms. "All of the people in your sketchbooks are familiar to me. You share my nightmares."

"That's impossible."

"Not if we share the Azcura—the Bond. The link is a rare occurrence, even in Centallian couples. We thought never to experience it with your species, yet what you and I share cannot be denied, nor would I want to." He nuzzled her neck, his breath warm. He yawned. "Sleep, *Rishka*. You need your rest." He settled deeper into the mattress. Within seconds his breathing deepened and his body relaxed.

She couldn't rest. Her thoughts wouldn't let her. He had complicated her life again when he'd explained their irrevocable connection—and he'd given her his baby.

She touched her stomach. Was it a boy with Rhyel's dark coloring and obsidian eyes.... or a tiny black-haired girl that resembled little Dzang? She wouldn't be able to surprise her bond-mate with the announcement of his pending fatherhood. He'd be as arrogant in his certainty of her condition as the Guardians she'd dealt with in the clinic. Now she understood the Guardians' persistence in seeing their mates inoculated as soon as possible.

With a silent apology to those fathers-to-be, she eased out of Rhyel's arms, quietly slipped out of bed, and made her way to the bathroom. After freshening up, she slipped her necklace over her head and traced the etched A with her thumb, and wondered if her grandfather would ever have a chance to hold his grandchild.

A few minutes later, she emerged, wearing the skirt and blouse she'd discarded earlier.

She could wait until morning, but Hiilani would ask questions, and she didn't feel ready to explain the quicksilver changes in her life.

34

The great hall lay in shadows, and Amber bumped into more than one table as she navigated the big room on her way to the clinic.

She switched on the clinic light, and crossed the room to the cooler where the vaccine was kept. She retrieved a small vial and moved to the cabinet for a syringe and alcohol swabs. Taking a seat at her desk, she filled the hypo, and rolled up her sleeve. A few seconds later, she was satisfied her baby was safe. She applied a Band-Aid—the little yellow ducks seemed appropriate—and started to dispose of the hypo and vial when she heard a noise and turned.

Tzorik circled the room, getting between her and the door to her old room. She swerved to make a run for the other door when Kaarz caught her waist from behind and a dry rag was forced into her mouth.

"Grab her arms," Tzorik ordered in a loud whisper. "Don't let her get loose."

Kaarz pulled her arms back so far she wanted to scream. He was close to tearing her shoulders out of their sockets.

She tried to spit out the gag, but a second later, Tzorik slapped a broad strip of cloth tape over her mouth. Her heart pounded in her ears. Were they crazy? Rhyel would kill them when he found out.

"I've been waiting for you to show up here," Tzorik said. "It didn't take long for word to spread through the colony. Did it surprise you to discover you were compatible with the commander after all, that your little ploy to stay untouched didn't work?

"Has he slaked his frustration, and spilled your virgin's blood on his mating rug?" The demon snatched her hair and viciously jerked her head back. She was sure he intended to break her neck. His eyes were full gold when he leaned in to growl, "Did he take what was mine?"

He backhanded her. Light exploded behind her eyes, and everything receded into a gray, quasi-reality. She sagged and would have gone to the floor if Kaarz hadn't jerked her upright.

Tzorik laughed. It was an evil, venomous laugh that twisted her insides. "Don't you have anything to say?" He brushed a finger across the tape over her lips. "I guess not. Unfortunately, your bond-mate's discovery complicates my plans. It won't take him long to connect Kaarz with the first scan's manipulation. He may already know. I have no doubt he will come after Kaarz, and he will eventually connect Kaarz to me. It necessitates moving our schedule forward a few months." He glanced over her shoulder. "Don't you agree, Kaarz?"

He grabbed her chin and forced her head up. "Of course, it's your fault, my dear. Choosing Rhyel over me set everything in motion. I can't allow that to go unpunished. Normally, I would refuse another man's leavings. But I intend to make you the exception, perhaps put a stain or two on my mating rug. And when I tire of you, Kaarz will have his turn. But I warn you, Kaarz's inclinations run toward the bizarre. He will not be as gentle as I."

Tzorik laughed as he moved to the medicine cabinet and riffled through the shelves. Kaarz forced her closer to her tormentor. Tzorik found the bottle he sought and held it up for her inspection.

"I've made a point of familiarizing myself with the medications you stock. I like to be aware of what's available. This should keep you from causing any more trouble."

Fresh adrenaline surged through her. She recognized the powerful tranquilizer he held. She'd seen it used in the hospital at home. One small injection had turned a violent, six-foot-five psychiatric patient into a near-zombie within minutes.

Tzorik found a hypodermic and tore the plastic away. He plunged the needle into the bottle's rubber cap and upended the vial.

Her breath quickened as he pulled the hypo's plunger back, filling the syringe to capacity. He had no idea what he was doing—unless he intended to kill her now. It was a potentially lethal dose.

He held the needle in front of her eyes, taunting her. She was transfixed, as though staring at a viper. That amount of serum was likely as deadly, too.

"Kaarz has the shuttle ready for our departure," Tzorik said, drawing her attention back to him. "This will keep you quiet for our little trip." She looked from Tzorik to the needle and shook her head violently.

"You look frightened, my dear. Do you fear discovery? Don't. Cintar leaves orbit for Earth soon. Shuttles have been transporting ore from the mines to the *Novaria* throughout the afternoon and evening. No one will notice one more departure." He shoved the sleeve of her blouse up.

She shook her head and twisted, trying to escape Tzorik's hand. She brought her knee up hard but he deflected the blow with his thigh.

"Hold her," he ordered Kaarz, "or you'll feel the bite of the needle." His fingers dug deep into the flesh of her arm as he jabbed the needle into the muscle and shoved the plunger to the hilt. He'd given her the full dose.

The drug hit her system in seconds. Tzorik's face blurred into a grinning, misshapen caricature.

Siikzo closed the entry doors to the great hall and breathed a heartfelt sigh of relief. He was exhausted. *Novaria* was due to leave orbit at dawn. When they'd discovered the loose beam in the mineshaft, all activity had been halted. It took over an hour to shore up the large timber. Once it was safe to return to the mine, everyone bent their backs to the task of filling the crates and loading them onto the ground shuttle.

There were more than enough men to see the crates transferred from the ground vehicle to the large cargo shuttle. No one argued with his decision to go on to the fortress. They knew he worried about his mate. A light under the clinic door caught his attention. Sonya.

He jogged to the clinic and knocked. No one answered. He knocked a little louder. This time, he heard someone moving, but still no answer. Something wasn't right. He turned the handle and pushed the door open.

Tzorik stood on the far side of the room. The healer hung limp in his arms, unmoving.

Siikzo barged into the room. "What have you done to the healer?"

Tzorik scowled. "How interesting that you assume I've done something to her. Did it occur to you that I might be trying to help her?"

Helping their healer was something he doubted Tzorik would ever do. "What's wrong with her?"

"She's sleeping."

"Tzorik, if you've—" He stiffened. The fine point of a deadly-sharp blade penetrated his shirt and pricked the skin between his shoulder blades.

Tzorik smiled. "Nicely done, Kaarz. Why don't you encourage our friend to move over here? Shut the door behind you."

The door closed quietly, the long knife never leaving Siikzo's back. Kaarz nudged him forward with the tip of his blade and a trickle of warm blood rolled down his spine. He stopped in front of Tzorik.

The healer looked as pale as death. She was breathing, though, each breath alarmingly slow. "What did you do to her?"

"Your concern for the woman is commendable, but you needn't worry. She'll wake up when the drug wears off. Take her." Tzorik practically tossed the healer into his arms. "We're going to take a walk to the shuttle pad. You hold the woman in such high esteem, you can carry her. Cooperate, and you both might live. Cause any problems and Kaarz will kill you—and after you are dead, I'll send him to kill Sonya. I can promise that she will suffer before she draws her final breath. Do we have an understanding?"

Siikzo nodded and the knife withdrew.

Tzorik shoved Siikzo toward the door. "Kaarz, see if the hall is empty. Turn out the light first."

The room darkened, and Kaarz stuck his head out the door. "It's clear," he whispered.

Tzorik didn't bother to lower his voice. "Let's go."

Siikzo pulled the healer close against his chest as they filed out of the clinic and through the hall to the main doors. Kaarz held the massive portal open, allowing Tzorik and Siikzo to pass through into the night.

35

At a nod from Tzorik, Siikzo sprinted toward the smaller ship, the healer snuggled close in his arms. He reached the protective shadows of the shuttle and turned to watch Tzorik cross the expanse at a run.

"Take her into the shuttle." Tzorik slapped his hand against the panel release. The shuttle door slid open, and he shoved Siikzo ahead of him into the shadowy interior. "Put her on the floor. We'll have to wait for the other shuttle to disembark before we can leave."

Siikzo scanned the craft for a clean spot among the debris and empty ore crates, then carefully placed her on the deck. He swung around. "Tzorik, you—"

Kaarz's huge fist caught the side of his head, and he went down.

Dazed, he watched Tzorik rip a heavy cord from the nearest empty crate and toss it to Kaarz. "Tie and gag him. I don't want to listen to whatever he has to say. I'll raise the blast shields and secure the entry."

Kaarz yanked Siikzo's arms behind him and bound them.

"Did you get *Novaria*'s orbital coordinates?" Tzorik asked.

Kaarz grabbed a greasy rag from the floor and stuffed it into Siikzo's mouth before turning to Tzorik. "Yes."

"And Celiiel's ship?"

"Your woman's ship is in the same orbit on the opposite side of the planet waiting for our arrival. I've entered its coordinates into this shuttle's navigation system."

Celiiel? Siikzo shook his head to clear it. He couldn't have heard them right. Celiiel was dead. Tzorik's mate had been on Centallus when it was destroyed.

"How long before the *Novaria* departs?" Tzorik called over his shoulder.

"Within the hour."

"Tie Siikzo's legs as well. Make sure he can't get to his feet."

Kaarz nodded and knelt in front of Siikzo, blocking his view. But when the large man bent to secure Siikzo's feet, Tzorik, long-knife in hand, advanced on Kaarz's back.

Siikzo jerked upright, knowing exactly what Tzorik intended. He pulled at the restraints as Tzorik drew silently closer. Kaarz punched him in the ribs for his resistance. Siikzo tried to push the gag away with his tongue. When that failed he tried to cry a warning around the cloth. Kaarz leaned back to look at him. Siikzo caught his gaze, then glanced at Tzorik who stood at Kaarz's back—smiling.

Tzorik lunged. Kaarz's wide, disbelieving eyes locked with Siikzo's as the blade found its mark. He stiffened, his eyes glazing before he slumped across Siikzo's legs.

Siikzo's every sense was focused on the knife and the dreadful anticipation of his own impending death.

Tzorik calmly wiped the bloody knife on Kaarz's tunic. "I do intend to kill you, but not with the ease of a knife between your ribs. Kaarz's only mistake was being found out—or he soon would have been. Rhyel is smart enough to link Kaarz to the manipulation of the genetic scans, and eventually I would have been implicated. Kaarz had become a liability. Of course I had to make him believe we were leaving the planet now. He would have questioned what we were doing otherwise.

"But you… you betrayed our association when you befriended her." Tzorik tilted his head toward the healer. "I've decided your death should be prolonged."

Tzorik scrutinized the litter of twine, cardboard, and shredded paper strewn around the deck. "I believe fire will be the appropriate means." He shoved a bulky crate close to Siikzo's side and began filling it with anything combustible. "This, of course, is strictly for your benefit. There will be an explosion later." As he spoke, he splintered a broken crate-lid and stuffed the pieces into the crate, then stood back to admire his work. "That will make a nice hot fire. We can't have the smoke killing you before you experience the benefit of the flames, can we?" He bent close and sneered with satisfaction. "The heat will blacken your flesh as you watch, and before death takes you, you will beg for a swift blade. It's a shame I won't be here to listen to your pleas." Tzorik straightened and moved to the shuttle's controls. He pulled a com-panel open and jerked a handful of wires loose.

"The blast shields are in place. And the alarm system is useless now. No one will notice a small fire—except you."

A few quick steps took Tzorik to a supply cabinet where he found a store of explosive cartridges used for blasting mine tunnels. From a separate cabinet he retrieved a detonator.

Close to panic, Siikzo twisted his hands, trying to free them, but the cord held fast. He glanced toward the healer.

"She isn't in any condition to help you," Tzorik said as he moved to the auxiliary fuel cell housing. He wrenched the front panel away, exposing the cell cluster, placed the explosive charge against the metal bands that bound the cells, and set the timer. "You will be dead long before that goes off," he reassured Siikzo as he returned to the front of the shuttle.

Tzorik knelt beside Amber's still form and sighed. "I had such erotic plans for her." He fingered the necklace she wore, then ripped it from her throat. "It will take a while for them to discover who is missing. This will give Rhyel a hint," he said as he slipped the piece into his pocket.

"I must be at the fortress when this shuttle explodes. There will be questions. Fortunately, with a little prompting from me, the Elders will surmise that you convinced Kaarz to help you take Amber home. Everyone on New Centallus knows you owe her a debt of honor. Too bad the shuttle exploded before you could accomplish your good deed.

"Enough talk." He rose and carried a handful of twine and rags to the front panel and held them against the sputtering com-wires. The combustible material ignited, loose pieces falling into the opening causing flames to lick at the inner panel.

Tzorik tossed the burning cloth into the crate, smiled as a spiral of smoke rose from the center. He calmly walked to the entry, activated the exit, and stepped out. He turned to smile before the door slid shut.

36

✧

The heat in the confined space intensified. Siikzo twisted and jerked his wrists in his panic to be free. He pushed against the gag with his tongue until the cloth finally fell away. "Heal—" he licked his lips and swallowed to bring moisture to his dry throat. "Healer, can you hear me? Wake up." He lifted his legs to free himself from Kaarz's weight.

The prone man groaned and Siikzo stilled. "Kaarz? Kaarz, if you don't help me, we all die."

Kaarz lifted his head, but his eyes failed to focus on Siikzo and he fell forward again. His hand fumbled at his side until he clutched his knife.

Siikzo watched, praying Kaarz had enough strength and mind left to free him. "Kaarz, don't go into stasis yet. There's a fire. Cut me loose and I'll get us all out of here."

The word fire roused Kaarz. His hand shook as he pulled the knife from its sheath. He coughed, and blood spattered the deck.

"Hurry. We don't have much time."

The wounded man dragged himself behind Siikzo. The knife clattered on the deck. Kaarz moaned and Siikzo heard him fumbling for his weapon. Then the cold handle of the knife pressed into Siikzo's palm, and he closed his fingers around it.

"You nee—" Kaarz's words degenerated into a strangled gurgle.

"Kaarz?"

Silence.

Siikzo twisted his hands to position the cord against the blade and inched the bindings back and forth until the blade took hold. A few more strokes and his hands were loose. As he freed his legs, he blessed Kaarz for keeping his blade laser sharp.

He jumped to his feet and kicked the burning crate away from Kaarz and the healer. The fire no longer posed an immediate threat, but the smoke was still a danger.

He bent to check Kaarz. The Guardian was dead.

The healer lay as still as Kaarz, but a slow pulse greeted his seeking fingers, and her shallow breathing gave him hope.

Disarming the detonator was out of the question. Siikzo lifted the healer over his shoulder and ran to the entry. The red light on the controls indicated the panel had been secured from the outside. Siikzo punched in the release code. Nothing happened. With painstaking care, he entered the code again. Still nothing.

A new shower of blue sparks erupted under the com-link panel and a tiny curl of smoke drifted through the seams around the door's release mechanism. He touched the wall and jerked his hand back. The interior wall was burning.

In angry desperation, Siikzo slammed his fist into the release mechanism— and the door slid open. The sudden rush of cool, fresh air was heady.

He hesitated at the entrance long enough to scan the area. Tzorik might be waiting somewhere in the shadows. And tonight, Siikzo had discovered Tzorik did not mind the cowardly act of stabbing a man in the back.

No one moved in the shadows beyond the landing pad. He stepped out and the panel automatically closed behind them. Siikzo paused, undecided. He could take the healer back to the fortress. But Tzorik's warning rang in his mind. First Tzorik would kill him and then kill Sonya. It wasn't an empty threat. Tzorik had proven he was capable of murder—with no remorse to prevent him from killing again. The healer was no longer safe on New Centallus.

He circled the smaller shuttle and sprinted to the larger cargo carrier. The crew hadn't returned yet. Opening the bay door, he carried the healer inside.

Thick, radiation-proof walls separated the cargo bay from the shuttle's main deck in order to shield the crew from potentially hazardous shipments. The walls were soundproof. He was satisfied they wouldn't be detected during the trip.

Since this was the last shuttle to go aboard *Novaria*, it wouldn't be unloaded into the ship's cargo bay. It would also be the first shuttle to depart the ship once *Novaria* orbited Earth. No one would enter the shuttle bay again until the ship landed on the healer's home planet.

By then he hoped to have a plan.

He made his way to the back wall. A dim interior light blinked on to aid his progress as the shuttle's engines rumbled to life. He settled the healer into his arms and sat down to ride out the shuttle's bumpy assent to the *Novaria*.

He glanced at the healer and wondered if she still lived. He touched her wrist. The erratic, weak pulse gave him only a measure of relief. He studied the young woman who had saved his Sonya's life and provided the means to save their new, unborn child. She might yet die. But if she lived, he vowed to see to her protection. As long as Tzorik thought the healer was dead, she was safe.

And Earth was where the healer wanted to be. He was returning her life to her, as she had done for Sonya. It satisfied his honor.

37

✧

"Amber!"

No light penetrated the veil of darkness that hid her. Each time Rhyel reached for his mate he clasped empty air.

Her fear consumed him. Her mind cried out for him. He turned, arms outstretched, seeking her, but their connection faded until only a thin line of awareness remained....

Thunder exploded. Shock waves bombarded the fortress. Glass shattered. Rhyel came awake and turned to Amber. She wasn't there. He swung out of bed, grabbed his pants, and shoved his feet through the legs.

The dream was still vivid in his mind and he fought back the surge of panic that took his breath away. Where was she? Pulling his boots on, he grabbed a tunic and yanked it over his head as he bolted for the door.

He took the stairs at a run, reaching the hall in seconds. His father met him at the bottom step. Zitan was visibly shaken and only half dressed. He carried his tunic and one boot in his hands.

"Do you think it's an attack?" he asked.

"It's a possibility, but not likely." Several Guardians stood by, waiting for orders. He nodded to one. "Find my mate and send her to me. Check the clinic first." He turned to his father. "Ask Aadrok to assess the damage while I find out what's happened. Send Kroyda and Hiilani to the clinic to see to anyone who's injured. Amber may already be there." He locked eyes with his father. "If she isn't found, I want to know." At Zitan's nod, he sprinted for the entry doors.

"Tinnar."

"Sir?" His third in command aboard *Novaria* fell in step. He wore only trousers and boots.

"You're with me." He opened the big door and they stepped out into the murky, pre-dawn morning. His gaze was immediately drawn to a brilliant red-orange glow that mimicked the sunrise. Iridescent blue fireballs spiraled skyward before splintering with ground-shaking force.

"A shuttle?" Tinnar asked.

"Yes." It was impossible to tell if more than one craft was involved. "How many shuttles were out there?"

"Only two. One of the small cargo shuttles and the ground shuttle."

"Who piloted the cargo craft?"

"Kaarz had volunteered for the duty, but his shift ended hours ago, before the *Novaria*'s departure."

He grabbed a passing Guardian. "Find Tzorik. Tell him to get out here."

Zitan came up beside him. The older man stood transfixed by the dreadful light show. Rhyel placed a hand on his father's shoulder. "Did you find Amber?"

Zitan shook his head. "She wasn't in the clinic. I have several Guardians and most of the women looking for her."

"Ask the Elders to help the women find her. She should have been in the clinic by now. Make sure I'm advised as soon as she's located. You heard Tinnar?"

"I heard." Zitan's attention remained on the glowing horizon. "Do you think Kaarz could have survived that?"

His gaze followed his father's. "No. But we don't know that Kaarz was in the shuttle. He shouldn't have been. Send the Guardians to me at the burn site."

Zitan nodded. "Valdon and I will join you soon."

✧

The shuttle was nothing more than a tangle of liquefying metal in the bottom of a fifty-foot blown-out hole. Metallic debris littered a charred circle that radiated out at least six hundred feet from the crater. Anyone caught within that area would have been vaporized by the fireball the blast produced.

"Have you ever seen anything like that, Commander?" Liiam asked when he reached Rhyel's side.

Rhyel forced his eyes away from the hole and looked at the Guardian. "Never." Men struggled to keep multiple fires along the perimeter of the burned-out site from spreading. "When the fires are controlled, return to the fortress with ten Guardians. Find Aadrok. The Elder will know what needs to be done. The remainder of the men will stay here until the fires are completely extinguished. Have someone cordon off the area."

Tzorik approached from the fortress-side of the crash site. "You wanted to see me?" He stared at the devastation in fascination.

"Was Kaarz on the shuttle?" he asked when the man finally reached him.

"How should I know?" Tzorik's tone was barely civil. "Do you think he was?"

"Possibly. When did you see him last?"

"Yesterday afternoon."

Zitan and Valdon had circled the site, assessing the damaged area.

"How many are missing?" Rhyel asked when they joined them.

"We won't have an accurate count until the men come in from the forest," Valdon said. "There's too much confusion."

"Aadrok checked the ship's crew assignments," Zitan said. "But we cannot be certain of any last minute crew changes until Cintar returns from his supply mission."

Rhyel turned to his father. "Has Amber been found? Is she safe?"

"She's still missing."

Rhyel stopped a Guardian as the man passed. "Go to the fortress. Everyone is to stop what they are doing and find my bond-mate. Make sure she is safe, and report back to me at once."

The man acknowledged his commander's order with a quick nod and a frown of concern, and raced toward the fortress.

"Do you believe something has happened to her?" Zitan asked.

"I don't know." Rhyel ran his fingers through his hair. "It's probably nothing, but I dreamed she was in danger. She was terrified. When the explosion woke me, she wasn't in our chamber."

"Do you still feel her fear?"

He shook his head. "No. The fear I sensed in my dream diminished slowly as I slept, until I lost our connection."

Zitan placed a comforting hand on his shoulder. "Your concern is understandable. However, since no one has suffered more than minor injuries, it is safe to assume she is well and tending a patient away from the clinic. I'm sure your man will return soon to assure you of her safety."

He nodded but found no comfort in his father's words. Still, he had to focus on the emergency at hand. Both men and women had rushed to the blast site to fight the fires. Now that most of the blazes were contained, a few people stood at the perimeter of the blast-crater, staring into the hole.

"Liiam," he said, "get those people back before someone is hurt, and put the barriers up immediately."

Valdon touched his arm, drawing his attention. "What caused the explosion?"

"We may never know, but my initial suspicion is the ISF propulsion unit."

"ISF?" Valdon asked.

"Initial Sequence Fuel. It's used as a backup fuel in the event our solar cells fail. The propellant is highly concentrated and volatile under certain conditions." He stared down at the pool of molten metal. It gurgled and plopped like a platinum geyser preparing to erupt.

"Commander!" Tiinar skirted the crater at a neck-breaking speed, his feet dangerously close to the rim.

"Slow down!" Rhyel bellowed, but the Guardian kept his pace.

"Commander," he gasped, skidding to a stop in front of Rhyel. "We found this on the other side of the rim at the edge of the burned area." He held his hand out, palm up.

Rhyel took the charred, misshapen piece of gold to inspect it. At first he didn't recognize the object, but when he turned it over, the misshapen A caught his eye.

"Nooo!" he lunged toward the smoking rim.

Liiam grabbed him. "Don't!"

The big Guardian couldn't stop him. He was too strong, too out of control. Tiinar grabbed him around the waist and hauled back. Still he pushed forward, dragging both men with him toward certain death. They held fast. Two more Guardians tackled him, finally bringing him to the ground. He struggled against their restraint. He had to get to her. He'd promised to protect her. He loved her. She couldn't die.

"Rhyel," his father shouted. "She can't be down there. Why would she be at the shuttle pad?"

He stilled as a measure of sanity returned. His father was right. Amber couldn't be down there—but if she were… pain washed over him.

"She could have lost the necklace earlier this week when she walked to the cliffs to draw. She came this way."

Rhyel wrapped his fingers around the locket and shook his head. "The necklace was in our chamber last night." He whispered the unsettling truth.

One by one the Guardians released him and got to their feet. Liiam was the last to rise, and he extended his hand.

He grasped the Guardian's hand and pulled himself to his feet. "My thanks. I owe you all a debt of honor."

Liiam didn't deny his declaration. To do so would have been an insult. "We will search the woods."

Rhyel nodded, and watched his friend signal two men and head for the wooded area beyond the burned ring. He didn't have much hope for Liiam's mission. If Amber were out there and conscious, he would know it.

He centered his mind on the woods, seeking some sign of her presence. Nothing. He expanded his thoughts, mentally calling her name.

She didn't respond.

His gaze fixed to the liquefied ship. She wasn't dead.

"I will find her," he said as he passed the two Elders on his way to the fortress. "I swear by my honor, I will find her."

38

✧

Something tickled her face. She reached up to brush it away. A high-pitched squeak and a skittering of tiny feet rewarded her effort. She opened her eyes. A deep-shadowed darkness enshrouded her. She was alone.

The thought comforted her, and she closed her eyes, seeking the delicious oblivion she'd roused from. Faces swept through her mind, like phantoms seeking recognition. But she ignored them.

When she opened her eyes again it was daylight. The crisp air blowing through a broken window pane smelled… like home. She leaned up on an elbow and looked around. But the dingy, filthy room was unfamiliar—and more than a little frightening.

Where was she? Her fuzzy brain refused to focus on the answer. "Is anyone—" She coughed. Her throat felt as if every drop of moisture had been wicked away from her mouth.

A new canteen sat on an old bench beside the bed. She reached for it, willing it to be full. It was. Unscrewing the lid, she sniffed the contents. It didn't smell like anything in particular, which probably meant it was water. Tipping the container to her dry lips, she took a tentative sip. Tepid water glided over her tongue. It tasted fresh, good, even if it was almost warm. She swallowed several mouthfuls before replacing the lid and setting the canteen down.

There were broken windows on three sides of the single-room derelict, and a broken door on the fourth that had been propped in place.

Streamers of sunlight gilded the dust motes that floated above her head. A layer of dirt covered everything except the clean blanket on the cot. It looked as new as the canteen.

A variety of small animal tracks created quilted patterns on the floor. The tracks were disrupted by large boot prints leading from the door to her bed, around the room, and back out. Since they were the only human footprints in the dust, she had to conclude the person who tracked through the room had carried her inside.

The man who belonged to the footprints obviously didn't intend to keep her prisoner if the condition of the door and windows was an indication.

Where was she? She couldn't remember getting here—couldn't remember much of anything. Her chest tightened and she took a deep, shuddering breath. What was wrong with her?

She sat up and swung her feet to the floor. She had shoes on, sandals. She looked at her skirt and blouse. At least she had on clothes, even if she couldn't say where they came from.

She buried her face in her hands, trying to force a memory—any memory. And suddenly, she remembered her name. Amber Donovan—*Doctor* Amber Donovan. It gave her hope. One memory would have to lead to another.

She looked around. The shack offered no amenities, no bathroom, no privacy. More than likely the only privacy she'd get would be a well-placed cluster of buck brush.

Buck brush. A new memory. Did it grow here? Was she from this area? She walked to the door and spent a considerable amount of energy shoving the listing barrier aside.

The sight that met her eyes when she stepped through the opening amazed her. Mountains dominated the landscape, and trees, huge, scaly-barked trees with cones the size of large tea cups. Pine trees. Another memory. Scattered throughout were smaller trees with short, fat, golden leaves that fluttered in the wind like thousands of saffron-colored butterflies. It must be fall.

A rutted road led down the steep hillside. The clearing gave her a breathtaking view of a valley far below, and that line of snowcapped mountains in the distance.

She didn't find any buck brush. But a four-foot-high clump of pungent bushes offered adequate privacy. There probably wasn't a soul within miles of the place, anyway.

She was returning to the shack when she heard bells in the distance. The tinkling sound reminded her of... sleigh bells, and instantly an image of a rosy-cheeked, white-bearded man came to mind. She remembered Christmas.

It was disconcerting, this acquiring of random memories in sudden flashes. She soothed herself with the reminder that her memory loss appeared to be a temporary condition.

The jingling grew steadily closer. She tensed, prepared to run. She bent and picked up a rotted branch at her feet. It wasn't much of a weapon. She held it like a baseball bat—another sudden memory.

The wearer of the bells stepped from the pine grove and stopped. "What the... *how* in the... *where* on Earth did you come from?"

She would love to be able to tell him.

He looked like an African-American version of Paul Bunyan—the memories were coming faster. Small, round bells dangled from the belt loops of the man's denim jeans. Lumberjack might have been a misnomer. She wasn't sure, of course, but she didn't believe any self-respecting lumberjack wore bells, or a backpack that looked like it outweighed her.

He hadn't said a word since his surprised outburst. She should probably let him know she wasn't wandering around out here half-crazed. The look on his face indicated that was exactly what he was thinking.

"Why are you wearing bells?" So much for impressing him with my sanity.

The man grinned. "It warns off the grizzlies."

She glanced around. She hadn't thought about bears.

He seemed to think that was funny. His chuckle eased her anxiety. "You're not from around here are you?"

"I don't know."

His smile disappeared. "What do you mean you don't know?"

"I woke up alone in that cabin a few minutes ago. I don't remember how I got here. I don't even know where here is."

"Do you know your name?"

She nodded. "Amber Donovan. Doctor Amber Donovan."

He seemed relieved she knew that much. "I'm Jacob Roberts. You can call me Jake." His eyes narrowed as he took a closer look at her face. "Does that place on your cheek hurt?"

She skimmed the side of her face with a tentative finger, and winced. "A little."

"What happened?"

She tried to force the memory, but finally gave up. "I haven't any idea."

"You can't remember anything but your name?"

She tilted her head up at him, feeling ridiculous. "I remember Santa Claus."

He laughed outright, a rich, companionable sound that invited her to join in. "The bells, right?"

She grinned, glad he'd made the connection and saved her a lengthy explanation. "Right. Do you know where buck brush comes from?"

That caught him off guard. "You remember buck brush?"

"I came out of the cabin expecting to see buck brush. The only bushy stuff out here smells like—Thanksgiving."

"That's sagebrush. There's lots of it up here. But buck brush?" He scratched the day's growth of beard on his chin. "My grandfather had a small farm about thirty miles northwest of Memphis, just over the Arkansas line. I remember him talking about clearing the buck brush off one of his pastures, so I know it grows in Arkansas and probably in Missouri. It might grow in Kentucky and Tennessee, too. Lots of the same type of country."

None of the places sounded familiar. "Where are we now?"

He took a deep, appreciative breath of air. "The Colorado Rockies. No finer place on Earth."

Under different circumstances she might agree, but her need to know how she'd ended up on top of this mountain was paramount in her mind.

"How close is the nearest town?"

He pointed to the rough lane that meandered down the mountainside. "That road leads to Dunston. It's not much of a town, but I'm sure we'll find someone who can help you." He shrugged out of his pack. "Do you mind if I look inside the shack?"

She shook her head.

He studied the leaning door with a jaundiced eye as he entered. When he emerged a few minutes later, his dark scowl made her take a step back. "I see a man's footprints all over the dust on the floor inside. But there's only one set of your prints. They lead from the cot to the door. Someone dumped you here, didn't they?"

"I think so."

He shook his head. "I thought you were just lost." He stepped closer, gaze focused on her cheek. "I bet that bruise didn't happen by accident."

"If someone hit me I can't remember."

"The sooner we get you to town the better." He handed her a granola bar. "You might need an energy boost before we get to the bottom. You ready?"

She nodded as she pocketed the bar. "Thanks. For everything."

From the cover of a large scaly-barked tree, Siikzo watched the healer follow the rutted lane down the mountainside. Her rescuer, who walked beside her, was definitely big enough to protect her, and though he couldn't hear their conversation, he sensed the man was genuinely concerned for her welfare. The healer was safe and eventually she would find her way home to her grandfather. His obligation to her was over.

With a last glance toward the healer, he backtracked to where he'd hidden Keeso's Jeep. Fortunately, Keeso had taught him how to pilot the simple machine when he was assigned to Earth duty. Also fortunate was their discovery of the old prospector's shack.

Now, he had an obligation to his people, and to Sonya. To fulfill that obligation, he had to reach Keeso's mine before the *Novaria* returned to New

Centallus. The Elders had decided to delay the next shipment until early spring in Colorado. He couldn't wait that long. If Tzorik's plan succeeded, Sonya believed he was dead. And Tzorik would be free to implement whatever plan he shared with his supposedly-dead mate, Celiiel.

39

✧

Dunston boasted a combination service station and convenience store, a cafe and a post office. Jake insisted Amber rest on a bench in front of the post office while he tried to find the nearest law enforcement officer. Twenty minutes later he handed her a cup of coffee and a cellophane-wrapped sandwich.

"We're in luck. One of the county deputies lives here. The girl at the convenience store sent her brother to find him. I told the boy to have him meet us here." He pulled another sandwich from his jacket pocket and sat down beside her. "Feeling okay? You still look a little peaked."

"I'm just short of breath." She took a sip of the coffee. "I think it's the altitude. If I were from this part of the country that wouldn't bother me, would it?"

"Sounds logical." He took a bite of his sandwich, chewed it slowly, and swallowed. "The deputy will want to take you to a hospital. They'll want to run some tests, check that bruise on your face."

She didn't feel up to being poked and prodded. All she wanted to do was find a comfortable bed in a clean place, go to sleep, and wake up knowing this was all a bad dream. "I'm fine. I don't need a doctor."

"I'll let you argue with him about that." He pointed to a white Chevy Blazer with an emergency-light bar on top of the cab. "That looks like our deputy."

The tall lean man who stepped out of the truck looked no older than thirty-one, or -two. He raked his hair back with his fingers and placed a Stetson on his head.

"I'm Deputy Stuart Scott." His voice was quiet and friendly. "Steve said you folks have a problem?"

Jake stood and shook the deputy's hand. "I'm Jacob Roberts. This lady is Doctor Amber Donovan. She needs your help."

She smiled as Deputy Scott tipped his hat. "I'm not sure where to start." She was suddenly nervous and uncertain. "I don't remember much more than my name." She looked up at Jake. "Mister Roberts found me at an old cabin a few miles up the mountain."

"You don't remember going up there?"

"No."

Jake placed a comforting hand on her shoulder. "From the tracks on the cabin floor I'd say someone carried her in. I think she was roughed up a little. She has a nasty bruise on her cheek."

The officer moved closer. "May I?" He bent forward and brushed the hair back from her face. He prodded the sore place below her eye. She winced and he pulled his hand away. "Sorry." He drew a small spiral notepad and a pen from his front pocket and scribbled a few lines. "Do you feel disoriented?" He slipped the pad back in his pocket.

"A bit."

"I think we should get you to a hospital."

Jake gave her an I-told-you-so look.

But she shook her head. "I don't think that's necessary."

"I'm concerned about your lack of memory. I can't make you go to the hospital, but I think you should."

"My memory is returning a little at a time. I'll tell you if I feel any worse. Right now, I need to find out where I'm from."

Deputy Scott sighed. "I have a laptop in my office at home. There's a tower on that mountain you came down from. I get a signal most days."

"You may want to include the mid-south in your inquiry," Jake said. "She remembers buck brush."

"Buck brush?" The officer shook his head and grinned. "It isn't much of a lead, but I'll take what I can get."

He drove them to his residence, and a pretty young woman met them at the door. "This is my wife, Ellie. Ellie, I'd like you to meet Doctor Amber Donovan and Jake Roberts. Doctor Donovan has had a little trouble. We're going to see if we can help her out. She could probably use a shower and a change of clothes if you've got something she can wear."

Ellie nodded and smiled at her. "I'm sure I can find something, and while you're showering I'll throw your clothes in the wash."

The deputy drew Amber's attention back to him. "While you're upstairs, I'll see what I can find online. How do you spell your last name?"

She wrote it down for him before following his wife up the steps.

Twenty minutes later, she found her way to his office. When the men looked up from the computer screen they were both smiling.

"You've found something? What?"

The deputy grinned. "We've found you. Apparently you've been missing for several months." He pointed to a picture from a missing persons site. The caption directly under the photo read Doctor Amber Donovan.

"It isn't protocol, but after checking my credentials, the law enforcement officer I contacted gave me the phone number of a Doctor Samuel Donovan. He said Doctor Donovan is your grandfather. They're going to his home to break the good news. I gave them my cell phone number. They'll give it to him. He should be calling soon."

Half an hour later the phone rang.

Deputy Scott answered on the first ring. He listened, then said, "Yes, sir. She's here with me." He paused, listening. "She seems to be fine except for a few memory problems. No, sir, she refused treatment." He paused again, then held the phone out to her. "He wants to talk to you."

She lifted the phone to her ear with shaking fingers. "Hello?"

"Amber, honey? Is it really you?"

Grandpa.

She recognized him. Tears streamed unchecked down her face. She wasn't sure how she knew, but it had been a long time since she'd last heard that beloved voice.

"Grandpa?" The word caught on a sob.

He was crying too, and talking at the same time. "Thank God, honey, thank God. Where have you been? Are you all right? Where are you now?"

She laughed for the simple joy of hearing his voice. "I'm in Colorado, Grandpa. A town called Dunston, and yes, I'm all right. We'll talk about everything once I get home."

"I'll arrange for your flight as soon as I hang up. I'll send you some money too. Let me talk to Deputy Scott. We'll figure out the details. I'll get his number and call you back with the flight schedule."

"Yes. Okay. And Grandpa, I... I love you."

"I'm glad everything's working out," Jake said when she handed the phone to the deputy. "Now that I know you're safe, I'm going to take off."

She ignored the hand he extended in farewell and gave him a fierce hug. "Thank you for everything. I'm sorry you had to interrupt your hike."

"I was planning to come down for supplies anyway." He handed her a card. "I'll be home in another week. Please let me know how you are."

She took the card and hugged him again. "I will."

Deputy Scott joined them. "I told your grandfather you'd stay with Ellie and me tonight, and that we'd take you to the airport tomorrow." He turned to Jake. "When you're ready, we can head out."

"After I buy my supplies, I'm taking the deputy to the shack," Jake told her.

"If this isn't an FBI case, it soon will be," the deputy said. "I'd like to gather as many details as I can before they get here."

Grandpa met Amber at the airport. He got the biggest hug of all, and a tear-stained shirt. "Are you really okay, honey? Did they hurt you?"

"I'm fine, Grandpa. I'm so glad to be home," she said as they crossed the airport parking lot to her grandfather's car and climbed in.

He maneuvered the Dodge Caravan into traffic and after a few minutes said, "I'd almost given up hope of ever seeing you again. Can you remember anything that happened?"

"Not yet, but my memory's coming back in bits and pieces." She swiveled to face him. "I remember the terminal."

Everything seemed to be falling in place. The back roads and lane to the house were familiar. So was the house. They entered through the kitchen. She stepped into the room and remembered her childhood, her youth, becoming a doctor. The memories were so quick and complete it was disconcerting, yet something nagged at her mind, so elusive she couldn't grasp it.

"I think I'll go up to my room and rest for a while, Grandpa."

"You remember where it is?" he asked hopefully.

She gave him a reassuring smile. "Yes. I remember."

Her bedroom was stuffy. She crossed to the window and opened it. A breeze drifted in carrying the scent of early fall. She studied the yard and woods beyond. The dogwoods were turning, their deep burgundy leaves standing out against the still-green oak and hickory. She'd missed summer. She rested her hand on the screen, and leaned forward.

The pressure of her fingers against the screen triggered a sudden, vivid memory. She staggered back and sat down hard on the side of the bed. Rhyel.

Scenes cascaded over her mind like water crashing over boulder-strewn falls. Exotic, unearthly trees and plants, a green sea and bluffs, a fortress.

Faces took form—so many, so fast—Hiilani, the Elders, Cintar, the women who'd depended on her medical abilities. The memories crashed on her mind like breakers on a shore.

Her breath caught when her memory centered on one, beautiful, life-changing experience. She cradled her flat stomach in her arms. She was pregnant.

Then she remembered Tzorik's hate-filled eyes and shivered. Somehow, he was the reason she was home again.

40

✧

"It has been five months since Amber's death. Have you considered taking another bond-mate?" Rhyel and his father had been inspecting the recently finished aquifer when Zitan posed the question. "Not all of the women have been spoken for as yet. I know of several who would welcome your claim."

Rhyel's mouth drew down in a tight line. "I know my duty, and I will honor it when the time is right."

"I'm concerned about you, son. You grieve for her as if she passed from our realm yesterday."

Rhyel withdrew Amber's necklace from its place in his vest pocket and closed his hand around it. "When I brought her to our world, she begged me to take her home for her grandfather's sake. The man still doesn't know what happened to his granddaughter. He will never know unless I tell him."

He placed a heavy hand on his father's shoulder and looked into his eyes. "I understand the pain he must have felt. I share that sense of loss. In truth, neither of us knows what became of the woman we love." He caressed the deformed locket before he slipped it back into his vest. "I cannot give him back his granddaughter, but I can tell him what happened to her. He needs to know what she did for us... what she meant to us. This is something I must do before I can make any decisions about my future."

Zitan frowned. "If you tell him the truth, you may compromise Keeso and our mine operation."

"It isn't necessary to tell him who we are, only that Amber was never harmed, that she was respected and loved, and she was mourned when an accident took her from us."

"Then you accept her death?"

"Amber's grandfather must accept her death, so I'll tell him what you believe."

Zitan did not pursue the subject.

"You've got to be kidding." Chris Anderson shoved the Stetson back on his blond hair and sat forward on the front porch rail. He laughed. "You don't really expect me to believe a story like that."

Amber adjusted the cushion to support the curve of her back and tried to find a more comfortable position in the big wicker chair. But comfort was just a memory. So was staying cool. Five months ago, when she'd come back home, the early fall heat hadn't bothered her as much as this winter thaw. In spite of the patches of snow in the yard, she swore this was the warmest February on record.

She finally looked up at her former fiancé. "Grandpa believes me."

He sobered. "You're not kidding about this, are you?"

She shook her head. "I can't marry you, not even to give my baby a name."

"You honestly believe you're married to this Rhyel fellow."

"We are married. I fell in love."

"With your alien kidnapper?"

"Alien is an overused term. I was kidnapped by a very human man who happens to live on another planet."

Chris shook his head. "Is that what you told the FBI?"

"No. I don't want the authorities to know anything about the Centallians."

"I can understand that."

"I'm not making this up, Chris."

He pushed off the rail and stuck his hands in his jean pockets. "I'm not accusing you of lying."

"What are you accusing me of?"

"I'm not accusing you of anything. I don't think you know what happened to you."

"You believe I'm delusional?"

"No, of course not." He squatted in front of her and took her hand in both of his. "But your blood test results showed traces of a powerful tranquilizer in your system. It could have caused hallucinations. Or your mind could have blocked out the truth. You know, people can block out violence or terror." He looked away. "Sometimes guilt will make a person forget what really happened."

She pulled her hand out of his grasp. "What do I have to feel guilty about?"

"Nothing." He glanced at her distended abdomen, and averted his eyes as he stood. "Absolutely nothing."

She placed a protective arm across her stomach, as if she shielded her baby from his contempt. "The baby bothers you."

"No, it…." The denial died on his lips. He retraced his steps and sat back on the rail.

She didn't have the patience to wait for him to gather his nerve. "Say it."

"Yes, it bothers me."

His admission felt like a slap in the face. In spite of everything, she thought they were friends. A friend wouldn't blame your baby for existing.

"You were my fiancée," he said. "The thought of another man's brat growing in your belly is driving me crazy." He pulled a pack of cigarettes from his coat pocket and tapped one free. "I'm trying to accept what really happened. But you have to accept it too."

He stuck the cigarette between his lips and bent away from the wind to light it, then took a deep pull and exhaled slowly. "Listen to yourself. You can't even get your story straight."

When she waved away the smoke that drifted toward her, he tossed his cigarette out into a snow bank. "Do the math. You were kidnapped nine months ago, almost to the day. Look at you. Your grandfather hovers over you like he expects you to drop that kid any minute. Now you're telling me you and this alien got it on just five months ago. You're the doctor." He pointed to her stomach. "Tell me how that happened in five months."

"I can't."

The time factor bothered her too. She'd seen the ultrasound at her last checkup. Her baby was nearing full term. At five months it should be in the second trimester, a recognizable baby, but not developed enough to survive outside its mother's womb.

Logically, she should question her memories, but those four months with the Centallians were too genuine to be fabricated. Rhyel was not a fantasy.

"Have you thought about my suggestion?" Chris asked.

"What suggestion?"

"Adopting out the baby."

"The baby belongs with me."

"Amber, that baby should've been aborted the minute you found out you were pregnant."

She awkwardly pushed up from the chair. "How can you suggest that when you know how I feel about abortion?"

"You were raped. Some brute held you down and took what was mine. Mine! I swear I'll kill him if he's ever found."

"Chris!" She took a deep breath, willing herself to calm down. "Our engagement ended long before I met Rhyel."

"I still want to marry you. I'll even claim the kid if that's what it takes."

"I told you months ago that I couldn't marry you. Now I've told you why."

"Because of your imaginary lover?"

"Because I'm already married to the father of my child. Respect that, please."

"Deep inside that confused mind of yours you know the man you thought you married doesn't exist."

"The FBI seems to think he does."

"You were kidnapped."

"I know I was kidnapped, but not by someone I want them to find."

"For the love of—" He turned his back to her but immediately swung around to face her again. "When are you going to face the truth?" His voice rose to a near shout. "You've turned some sicko into a bigger-than-life hero I can't compete with."

"Chris!" Her grandfather stepped out the front door. "I warned you not to upset my granddaughter." Before Chris could respond, the old man turned to her. "You look a little tired, honey. Why don't you go upstairs and rest a while?"

Grateful, she nodded and walked into the house. Before she closed the door, Chris said, "Sam, we need to talk about this."

She lay across the top covers, too warm to crawl under them. Maybe Grandpa could talk some sense into Chris. She certainly didn't feel up to the effort.

As usual, the baby started kicking as soon as she was prone. Rhyel's son. The ultrasound had confirmed it was a boy. Would he have the dark hair and eyes of his father?

Rhyel, you have a son and you'll never know he exists if you don't come for me. Why hadn't he? What was wrong?

41

From the seclusion of a large cedar, Rhyel watched the two men standing on the cabin's porch. He recognized Amber's grandfather from her drawings, but she had never drawn the younger man.

He couldn't hear what they were saying, but the tone of their raised voices indicated a disagreement of some type. When they went inside, he hunched beneath the tree's sprawling branches to wait until her grandfather's visitor left.

His eyes were drawn to the upper window at the side of the cabin. He remembered her standing at that window. The ever present sense of loss focused into true pain.

He had shared the Cup of Sorrow at Amber's memorial, though he swallowed none of the bitter wine. He'd spread the Sands of Eternity before the wind on New Centallus, but refused to speak the sacred words of farewell. It would be fitting to say his final goodbye here on her world. But his heart wasn't ready to free him from the bond he shared with her. She seemed too close.

Amber wrenched up from the bed, her sense of anticipation overpowering. She sat on the edge of the bed and pushed the long strands of hair out of her face.

The baby kicked so hard she winced. She patted her swollen tummy.

"It's okay, baby."

Her agitation must have shot a fair dose of adrenaline into his little system. He had every right to kick up a fuss. She braced her hands on the mattress and pushed to her feet.

Not given to speed in her condition, she moved with ungainly grace to the window. Rhyel's presence was as strong and undeniable as it had been the night he'd kidnapped her. She looked out in time to catch a glimmer of movement at the corner of the cabin. Someone was walking to the porch. A sudden giddy excitement caught her off guard.

She didn't bother to slip on her shoes before going into the hall. By the time she reached the stairs, Grandpa stood at the door. He stepped aside to allow their guest to come in.

"Rhyel." Her lips shaped the word, though no sound escaped.

His head jerked up as if she'd screamed his name. He walked slowly, almost cautiously, to the foot of the stairs, as if he feared she might disappear.

He's here. He's really here. She gripped the banister with both hands. Tears rolled down her cheeks. Her knees buckled. Black wraiths shadow-danced into her vision and blinked everything out.

Rhyel took the stairs two and three at a time, bellowing her name when she began to topple. He lunged over the last few steps, came down hard on his knees, and reached out. She sank into his arms.

She was pale as death. He cradled her in one arm and felt for a pulse. His heart hammered so hard he had trouble separating the beat of her pulse from his own. But it was there, a little fluttery, though strong. He put his forehead against hers, closed his eyes, and breathed a prayer of thanksgiving. She was alive, and in his arms again, where she belonged.

"Bring her down here, young man," Samuel Donovan called. "There's a sofa in the next room. Hurry—no don't hurry. Be careful on the stairs."

He didn't think he could hurry. He wasn't even sure he could stand, but her grandfather was also a healer, and she looked as though she might need one right now.

He snuggled her against his chest, and tested his legs, then cautiously carried her downstairs.

"What's going on?" A man stood a few feet away, his fists balled, and lips drawn down in a thin, belligerent frown—the man on the porch. "What are you doing with her?"

"Get out of the way, Chris." Doctor Donovan nudged the man aside. "Let him pass. Amber fainted. Put her over there," he told Rhyel, and bustled ahead to toss small pillows off the long piece of furniture he indicated. "Let me see her."

Rhyel gently settled her into the soft cushions, but didn't relinquish his place by her side.

Chris had followed them into the room. He hovered as close as Rhyel's presence allowed. The older man managed to work around them both.

"It's just a faint," he finally said. "Her mom did the same thing when she carried her." He patted Rhyel's shoulder. "Glad you caught her, though."

A nod was all he could manage. He still couldn't believe she was here, safe. He knelt on one knee beside her and covered her hand where it rested on her rounded stomach. The baby kicked hard enough for him to feel it. His child. He slid his hand beneath hers and waited for his baby to move again.

Hard fingers dug into his shoulder.

"Get your hands off her," Chris growled. "Who are you?"

He leveled his gaze on Amber's grandfather. "I am her mate."

Chris drew back a fist. "You son of a—"

Rhyel pivoted and blocked the blow.

"The baby's mine." Chris swung again.

He grabbed Chris's wrist, pulled him off balance, and twisted his arm behind his back.

"We both know that is a lie."

✧

Amber came out of her faint, dazed, but aware enough to understand what was happening. She struggled to push herself up from the deep-cushioned couch.

"Rhyel, please let him go."

He complied immediately.

She tried again to sit up but the cushion was too soft, and she was too clumsy. "Will someone help me up?"

Three hands reached down to her. She took Rhyel's. She didn't miss the hate-filled look Chris directed at her bond-mate, and her questioning gaze moved to her grandfather.

"You fainted," he said, "but you didn't fall." He nodded toward Rhyel who had joined her on the couch, his arm around her. "He moves fast for a big man."

Did her grandfather know who this man was? Chris obviously did. He stood close by, fists clenching and unclenching, face scarlet with obvious rage.

Rhyel drew her closer. "Are you feeling better?" he asked softly.

Nodding, she raised her face to his, and was caught by the depth of emotion in his eyes.

"I don't have much time before the *Novaria* makes contact," he said. "I need to speak with you, privately."

"If you think I'm leaving you alone with her you're crazy," Chris interrupted. "She's my fiancée, and that's my baby."

She gasped. Chris had barely acknowledged her child's existence. She looked up to gauge Rhyel's reaction to the absurdity. His stoic features gave nothing away. But his words were clear.

"The child is mine." He'd made his claim in a firm, confident voice. She was satisfied he had no doubts about who had fathered her baby. She glanced at Chris. He looked ready to kill someone.

Sam Donovan stepped in front of the angry young man. "Maybe you should go home. I'll call you later."

"And tell me what, that Amber's been kidnapped again? I'm not leaving you and her alone with him."

The older man took a deep breath and sighed. "All right. You can stay. Just back off a little. Let Amber handle this."

"You and I both know she isn't capable of making a rational decision where that man's concerned. She still thinks she was kidnapped by someone from another planet."

"She was," Rhyel said.

Chris took a step back. "He's as crazy as she is."

"Crazy!" She did a little bellowing of her own. She tried to stand and confront Chris, but Rhyel's hand tightened on her waist, keeping her beside him.

"Chris, I think you'd better go," her grandfather said. "You're upsetting Amber and I won't have it."

Chris looked from her grandfather to her and back to her grandfather before he stalked to the front door and yanked his Stetson off of the hall-tree.

"He's a *felon*." He slammed the hat on his head as he charged back to the couch to confront her grandfather again. "I can't believe you're throwing me out and letting him stay. He kidnapped her. How do you know he won't murder you both?"

The doctor looked at her.

It was a reasonable question.

"He won't," she said without having to think about it.

Her grandfather nodded, satisfied.

"You can't know that," Chris told her. "If I'm leaving so are you." He reached for her arm.

Rhyel's hand snaked out and clamped Chris's wrist. "You will *not* touch her. *Ever.*"

Chris flinched. "All right. I'll go." As soon as Rhyel released him, Chris retreated through the kitchen. The back door slammed. A moment later his truck threw gravel as it pulled away.

She slumped in relief.

"Are you all right?" Rhyel asked.

She gave him a weak smile. "I am now."

Rhyel looked at her grandfather. "May we have a few minutes alone?"

"I won't have her upset."

"I'm already upset, Grandpa. And I'm not going to calm down until I've talked to Rhyel." She tried to give him a reassuring smile. "Please let us have a few minutes alone. I promise it will be okay."

Doctor Donovan parked himself in a chair beside the kitchen entry, out of hearing range if they kept their voices low. The look he gave Rhyel told them this was as private as it was going to get.

Neither spoke at first. They simply looked at each other. Then, in spite of her grandfather's presence, Rhyel cupped her cheek in his hand and kissed her. The kiss was extremely gentle, filled with restrained passion. His fingers trembled against her skin. She didn't deny herself the reassurance of his touch, but drew back. She had so many questions.

His face clouded with concern. "What makes you so uneasy?"

"Why didn't you return for me months ago?" she blurted out, unable to keep the hurt and uncertainty from her voice.

"There was a shuttle accident on New Centallus." He pulled something from his pocket and handed it to her. She recognized the mangled necklace immediately. "It was found near what was left of the shuttle. Everyone believes you are dead."

"Did you believe I was dead?"

"I refused to let myself believe it, *Rishka*, but as time passed, and I still couldn't find you...."

"I need to talk to you about my pregnancy. I'm troubled by it."

"You don't want my child?"

"Of course I want him. That's never been in question."

"Him?" His eyes widened in wonder. "You carry my son?"

She remembered the ultrasound—her quick nod when the doctor asked if she wanted to know the sex of her child. She had welcomed one certainty in her life. No one knew she carried a son, not even her grandfather. Rhyel was the first to share her secret.

"Yes," she whispered, caught in the wonder herself. "My doctor tells me he is strong and healthy, and—ready to be born."

She expected him to react to that last announcement. The baby shouldn't be due for at least four more months. But he only nodded.

"Rhyel, the night we made love, I remember it vividly."

"As do I." His low, husky voice attested to how well he remembered.

Heat flushed her cheeks. "You took my virginity that night."

"That I also remember."

"It takes nine months for a baby to develop. To be this far along in my pregnancy, I had to have conceived within days of my kidnapping—not five months ago. If that memory is wrong, I can't be sure of anything."

His hand covered hers. "I gave you this child the night you gifted me with your innocence—the same night you left our bed and disappeared."

She pushed awkwardly to her feet. His hand slipped to her elbow to support her as they rose together.

"Look at me," she demanded. "This baby is full term."

"As it should be." He bent and kissed her. "Your worry is unfounded, *Rishka*. A child born of Centallian parents is fully developed after five of your Earth months. Apparently the Centallian gestation timeline is dominant. Hiilani had the situation figured out and under control before Sonya's child was born."

"Sonya had her baby? Was it a boy or a girl? Is she okay?"

"A boy. They are both fine."

"Why did you leave me?"

She immediately reacted to the pain in his voice. "I didn't leave you."

"Yet you are here."

'I'm not sure how that happened, I—"

The kitchen door slammed. Rhyel looked over her shoulder and stiffened. Then came the unmistakable sound of a rifle being cocked and she swung around.

42

✧

Chris stood in the kitchen doorway, the rifle pointed at Rhyel's head.

"Chris, what are you doing?" she cried.

"Get away from him."

"Do as he says," Rhyel spoke softly, but there was urgency in his voice as he nudged her toward the stairs. "Go now."

"No." She planted herself in front of him and glared at Chris. "Put the gun down. Rhyel isn't going to hurt me."

Rhyel grabbed her waist and pulled her to his side.

She resisted when he tried to move her behind him.

Chris moved into the room, his eyes on her. "I told you to get away from him. I'll make sure he won't be able to take advantage of you or any other innocent woman again." He glanced at Rhyel. "I called the sheriff."

She grabbed Rhyel's hand. "You have to leave. If they arrest you—"

"He's not going anywhere except to jail where he belongs." Chris braced the rifle against his shoulder, his finger resting on the trigger. With his free hand, he motioned to her. "Be a good girl and come over here out of the way."

"Do it," Rhyel ordered through clenched teeth. But he didn't look at her. He didn't look at her grandfather either, but she did and her breath caught in her throat.

Grandpa reached out, touching Chris's shoulder.

Chris swung around and her grandfather grabbed the side of the rifle barrel to keep from getting hit. Chris wrenched the gun back, dragging the older man with it.

She moved closer to Rhyel, stepping between him and the danger.

"No!" Rhyel grabbed her arm, jerking her behind him as a sharp crack echoed off the walls.

Rhyel's body slammed into hers and they both went down. He twisted and hit the floor first, cushioning her fall, but the landing was still hard. She held her stomach, cradling the baby, and waited for the twinge that would tell her something was wrong.

Rhyel's body shook but he still held her protectively. "Are you hurt?" His voice sounded strained.

"I don't think so."

"The baby?"

"He's kicking again. I think he's okay."

"Good." The word was no more than a raspy whisper.

She shook herself out of her stupor and sat up. She edged around and took a good look at Rhyel. He lay on his side, eyes closed, complexion pasty. The right side of his tunic had a hole in it. Blood spread around the tear and dripped onto the floor.

He'd been shot.

"Rhyel?" Panic clawed at her throat, her cry high-pitched, and frantic.

He opened his eyes, but she wasn't sure he saw her.

"How bad is it?" she demanded.

He closed his eyes again and shuddered.

She pulled at the ravels of his tunic, and he tensed against the pain. "I'm sorry. I need to see your wound."

"Get away from me before you get hurt," he warned. "Your grandfather lost his battle for the weapon."

Grandpa?

Everything had happened so fast that she'd forgotten. She looked up.

Chris stood, gun in hand, staring in disbelief at the widening bloodstain on Rhyel's shirt.

Her grandfather picked himself up off the floor and moved toward her. "Amber, honey, are you hurt?"

"I'm fine, but Rhyel's been shot."

Grandpa knelt beside them. In spite of her assurances about the baby, he gave her an assessing glance. Satisfied, he turned his attention to Rhyel, took one look, and shouted, "Chris call the paramedics, and you better pray they get here soon."

Instead of picking up the phone on the counter, he whirled and made for the kitchen.

The doctor pushed to his feet. "I'll get my bag and some towels," he said, heading for the kitchen, "and I'll see that Chris makes the call."

She waited until they were alone before she whispered, "Rhyel, can you hear me? You have to go into stasis. Do it now before you lose any more blood."

He shook his head and felt for her hand. She laced her fingers through his. "The *Novaria* is monitoring my life signs. They'll know something is wrong. Cintar will transfer me to the ship within minutes. You won't have any warning. Anyone within four feet of my proximity will be transferred to the ship. I love you and our child, but this time the choice to stay or go must be yours." He leaned back, and closed his eyes. "I won't force you to give up your home again."

He said nothing more.

43

✧

"I didn't expect to see you until spring," Keeso gave Cintar what the locals called a bear hug. "Has something happened? Hiilani?"

"Hiilani is well," Cintar quickly assured his friend, knowing Keeso still worried about his former mate. "Rhyel had a private matter to see to here. We brought a shipment of ore. The men are unloading it now. Do you have any supplies to go back?"

"A few crates for the clinic. Come in and sit down. I was boiling coffee when you arrived. Share a cup, and tell me the news of the colony. It's good to hear a voice from home."

Keeso had learned to make coffee from the old prospector who'd sold him the played out mine. Keeso had told Cintar the old man's idea of making coffee was to fill a pot with water, dump in a quarter pound of coffee, boil it, and crack a raw egg into it to settle the grounds. Cintar had tried Amber's coffee, and he'd tried Keeso's. Amber's had been better.

Though not by much.

"I've never developed your appreciation for the beverage, but I do need to talk to you."

"You sound serious."

"It is a matter of honor, and it concerns Hiilani." Cintar leaned forward and rested his arms on the table. "As her former mate you have the right to know I intend to ask her to become my mate."

Keeso poured himself a cup of coffee before he sat down at the table. "You don't need my permission to bond with Hiilani, but you have my congratulations. Hiilani is a good woman who cares about what we're trying to accomplish. She will always hold a place in my heart, but I knew she would eventually choose another mate as I must also do. I've found peace with that. I am relieved it is you. I know you will care for her. Tell her I wish her happiness."

"Ah… sir?" Liiam stood in the doorway, unmindful of the freezing air that gusted around his big frame into the room. His face was stark white except for the blotches of red on his cheeks from the cold wind. He opened and closed his mouth a couple of times, then simply stepped aside.

Siikzo walked into the room.

Cintar vaulted to his feet. "You're dead."

"Not yet," Siikzo answered. "I need to talk to Rhyel."

"Is Amber also alive, and Kaarz?"

"Amber lives. When will the *Novaria* return to New Centallus? I need to talk to Rhyel."

"Rhyel is here and should contact us within the hour. You can talk to him then. You failed to mention Kaarz."

"Kaarz did not survive. I will explain everything as soon as Rhyel is here."

"Rhyel has returned to Amber's home to speak with her grandfather. Is she there, as well?"

"It is likely, though I cannot say for sure."

"How did you get here?"

"The healer and I arrived on *Novaria* when you brought your last shipment to the mine. She was in danger on New Centallus. Bringing her to Earth was the only way I knew of to keep her alive—and by doing so, I keep Sonya safe as well."

"What kind of danger?"

"I respect you, Cintar, but Rhyel should be the first to hear my report." Siikzo's voice softened. "Is Sonya well?"

"Sonya believes her bond-mate is dead and still grieves. The Elders have advised her to accept a new mate in order to give her child a father." Cintar sat down. "They are well, thanks to Hiilani. Your son is strong and healthy."

"I have a son?"

Cintar nodded. "Elder Tzarn stands as his mentor in your absence. Sonya works with Hiilani in the clinic. The new babies keep them both busy. It is good for her to stay active."

Cintar turned to Keeso and grinned. "Hiilani complains to me about the number of babies, as though I am personally responsible."

Keeso frowned. "Hiilani is not overworked is she? Being around the babies doesn't trouble her?"

"Hiilani has five women helping her. Be assured I will not allow her to exhaust herself. As for the babies, sometimes I see sadness in her eyes when she looks at a newborn, but it is soon replaced by satisfaction. Her spirit is healing."

"Good." Keeso smiled, but Cintar noted a little of the same sadness in Keeso that he occasionally saw in Hiilani.

A second Guardian burst through the door, skidding to a halt in front of Cintar. "Sir, Rhyel's bio-readings tripped the warning beacon."

Cintar leapt to his feet again. "Has he gone into stasis?"

"No, sir."

"He hasn't made contact with the ship yet?"

"No, sir."

"Keeso, have the men load the supplies in the shuttle but don't send it to the *Novaria* yet. When I know what's happened, I'll contact you. Siikzo will go aboard with me now."

Amber placed her hand over Rhyel's heart and was relieved to feel the beat slowing. He had finally given in to her pleas and placed himself in deep stasis.

Her grandfather brought a pan of water and towels, and knelt beside them. "What did he say?"

She looked toward the kitchen doorway to make sure Chris wasn't in the room before she answered. "His crew monitors his life signs when he's down here. He'll be transferred to his ship any minute. He warned me to keep my distance or I'll be caught in the transfer beam."

She placed her hand over her grandfather's when he reached for a towel. "Grandpa, he could have forced me to go back with him simply by keeping silent. He's letting me make the decision this time."

Her grandfather studied her face then said, "I don't see you moving away from him."

"No you don't. I'm sorry, Grandpa." She leaned over and kissed his cheek. "I can't stay. I don't want to leave you, but—"

"I know," her grandfather said, patting her hand like he used to when she came to him for advice. "We both know you belong with him."

"They can bring me back to visit. I'll insist they bring me back." She pulled away from him. "You should get out of range. Rhyel said four feet."

"Did he?" Her grandfather lifted Rhyel's shirt.

The torn flesh and gaping hole in Rhyel's side made her forget everything else. After two years in trauma, she shouldn't have been affected by the sight. She gagged.

Her grandpa dropped a towel over the wound and reached for her. "Hey, what's this?"

She took several deep breaths to calm her gyrating stomach. "I'm okay now." He didn't look like he believed her. "It's okay, really."

"It's serious, but I don't think it's life threatening," he told her. "Your young man has lost a lot of blood, but a transfusion should take care of that."

A siren wailed in the distance, growing louder by the second. She gripped her grandfather's arm. "If they find out who he is...."

Tires skidded on the rocks outside. Doors slammed.

"I know," Grandpa said.

"Please stall them for as long as you can. We have to have time for the transfer."

"I've already stalled them, honey."

Someone pounded the kitchen door. Her grandpa grinned. "Chris was out by his truck—probably waiting for the sheriff. I locked him out when I went for the towels. Didn't care for his attitude. Locked the front door too."

She felt a slight tingling. "Grandpa, I love you. Get back. I think the transfer is beginning."

He put his arm around her. "I don't intend to lose track of you again. I have a great-grandchild to spoil."

There was a crash. Someone might have kicked in the kitchen door.

"He's in here," Chris shouted.

There were running footsteps. The whole room swam in blue.

Chris slid to a halt, mouth agape, eyes growing wider.

She reached over and touched Rhyel as the room disappeared.

"Stop," Chris shouted. "Wait…." His cry faded with the haze that dissolved around Amber and the others.

They evaporated. They just plain evaporated in front of his eyes.

"You'd better give me that rifle," an agitated voice called. "Real slow like."

Chris stared at the puddle of blood on the floor, then looked down at his recently fired rifle and groaned.

He slowly laid the weapon on the floor and placed his hands behind his head—like he'd seen felons do hundreds of times in the movies. Cautiously he turned and faced a nervous-looking deputy.

"Did you see them disappear?"

The deputy leveled his sidearm on Chris's chest. "The only thing I've seen is you kickin' in that back door." The young man's gaze dropped to the floor behind Chris. "Sheriff!"

"I can explain," Chris said, knowing no one would believe what he'd just seen.

"Looks like you've got a lot to explain," the sheriff said from behind his deputy. "You can start with where Doctor Donovan and his granddaughter are."

44

Cintar and three Guardians were waiting when Amber, her grandfather, and Rhyel materialized aboard the *Novaria*.

Grandpa squeezed her shoulder. "That was interesting. Are you and the baby all right?"

"We're fine. You?"

"I guess they put everything back together right. They could've left my arthritis out in space though."

Cintar knelt by Rhyel's side. "What happened?"

"He was shot." Her voice shook. She wasn't sure if it was from worry or anger.

Her grandfather knelt beside Cintar. "He's in shock. He's cold, and barely breathing." The doctor shook his head as he lifted Rhyel's hand. He looked up at her. "Honey, I can't get a pulse."

"It's all right, Grandpa, You're looking in the wrong place. Let Cintar check him."

Cintar examined Rhyel's eyes, pulse, and breathing.

"Is this man a doctor?" her grandfather asked, confused.

"No, he's Rhyel's second in command."

"Then why are we letting him take care of your husband?"

"He's making sure Rhyel is in full stasis."

"He is," Cintar assured her. "And he's strong. In a day, possibly two, we can wake him. It's good to see you, Healer." He extended his hand to her grandfather. "I assume from your conversation you are Doctor Donovan. Welcome aboard *Novaria*."

Grandpa accepted the large man's hand. "Thank you. Can we get this man to a medical facility?"

Cintar nodded. "Liiam, have the men move Rhyel to the infirmary."

Grandpa tilted his head toward Cintar as he and Amber moved back to give the men room. "What language is he speaking?"

"It's Centalese. They're moving Rhyel to their infirmary."

"You understood that?"

"With a little help." She touched the gold square in her earlobe. "We'll have to get you outfitted with one of these."

He suddenly looked horrified. "You want me to wear an earring?"

She laughed. "Trust me, Grandpa. They're the rage on New Centallus. Everybody has one."

"If you will follow me?" Cintar led them from the transfer pod to the infirmary. Rhyel had been placed on the exam table, and she immediately went to his side.

Her grandfather joined her. "How is he?"

"We'll have to remove the bullet, but he's going to be all right."

"You're awfully calm about this."

"If Cintar says Rhyel will be okay, I can depend on it." She brushed Rhyel's hair out of his face. "It didn't take long to learn that the Centallians have an amazing ability to heal themselves. They also have a code of honor that won't allow them to hide the truth."

"They sound like good folks. So who's going to remove the bullet?"

"You do the surgery. I'm too emotionally involved." She did hover, though, explaining a Guardian's stasis reactions and readings as her grandfather skillfully removed the bullet. He held the misshapen piece of metal up for Cintar's inspection.

"Barbaric," was all the big Centallian said.

She tended to agree with him.

"My granddaughter needs a place to rest," Grandpa reminded Cintar.

"I won't leave Rhyel," she insisted. "The trip to New Centallus is short. The chair will be fine."

"Now Amber—" He didn't bother to finish when she gave him "the look."

Cintar made them both happy. He had a cot brought in before he left for the bridge.

"Sleep," her grandfather ordered, before following one of the Guardians to the room assigned to him.

She gave her grandfather enough time to reach his room, then quietly slipped out of the infirmary. She was stopped in the corridor by Liiam.

"You are supposed to be resting."

"Did my grandfather ask you to watch me?"

"No, Healer. Cintar ordered me to stay close should you require assistance."

"I need to talk to Cintar. Is he on the bridge?"

"He is. I'll take you there."

"I know my way. I was hoping you'd stay with Rhyel while I'm gone."

"The commander is in stasis. He does not require watching."

"Humor me."

She stepped onto the bridge.

Cintar was on the upper deck issuing orders to the bridge crew. He turned when she entered and shook his head. Sighing, he swiveled one of the command chairs around to face her.

"Please sit down."

She took the seat, and smiled at Siikzo, who stood with Rhyel's second in command. She looked over at Cintar. "I need to warn you about Tzorik before we reach New Centallus."

"Is Siikzo involved?"

She looked from one man to the other. "Why would you ask me that?"

"I'll explain later. Please continue."

She shrugged and took a deep breath. "I'm here because Tzorik drugged me. I'm not sure how, but I think he had something to do with my being on Earth."

Siikzo shook his head. "Tzorik didn't bring you here. He intended to kill you, and tried to kill me as well. He succeeded in murdering Kaarz."

She shook her head. "Why would he kill Kaarz? He helped Tzorik drug me."

Siikzo shrugged. "He helped Tzorik tie me up and got a knife in the back for his trouble. I think Kaarz became a liability Tzorik had to get rid of. He rigged a shuttle to explode and locked us inside. Kaarz used his last minutes of life to free me. I smuggled you aboard another shuttle bound for *Novaria*, and returned you to Earth where I knew you would be safe."

"You left me alone in that shack?"

"Not alone, Healer. I waited until you were on your way down the mountain before I returned to Keeso's mine. I needed to warn Rhyel, but I didn't make it back before *Novaria* left orbit."

Cintar folded his arms across his chest and studied the Guardian. "Until Rhyel recovers, I would prefer you remain on deck," he said at last. "You can stay in the map room until we reach New Centallus."

Siikzo nodded and walked to the map room door. He stopped to smile at her. "Healer, Cintar tells me Sonya has gifted me with a son. For that I thank you."

She watched Siikzo close the door behind him then turned to Cintar. "He saved my life didn't he?"

"If we believe what he says, yes."

"If Tzorik is guilty, what will the Elders do?"

"Tzorik deserves a slow death."

"Is that what will happen to him?"

"No. If Tzorik is guilty he will be banished. There are islands on New Centallus that can serve. He will live alone for the remainder of his life, his survival dependent on his abilities."

She nodded, satisfied.

45

✧

No one had ever been harmed on a mission to Earth. When Cintar transferred ahead to warn the council of Rhyel's injuries, chaos resulted. Cintar's assurance that Rhyel's wound was not life-threatening failed to calm them. The entire council headed for the clinic to await Rhyel's arrival.

The familiar blue aura circled the center of the clinic's main room, and two Guardians bearing Rhyel on a stretcher materialized.

"Let's get him to a bed," Hiilani ordered, but Zitan stood in their path.

"I would see my son." No one questioned an Elder, so the men waited until Zitan was satisfied Rhyler was as Cintar had maintained.

Zitan started to follow the men as they carried their commander to the bed Hiilani indicated, but Cintar delayed him.

"I need to speak with the council," he said, "but I want to talk to you alone first." He led the Elder to a secluded corner. When they were standing alone, Cintar simply said, "Amber is alive."

Zitan stared blank-faced for a full minute before asking, "You are positive?"

"She and the child she carries are well and aboard *Novaria*. I felt you should be told before I spoke with the council."

"A child too? This is joyous news."

"It is, but for now only a few must know."

"I will call the council together immediately."

Cintar watched Zitan leave the clinic, then spoke with Hiilani about Rhyel's condition. "I'm sending two Guardians to keep anyone from entering the clinic."

"But my patients—"

"Will be allowed inside only if there is an emergency." He smiled when she frowned at him. "You will not be inconvenienced for long," he promised as he walked out the door.

Cintar's meeting with the Elders was brief. He tried to find the right words to tell the council of Tzorik's deception but there was no gentle way to tell this truth.

"The healer is alive. Tzorik and Kaarz were involved in her disappearance."

Valdon was quick to respond. "My son could never be so dishonorable."

Cintar hated to cause the Chief Elder additional pain, but it was unavoidable. "I'm sorry, Elder, but there is more. Siikzo also lives and has accused Tzorik of killing Kaarz and leaving Amber to die in the shuttle explosion. Siikzo claims he was able to get the healer out of the shuttle and onto *Novaria*.

"Amber's been living on Earth since her disappearance, and is now safe aboard *Novaria* with her grandfather. Siikzo is being detained aboard the ship. I must ask for a judgment to confine Tzorik as well, until we ascertain the truth."

He got his judgment.

Cintar returned to the clinic and saw Hiilani bending over the captain, pressing a stethoscope to his chest. "I thought you'd given up trying to make sense of stasis readings."

She hung the stethoscope around her neck. "When it is the commander, I take extra precautions. Something's happening isn't it?" She pointed to Rhyel's bandaged side. "I've seen wounds dressed by amateurs before, and this isn't one of them."

"I'm not an amateur."

"You're not the one who dressed this wound either."

"That is true."

"It looks like a doctor's work."

"It is."

"That bandage is too fresh to have been applied on Earth," Hiilani pointed out.

"It wasn't."

She tossed the stethoscope on the desk and practically got in his face. "Are you going to waste the rest of this conversation on two word sentences, or are you going to tell me what's going on?"

"Amber's grandfather is on board *Novaria*. He saw to removing what he called a bullet, and bandaging Rhyel's wound."

"A bullet? Rhyel was *shot*—wait a minute—did you just say you *kidnapped* Amber's grandfather?"

Cintar let her see his irritation. "I did not kidnap an old man. He came willingly. In fact, he insisted on coming with us."

Hiilani tilted her head. Clearly she didn't believe a word he'd said. "Why would he want to do that?"

"To be close to his granddaughter and the baby she carries." He caught her before her knees completely buckled. "Are you fainting?"

"Of course not," she huffed. "Let go of me."

He did, and when she wobbled, he caught her again and swung her into his arms.

"Put me down."

"No."

"Cintar, did you just tell me Amber is alive?"

"Yes."

"Put me down and tell me why Amber isn't dead." She blanched. "I didn't mean that the way it sounded."

He leaned forward as he sat in the large chair they now kept in the clinic.

She instinctively threw her arms around his neck to keep from falling. "Amber is really alive?"

"Yes." He settled her in his lap before continuing. She didn't seem to mind. "She may need your help soon. Her baby is nearing full term. Actually, it is due—"

"Any minute. Why didn't she transfer down with Rhyel and why have you set guards at the clinic door?"

"I will explain soon. Remain at the clinic. Sleep in the infirmary tonight. I have guards at that door too."

"Are you expecting trouble?"

"Just being cautious." He stood and set her in the chair. "Don't worry."

He bent and touched his lips to hers in a kiss so quick she didn't have time to stop him. Her wide-eyed, bemused expression satisfied him—for now. He left the clinic savoring the taste of her.

46

✧

Tzorik watched the Elders cross the hall and enter the council chamber. Cintar posted guards at the clinic and infirmary doors, then joined them.

Something was wrong.

He moved to the council door, but a guard blocked his entry. "I'm sorry, sir, but you cannot go in."

"I'm presently in command of this fortress," he said. "Open the door."

"I cannot, sir," the Guardian said respectfully. "The Elders have forbidden entrance to anyone."

A strong sense of self-preservation warned Tzorik not to press the issue. It also caused him to detour to the transfer chamber. There could be only one reason for a closed council meeting.

Cintar had discovered Celiiel's ship.

There were times when he regretted having to kill Kaarz. Without Kaarz's expertise to cover their transmissions, every communication with her ship had been a risk. They'd been careful, but apparently not careful enough. He needed to warn Celiiel. It meant yet another transmission.

Novaria was equipped to intercept indirect signals, but the com system at the fortress wasn't. He would have to chance contacting Celiiel from the ship. Tzorik set the coordinates on the transfer unit and stepped into the blue haze.

Fortunately, all but the most essential crew members transferred to the fortress when *Novaria* was in orbit. Tzorik moved out of the transfer pod into an empty hall.

Rhyel would be on the bridge if there was trouble. The com in his chamber was the best option for making the call. He could have Celiiel's men board the *Novaria* before Rhyel knew what was happening. Tzorik jogged to the captain's quarters and ducked into the darkened room.

"Grandpa?" a woman's voice came from the depths of the chamber. Tzorik stilled, his fists clenched. It wasn't possible.

"Grandpa, is that you?"

His hand trembled as he pressed the panel lock.

"Who's there?"

He followed Amber's voice, thankful for the total darkness of a starship's inner chamber. His passage was silent, and confident. He knew the location of the table, chairs, and bed. The ship's rooms were uniform, the furniture secured to the floor for safety.

"Who's there?" Amber's voice was calm and unafraid. She obviously felt safe on Rhyel's ship. He would disabuse her of that assumption—just before he strangled the life from her body.

Amber activated the lamp, and looked up at him.

"Scream if you wish," he said almost pleasantly. "The walls are soundproof."

"What are you doing here?"

"I was about to ask you the same question. Aren't you supposed to be dead?" He sat down on the bed beside her. She scooted as far away as the wall permitted. It wasn't far enough.

"You told Cintar about our little rendezvous didn't you? That was the reason he called the council together. Get out of bed." She didn't move fast enough to satisfy him. He dragged her to the edge. "I said get up."

She struggled to climb over the side and plant her feet on the floor.

His eyes narrowed at her extended abdomen. "I see Rhyel planted his seed in you that night. It's a shame I didn't do the same. You'd be wondering whose brat it is."

"I would have died to prevent you from touching me."

His fingers gripped the back of her neck like talons, digging into the muscle until tears showed in her eyes. "You were supposed to die that night. Where's Rhyel? I doubt he'd leave you alone for long."

"He's on the planet."

"You're lying. I came from the planet. He isn't there." He shoved her toward the exit. He pushed her into the wall beside the panel, disengaged the lock, and propelled her into the corridor ahead of him. One hand grasped her hair to hold her while he unsheathed his long-knife and pointed the weapon toward the end of the corridor. "Walk, and don't think about drawing attention to us by screaming. Your only value to me is as a hostage. I can take another hostage."

Amber believed him. He looked crazy enough to use that gruesome knife. Siikzo vowed Tzorik had used it before—on Kaarz.

Two Guardians stepped out of a lift into the corridor. Tzorik pulled her against him and pressed the knife to her jugular. "Drop your weapons," he ordered the surprised men. "Turn around." They didn't argue.

She breathed a small sigh of relief when the pressure of the blade eased.

"Put your hands on top of your heads and walk to the bridge," Tzorik ordered. "Not too fast. We want to arrive together."

At the bridge door, the knife pressed her throat again.

"Open the doors," Tzorik said. "Go in first."

The men stepped onto the bridge, but he stopped her at the entrance. Three Guardians manned the consoles of the upper level.

"Drop your weapons if you value the healer's life."

She stumbled as he forced her forward. One of the two Guardians automatically reached for her. Tzorik slashed the knife across the Guardian's wrist, and had the blade back at her throat before she realized what had happened.

The crewman cried out and grabbed his wounded arm. Blood pulsed from the slit artery.

Tzorik prodded her past the bleeding man to the center of the upper deck. "Please let me help him," she pleaded.

"He can go into stasis if he wants to live." He pointed the bloody knife toward the man at the communications panel. "You. I want every man aboard this ship on the bridge now. If you warn them in any way, I will kill the healer."

Within minutes nine additional crew members stood beside the bridge crew. The wounded Guardian had gone into stasis and was lying on the floor.

"Is this all of them?" Tzorik demanded.

"Yes, sir," the Guardian at the com confirmed. "Everyone else returned to the planet after we gained orbit."

"I swear the woman will suffer if you lie."

"Every Guardian onboard is here," the man promised. "I would not jeopardize our healer's life."

"You." He pointed the knife toward the Guardian standing next to the wounded man. "Carry him to the cargo lift. The rest of you follow him, and remember, the healer and I will be close behind."

The cargo lift? She remembered riding in it when Rhyel first brought her to the lab. It was big enough to accommodate them all. It went down to the cargo hold—and the shuttle bay. Did he plan to steal a shuttle? Siikzo believed there was another ship out there. Was that his destination?

The crewmen were herded like cattle down the long corridor. The lift was larger than she remembered, giving Tzorik adequate room to control the Guardians.

When they reached the cargo hold Tzorik ordered them into the shuttle bay, and onto the larger shuttle. "Return to New Centallus, and tell Rhyel I have his mate. He is to wait for my instructions."

The shuttle door closed and he forced her toward the safety of the shielded observation deck. He shoved her into a corner. "If you move I'll cut you."

She stayed put. The man had clearly lost his hold on reality, and the room was too narrow for her to avoid him.

He moved to a small panel and pressed several lighted squares. Alarms rang as the huge bay door rose, allowing the shuttle to disembark. He grabbed her arm and half dragged her back to the bridge.

47

✧

When the bridge door opened, Amber's heart lurched to her throat. Grandpa stood on the upper deck of the empty bridge, his back to the door.

"Who are you?" Tzorik demanded. He snagged her hair, yanked her head back, and pressed the knife so tight against her throat she didn't dare swallow.

Her grandfather pivoted, and froze in place. Slowly, painfully so, he lifted his hands in the air. "I'm Samuel Donovan, her grandfather. Please don't hurt her."

Tzorik nudged her into the room and waved the knife toward the side wall. "Get over there."

Grandpa moved to the wall and stood with his back against it, watching.

"Two hostages," Tzorik said. "Is that a benefit, or a detriment, I wonder? I suggest you both remain on your best behavior while I decide." The threat wasn't subtle.

"Tzorik," she said, "If you let us go—"

"I'll be dead within the hour."

"Your father won't let that happen."

"I'm already dead to him."

"I don't believe that."

"What you believe or do not believe is of little value to me. Go stand with your grandfather." He shoved her toward him and moved to the center console.

"Are you all right, honey?" her grandfather asked.

"I think so, but I'm scared to death."

"That man of yours won't let him hurt you."

"Rhyel's in stasis, Grandpa. They can't wake him right now. It's too soon."

Her grandfather inclined his head toward Tzorik. "Is he the one who tried to murder you?"

She nodded.

"If he turns his back—"

"No, Grandpa."

Tzorik glared at them. "If you're up to something, old man, it will get you killed, and her with you." He returned his attention to the holographic screen in front of him.

The image of a tall, striking woman with long dark hair appeared. A tight fitting uniform flattered her reed-thin body.

She frowned. "You're taking a risk contacting me."

"Not much of a risk, considering."

"Considering what?" Her frown darkened when she saw Amber and her grandfather. "Who are they?"

"Hostages."

"Hostages! Are you crazy?"

"Not crazy, Celiiel—found out. We have to act quickly or lose everything. Ready half your crew to board the *Novaria*."

"You're taking the ship? Is Rhyel dead?"

"Not dead," He glanced toward Amber. "In stasis. He won't bother us."

"What did you do, stab him in the back?"

"You don't think I can defeat him in a fair battle?"

"I don't think you'd take the chance. Have you found the *Acqeli*?"

"All in good time. Prepare your ship, and choose the men you'll send to me. I'll contact you as soon as I have the crystal." He cut the link.

She stared at the empty space where the woman's image had been and everything fell into place. The Centallians had been right to suspect the ghost signals. There had been another ship out there.

Tzorik initiated a second call and the holographic screen blinked on again.

Cintar's face appeared. "Transfer Amber and her grandfather to the fortress, now. We can talk when they are safe."

"You and I have nothing to talk about. Where are the Elders?"

Valdon stepped into view. The remaining Elders moved up behind him. "We are all here, son. Please don't hurt anyone else."

"Does it pain you to call me son?" Tzorik sneered, and shook his head when Valdon started to speak. "I don't have time for your placating lies. Give me the *Acqeli*."

Valdon staggered back. Tzarn reached out to brace him. "How do you know about the *Acqeli*?"

"I'm not stupid, and you are too trusting." Tzorik laughed. "I eavesdropped. I discovered your secret, now I intend to possess it."

"Don't dishonor yourself and our family, Tzorik."

"Enough. Give me the *Acqeli* now."

"We cannot. It isn't here."

"I know you lie." Tzorik reached over, yanked Amber away from the wall, and dragged her in front of the com. He held the knife to her throat once more. "I will kill her now."

Valdon shook his head "No, don't. I'm telling you the truth. Only Rhyel knows where it's hidden, and he is in stasis."

Tzorik pushed her back toward her grandfather. "Wake him. If he wants to save his mate he'll crawl to a shuttle if he has to. He will bring the crystal to me, and he will come alone. If he cooperates, he can have her back." He slammed his palm down on the controls, disengaging the connection and slowly turned toward her, his grin demonic. "I lied."

48

✧

Rhyel's body shook with weakness—and fury. Tzorik was unpredictable. Amber was in grave danger.

"Is the *Acqeli* still hidden on board?" Valdon's voice lacked emotion.

"It is."

"You must regain control of your ship... at any cost."

He understood the unspoken message, the silent permission the father had given regarding his son. "I will see to the *Acqeli* after Amber and her grandfather are safe on New Centallus."

He winced as he pulled the tunic over his head. The bullet wound was closed, but the scar tissue was a vivid pink, and swollen. "Cintar, walk with me."

"Rhyel," Zitan called before he could leave. "Be careful."

He gave his father a quick nod as he and Cintar left the clinic.

"How did Amber's grandfather end up aboard *Novaria*?" He asked as the two men sprinted toward the shuttle pad.

"He transferred up with you and Amber."

"I wish she'd stayed on Earth. She'd be safe now."

"She seems to think she belongs with you. You can't blame yourself for what's happened. You were in stasis." Cintar paused a moment. "You should know that Siikzo is alive and still aboard *Novaria*. He didn't return with the crew."

He was only mildly surprised. If Amber had survived, it was reasonable to assume the others might have.

"Is Kaarz alive?"

Cintar shook his head. "If Siikzo can be believed, Tzorik murdered Kaarz, and intended to dispose of Siikzo and Amber in that shuttle explosion."

Gut-tight rage clenched his body and seized his throat.

"Amber didn't tell you about Tzorik, did she?" Cintar asked.

"There was no time."

"Tzorik kidnapped Amber the night she disappeared. She was drugged before they left the fortress, so she doesn't remember much. There's one more thing you should know," Cintar said as they reached the shuttle. "According to Siikzo, Tzorik's mate, Celiiel, has a ship out there."

His only reaction was a raised eyebrow. "That would explain the transmissions, then."

"You might be flying into a trap."

"I doubt it. Tzorik wants the *Acqeli*. He won't do anything until it's in his possession. Count upon it."

"I should go with you."

Rhyel activated the shuttle door and stepped inside. "He wants me alone."

The *Novaria's* docking bay was empty when Rhyel stepped onto the deck. He eyed the nearly empty expanse and wondered what Tzorik had planned for him. He didn't have to wonder long. The ship's communications system activated, and Tzorik's voice filled the huge room.

"Bring the *Acqeli* to the bridge."

He didn't respond. He took the cargo lift to the main deck and walked down the central corridor. The bridge door was open. Tzorik and Amber stood on the upper deck, facing him. She was pulled against Tzorik's body, his knife at her throat. Her grandfather sat on the floor to their left.

"I think you're close enough for now."

He stopped just inside the entry.

Amber tried to smile, but her wide eyes revealed her terror. Once she was out of danger, he'd enjoy taking Tzorik apart.

"Let her go, Tzorik. Your fight is with me. It has nothing to do with her."

"Only a fool relinquishes his advantage. As long as I have your woman and your child, I am in command. Give me the *Acqeli*."

He slowly shook his head.

"You will, or your mate dies." The communication alert piped. Tzorik glanced over his shoulder and his eyes narrowed as he backed Amber toward the com-panel. He leaned back and activated the hollo-screen.

"Celiiel," Rhyel growled.

"Rhyel." The woman's eyes traveled the length of him. "You seem fit. I was told you were in stasis."

"You look far better than expected... considering we thought you had died on Centallus."

"Not so." She laughed, apparently enjoying the byplay.

Tzorik showed no enthusiasm for the woman's humor. "Are your men ready to board?"

"Do you have the *Acqeli*?"

"I will soon. Rhyel is proving reluctant to part with it."

"Show him how serious we are, and rid yourself of that burden as well." She nodded toward Amber. "Slit her throat."

Tzorik flicked a nervous glance at Rhyel's tense stance. "You have eyes, Celiiel." He managed a bored attitude, but his quivering knife-hand spoiled the effect. "Amber is the only reason my friend here hasn't killed me."

Rhyel's tight-lipped smile confirmed Tzorik's assessment of his situation. Tzorik's fear kept Amber alive.

Celiiel's eyes rounded, mimicking surprise at Tzorik's admission. "You don't believe you can defeat Rhyel?"

"I prefer an edge."

"Like a knife in your opponent's back?"

Tzorik smiled. "It does have its advantages."

"I think we've enjoyed enough banter," Celiiel said when Tzorik refused to be baited. "Give us the *Acqeli*, Rhyel, or your mate will suffer the consequences."

"Honor forbids me to do so," he calmly told her.

"Even if Amber dies?" Tzorik said.

He shook his head. "We both know your threat is hollow."

Tzorik glided his knife to Amber's stomach. "Perhaps, but what of your child? If I'm careful, I can rid you of your heir, and still keep your mate alive—for a time at least. Imagine the agony she will suffer when the child is impaled in her womb."

Amber's arms slid between the knife and her child. Tzorik grazed her forearm with the blade in warning, but she held fast, in spite of the blood oozing from the shallow cut.

"Hurt her again and I'll kill you."

"You have more to lose than your mate," Celiiel said. "Give us the key, or your fortress and the pitiful remains of your society will share the same fate as Centallus."

A mind-numbing suspicion gripped him. "Explain yourself."

"Celiiel, shut up," Tzorik warned, lifting the knife to Amber's throat again.

"Why keep secrets? We have the *Novaria*, and when we leave orbit, their pitiful colony will be stranded forever." Her eyes slanted to Rhyel. "Tzorik tells me you have no idea as to the identity of the ones who destroyed Centallus. But you do suspect the *Acqeli* was involved. It was the target, but those who attacked Centallus were not strangers. They were as familiar to you as… Tzorik and I."

"Celiiel, don't."

But he understood. "It was *you*."

"Yes… though, in my defense, destroying Centallus wasn't my intention. All I wanted was the crystal. Tzorik and I had devised the perfect plan. Our leaders had grown complacent. They felt safe enough to shut down our fleet of ships during the holy celebration. It was easy to acquire a ship no one could identify and hire a crew from off-planet. I targeted the Elders' sanctuary. Tzorik should have been there to encourage his father to relinquish the *Acqeli*.

"Unfortunately, Tzorik didn't have time to warn me that he and the Elders had left Centallus. I was on my own.

"When the Elders at the sanctuary refused to cooperate, I decided to encourage them by laying waste to a small city. The city was vaporized, of course, which suited my purpose. But the blast must have ignited a massive pocket of natural gas. Successive explosions vented the planet's molten core.

"Even from a safe distance it was quite a show. Massive volcanic eruptions spewed lava, ash, burning away the atmosphere." Celiiel shrugged her shoulders. "No one survived." It was a cold statement of fact.

Tension crackled in the room.

"Millions of Centallians died because of you… my mother, my sister, little Dzang… and you're willing to sacrifice what is left of our species—your species—to possess the power of the *Acqeli*?"

"Relinquish the *Acqeli*, and you can save them."

"Let Amber go, Tzorik."

"She stays until the exchange is complete."

He caught a glimpse of movement to Tzorik's right.

Amber's grandfather suddenly jumped to his feet. "My granddaughter's in no condition to endure the strain you're putting her through."

The doctor had been so quiet Rhyel had forgotten he was there. Tzorik must have done the same. He started at the unexpected voice. His knife wavered close to Amber's neck.

"Please," her grandfather said when the crisis had passed, "allow her to sit down. Use me as a hostage."

"You are a hostage, old man." Tzorik turned to keep both men in his line of vision. "I think we will continue as we are."

Rhyel had little doubt Amber's grandfather had purposely distracted Tzorik.

A man moved on silent feet out of the shadow of the map room. Tzorik's back was now to him.

Rhyel controlled the urge to turn his head and identify the person who seemed intent on helping them. He gritted his teeth. If there was a fight, Amber would be in the middle of it.

"You're too quiet, Rhyel," Celiiel said. "You aren't considering something foolish are you?"

Rhyel used Celiiel's question as an excuse to look away from Tzorik, toward the com and the man just out of Celiiel's line of vision.

"Not when Tzorik holds my mate."

He dared a brief glance at the man. Siikzo never took his eyes off of Tzorik, but quickly nodded to his commander.

"Then give us the *Acqeli*," Celiiel said.

Tzorik extended the knife toward Amber's grandfather when the older man shifted his feet, and motioned him toward Rhyel. "Move."

Siikzo lunged, grabbing the arm that held the knife.

Rhyel rushed forward, putting himself between Amber and the weapon. He jerked Amber from Tzorik's grasp and pushed her into her grandfather's waiting arms.

He spun around as Tzorik broke Siikzo's hold and blocked the knife plunging toward him with a solid chop to his wrist. The knife clattered to the deck. His fist smashed into Tzorik's jaw, and the man crumpled. He waited but his adversary didn't get up. It hadn't been a very satisfying confrontation.

He reached for Amber, pulling her into his arms. "Did he hurt you?" When she shook her head he turned to Siikzo. "My thanks."

"You have one minute to produce the *Acqeli*, or I'll fire on your ship," Celiiel shrieked, drawing everyone's attention to the holographic image.

His hand came down hard on the com-panel and Celiiel disappeared. "Siikzo, take Amber and her grandfather to the shuttle. It isn't safe to transfer to the planet. Celiiel will be transferring her men to *Novaria* if she can. Head toward the planet. Keep us between the shuttle and Celiiel's ship for protection. I'll keep them occupied until you make it down."

Amber tightened her hold on him. "I don't want to leave without you."

He kissed her. "You have to go, and I don't have time to argue." He hugged her, then gently thrust her toward Siikzo. "Get her out of here."

49

✧

"Siikzo," Amber cried, "you can't leave Rhyel alone to face that woman and her men." He held her arm to support her as they ran through the corridor. "He hasn't had enough time in stasis. I saw the way he favors his side."

"Celiiel's men could be in the transfer chamber already. I have to get you off this ship now. Rhyel knows I'll return with more men as soon as you're safe."

"Radio Cintar," she persisted. "Have him transfer his men to the *Novaria*."

Siikzo was already shaking his head. "A transfer unit holds no more than five men. A personnel shuttle makes more sense. It can transport a substantially larger number of Guardians to the ship in less time than it takes to transfer them."

They took the cargo lift to the hold, and hurried to the shuttle bay. He lifted her into the ship's open doorway and steadied her grandfather as he climbed in behind her.

"Find a seat and fasten yourselves in," he told them as he secured the door. "Healer, use the shoulder harness that snaps across the upper chest. It won't endanger the baby."

She nodded, remembering the harness from her shuttle trip with Rhyel.

He strapped himself into the pilot's chair. "We'll be at the fortress in minutes."

He activated the control panel, tapped a few lighted squares, and the *Novaria*'s docking portal raised. The shuttle vibrated to life.

"What if that she-devil sees us leave?" Grandpa asked.

"I'm depending on Rhyel to keep her too busy to notice."

A thunderous roar vibrated the ship, and *Novaria* lurched.

"What was that?" she demanded, grabbing the arms of her chair.

"Celiiel fired on *Novaria*." Siikzo nosed the shuttle through the bay doors.

Vertigo swept over her as the ship rocked from another blast while their hovering shuttle remained half in and half out of the portal.

Siikzo's hands flew across the command board and the shuttle shot away from the bay. It was like being tossed off a skyscraper. He kept *Novaria* between their shuttle and Celiiel's ship. The *Novaria* pitched.

"Is Rhyel's ship being fired on again?" her grandfather asked.

"Yes, sir, but Rhyel knows what he's doing." As they descended toward the planet, Celiiel's ship came into view. Rhyel fired and hit the other ship's aft.

"Celiiel's ship is a familiar design," Siikzo said. "Rhyel's aiming for the transfer units. He's trying to keep them from boarding the ship."

Celiiel returned fire, grazing the *Novaria*'s forward hull. Rhyel prayed the shuttle was well on its way. He spared Tzorik a glance. The man hadn't moved since he'd hit the deck.

The holographic projectors were off-line but they could still hear each other. "Celiiel, Tzorik will die with me if you blow up this ship."

"I will offer a prayer for his soul. Provided he has one."

"I'm sure he has one, Celiiel, just as black as yours."

"If you're so concerned for Tzorik's life, give me the *Acqeli*. I'll take the crystal and you can have him. Refuse me, and my next target will be the fortress."

He fired as her ship came about. The shot soared high over her ship's bow and disintegrated.

She fired.

He took evasive action, but her volley struck navigation control. All he had left were weapons.

A noise from behind alerted him and he swung around.

Tzorik took a wild swing before turning to run from the bridge.

He didn't go after him. Celiiel had brought her ship around. Her laser cannons moved into position—one aimed at *Novaria*, one at the planet below.

He transferred every ounce of power to weapons. He had one chance to stop her—only one. He targeted Celiiel's bridge, held his breath, and fired.

Tzorik raced through the corridor to the closest transfer unit. Skidding into the small room, he closed the door and locked it. He swung around to the control panel, quickly entered the coordinates to Celiiel's ship, and stepped onto the transfer pad. He took a deep, relieved breath as the glass panel glided around him, and the familiar tingle coursed through his body as his surroundings dimmed into blue.

He had enough time to recognize the charred and melted debris hurling around him—Celiiel's ship. Time to see mangled bodies flying past. He had time to feel his lungs crave air. There was time to feel the moisture in his mouth boil—time to know his last breath had been drawn aboard *Novaria*.

He didn't have time to scream.

Rhyel watched the ship explode. Wreckage spread outward in a spiral of tangled steel. *Novaria* was directly in the debris path, and too crippled to avoid the impending collision.

With luck, he had a few minutes before *Novaria* was destroyed. He tore the front panel loose beneath the com-board and reached into the dark, filament-strewn recess. The box he retrieved was small and plain. The black crystal inside was equally plain. The *Acqeli*.

The ship lurched as the first boulder-sized chunks of debris pelted her like hailstones. She moaned as metal ripped through metal.

He removed the crystal from its resting place. Its potential for good had encouraged the Elders to protect it. He thought of his dead world, of the evil engendered by the desire to possess the power of the *Acqeli.*

Something large slammed into his ship, knocking him to the floor. Alarms sounded. The ship was losing orbit.

He struggled to his feet, and braced himself. The shuddering deck dipped and swayed as if the ship were an ocean-bound vessel caught in a gale.

He clasped the crystal tight in his fist. He had vowed to protect the *Acqeli's* secret, not the crystal itself. He tossed the source of so much misery to the deck. The secret would disintegrate with the ship.

Acrid smoke furled up from life systems vents. The ship tilted and plunged into the Centallian atmosphere. He bolted for the transfer pod, using the wall for balance as the ship listed to one side. She rumbled now, vibrating with atmospheric friction. He stumbled to the transfer pod and pressed the entry pad.

Nothing happened.

He punched in the numeric code.

Nothing.

In desperation, he clawed at the thin line where the panel joined the wall, forcing his fingers into the slot, then his hands. He strained against the balking door, reversing position to push it open inch by agonizing inch.

The ship careened and the door suddenly opened, catapulting him into the small room. The floor and walls shook. His ship was being wrenched apart.

He lurched to the controls, punched in the first coordinates that came to mind, and prayed the auxiliary power would hold.

Metal screeched. The glass panel on the transfer pad imploded.

He lunged into the transfer beam as the *Novaria* disintegrated around him.

50

✧

Cintar stood at the shuttle door and lifted Amber out of the ship.

"Are you all right?" he asked as soon as her feet touched solid ground.

She grabbed his arm before he could pull away. "You have to take the Guardians to the *Novaria*. Rhyel's alone up there and Celiiel's sending men to take over the ship."

Cintar looked over her head.

She turned and saw Siikzo assisting her grandfather from the shuttle.

"It's true," Siikzo said. "She and Tzorik want the ship, and something called the *Acqeli*."

Cintar gently pushed her into her grandfather's arms. "*Guardians*," he shouted toward a large group of men who were already assembled, battle armed with very futuristic-looking hand weapons. They reminded her of every science fiction movie she'd ever seen. "Man the shuttles. Everyone else clear the landing pad. You" —he grabbed the first Guardian that passed him— "return to the fortress. Alert the Elders that communications are jammed. Tell Liiam to set guards at the transfer unit. Celiiel may decide to take the fortress as well as the ship. Siikzo, escort the healer and Doctor Donovan to the fortress."

She pulled away from her grandfather and placed a hand on Cintar's arm. "Oh, please…."

She couldn't voice her fears.

But he seemed to understand her need for reassurance. "Be easy. Rhyel is a capable warrior, and he knows that all we have, and all we are, is at risk. He'll hold them off until we get there."

A brilliant flash of light overhead wrenched cries from the Centallians. Cintar pulled her into the protective circle of his arms.

"What was that?" Grandpa yelled.

"I'm not sure," Cintar said, gaze riveted on the fiery streamers that burned out in the atmosphere. He had a grim set to his mouth. Something devastating had happened up there.

She couldn't breathe.

The baby kicked, hard. Her lower abdomen tightened. She placed a protective hand over her child. "One of the ships is gone, isn't it?"

"I think so." Cintar met her gaze without wavering. "But I will wager all that I am that it was not the *Novaria.*"

She seized the hope he gave her like a lifeline. Rhyel had to live. She couldn't survive without him.

A sonic blast erupted, ending in a unified moan from the crowd.

She lifted her eyes to witness the shooting star descent of a huge fireball. It skirted the low horizon, then exploded with ground-jolting force. Shock waves shook the trees.

Cintar tightened his hold on her, keeping her from being knocked down.

Her body shook in reaction. Tears blurred her vision. A black shroud of despair threatened to smother her, and she sucked in great lungsful of air. Each breath made her desperate for another.

"Tell me that's the same ship," she pleaded between gasps. She clutched Cintar's arm with both hands, her nails digging into his flesh. "Tell me that wasn't the *Novaria.*" She didn't like his silence. It terrified her more than Tzorik had. "*Cintar,*" she yelled when he still failed to respond, "please tell me that wasn't Rhyel!"

Cintar dislodged her fingers from his arm and trapped her hands against his broad chest.

She felt his heart slamming into his ribs.

"I cannot," was all he said.

"No!"

"I am sorry."

She reached for Siikzo. "Take the shuttle back up. Rhyel needs help."

Cintar pulled her back into his arms, and pressed her head against his chest. He refused to let her pull away from him again. "Amber, the shuttle cannot go up, There's too much debris." He didn't let her look up to see his face, but she heard the anguish in his voice.

"Let your grandfather and Siikzo take you to the fortress. Check the transfer unit. He may have transferred down. We'll take the shuttle up as soon as it's safe."

"He's alive," she said, as much to convince herself as him. "I'd know if he were dead."

The tightening in her abdomen escalated into true pain. Her fingers curled into her knotted stomach, and she couldn't stop a groan.

"Here now," her grandfather said, "was that a contraction?"

"No." Beads of sweat moistened her brow, and she took another shuddering breath.

"You never were a good liar," he grumbled. "Let's get you to the clinic."

"I'm fine," she insisted, trying desperately to regain her composure. "I'm not going anywhere until I know what's happened to Rhyel."

"I'm afraid you are." Cintar scooped her into his arms and strode toward the fortress.

"Put me down, Cintar. I'm not having this baby until Rhyel is back."

"You can wait for him in the clinic."

Hope welled in her heart. "You do believe he's alive, don't you?"

Cintar avoided her gaze. "As long as you believe he is alive, I will believe."

It wasn't the pledge she wanted, but she blessed the loyalty of this big man.

"Thank you," she whispered, and hugged his neck.

By the time Cintar carried her into the clinic, a bed was turned down and waiting. Her grandfather grabbed a nearby blood pressure kit and wrapped the sleeve around her arm.

"You must take care of Rhyel's child," Cintar said quietly.

She looked up. "Are you going to search for Rhyel now?"

"Yes."

"Please don't try to keep the truth from me. The waiting is harder than the knowing."

"I will not return until I have news for you."

"You've got a nice little clinic here," her grandfather said, drawing her attention away from the closing door. His eyes took in the room. "You have everything you need. How are the supplies?"

"We have updated medical equipment," Hiilani said, moving to his side, "and a full stock of basic medications." She extended her hand. "I'm Hiilani."

He took her hand in both of his. "I'm delighted to make your acquaintance, young lady."

"Thank you, Doctor Donovan." Hiilani bent to give Amber a gentle hug. "I'm so glad to see you again. I have a gown ready for you to put on."

Hiilani pulled the curtain around the bed area and Amber's grandfather stepped out to give her privacy. Hiilani helped her get undressed and into the hospital gown.

By the time she was finished, another contraction began, this one not quite as intense as the last. She rode out the pain, forcing her mind to go blank, and her body to relax.

A light tap sounded at the clinic door as she slipped into bed, and the nurse pulled the drape back a little. Someone entered the room, but she couldn't see the door. A surge of adrenaline made her heart race. "Rhyel?"

"No, child." Zitan peeked cautiously around the half-opened curtain. "Are you well enough for a visitor? I promise I won't stay long."

She pushed herself up against the pillows. "Please come in. Have you heard from Rhyel?"

"I'm sorry, no." Zitan's words bespoke deep sorrow, and she ached all the more. Rhyel's father looked older. The worry lines she remembered from five months ago were more pronounced, his back not quite as straight. He had lost so much. Now he faced the possibility of losing his only son.

"Child, I thought never to see you again," he said. "When Cintar told me you were alive, I felt such joy. If only Rhyel…."

"Rhyel is alive," she insisted. "I know he's alive."

Zitan nodded, and smiled. "When everyone thought you dead, my son refused to accept what seemed obvious. He did not feel your death. Your bond with him is strong. Your words give me hope."

She prayed the hope she gave him wasn't false. The next contraction didn't allow her much time to think about it. She gave her full attention to controlling the pain, to mentally staying on top of it.

Hiilani introduced the two expectant grandfathers. "Doctor Donovan could use something to eat and drink," she suggested.

Zitan nodded, but her grandfather balked at leaving his granddaughter.

"I'm sure you know it will take a while," the nurse persisted. "This will give Amber and me time to catch up on things. I won't leave her side, I promise. And I'll keep you both updated."

The pains that had set in so quickly due to her anxiety subsided into a routine of mild contractions with prolonged periods of waiting in between. The afternoon faded, and the evening sun's rays slanted across the clinic's ceiling—and still no word of Rhyel.

With the passage of time, she became less certain of his survival. In the calm moments between contractions her imagination painted horrifying pictures of his fate.

Doubt robbed her of the serenity so important during childbirth. As the contractions strengthened, her ability to control them diminished. Her life centered on the pain and her overwhelming fear for Rhyel.

Dawn brightened the sky. Hiilani opened the thick curtains to help dispel the night's shadows.

Amber roused from the haze of pain and fear that engulfed her and realized, with some surprise, that the night had passed. "Hiilani, has Cintar found him?"

Hiilani shook her head as she straightened the sheets on Amber's bed. "But he hasn't returned, so they haven't given up looking."

"But they will soon, won't they?" Tears trickled down the side of her face.

"We can't know that, and I don't want you thinking negative thoughts right now. You have to conserve your energy."

Amber felt a slight ping, and suddenly her gown and the bed were soaked. A deep, wrenching contraction clawed the middle of her body. She moaned and grabbed the bed rail.

Hiilani was beside her instantly, taking in what had happened. "This is what we've been waiting for," she assured Amber, then grinned. "But I guess you know that. We'll get your clothes and the bed changed, then send for your grandfather."

Grandpa had been given a room on the first floor and from the rumpled hair and sleepy-eyed look of him, it was obvious he'd been resting when he was summoned. He glanced around the room. When his eyes met Hiilani's, she shook her head. He'd been hoping to see Rhyel. How often throughout the night had she roused from a fitful sleep and done the same?

The contractions came one on top of the other, now, each growing in intensity. She concentrated on her breathing, and tried to control the desire to push the child from her body. She spent the seconds between contractions arguing with Hiilani and her grandfather about Rhyel.

"I'm not having this baby without him. Find Cintar. I have to talk to him."

Hours after her water broke, her child had yet to make an appearance, and her threat of not having the baby unless Rhyel was with her seemed frighteningly prophetic. The pain was too intense to ride out.

Sonya arrived. She bathed Amber's face with a cool, damp cloth. "You will make it through this. You must have faith the commander will return to you. Think of how pleased he will be to see his son."

She tried to find the faith Sonya spoke of. She desperately wanted to believe Rhyel was still alive. But she was so tired, and it had been so long.

Pain consumed her, a wrenching, tearing pain that clawed at her belly like some ravenous, taloned predator. *Rhyel, I need you. How can I survive if half of me is dead? Where are you…?*

✧

Rhyel materialized at the second mine. He heard the blast and looked up to see the streaking fireball that had been his ship. His regret at losing *Novaria* was tempered by his gratitude at being alive.

Amber was his main concern now. He needed to get to the fortress, to make sure she was unhurt. He grabbed a couple of filled water pouches from the supply shed. It was a two-days' walk to the fortress, maybe more given his weakened condition.

Hopefully, someone would be looking for him.

51

✧

"*Rishka….*"

Amber's writhing body stilled. Time and pain were suspended as her entire being centered on the endearment.

"Rhyel?" She prayed his name, willed him to be real. But she was afraid to open her eyes and find out the truth.

"I'm here, *Rishka.*" Familiar arms enfolded her. He buried his face in the damp hair at her neck. "I'm here."

She breathed in his wonderful scent, turned her head, and touched his skin with her lips. He was real. He was alive!

She wanted to laugh and cry at the same time. Instead, she pulled back and cupped his face in her hands… looked at him… looked at his rugged, beloved face. He was bruised and sunburned, his clothing covered with dust—he was the most beautiful sight she'd ever seen.

"Rhyel." She whispered his name like a prayer. Thank you, God.

"Don't cry, *Rishka.*" His voice was rough. His fingers brushed the moisture from her cheek. She leaned forward and touched her lips to his. They tasted salty—from his tears.

The contraction caught her off guard. She grabbed Rhyel's shoulders and moaned—a deep guttural sound.

✦

Amber's jaw was clenched tight, her brow furrowed with pain. Rhyel straightened and looked across the bed to her grandfather.

Samuel motioned him to the far side of the room. Hiilani took Amber's hands in hers and murmured encouragement as she endured the torment.

"What's wrong with her?" He demanded as soon as they were out of Amber's hearing.

Samuel handed him a blue shirt and pants he'd grabbed from the counter. "Put these scrubs on over your clothes if you're going to stay."

He jerked the shirt over his head and shoved his feet into the pants. "Tell me what's happening," he said again as he tied the drawstring belt.

"We've run into a small problem." The doctor held up a hand, forestalling his respond. "Don't panic. It isn't serious yet. And if it gets serious we have options."

"Tell me the problem."

The doctor tried to smile. "If I didn't know better, I'd swear it's pure stubbornness on that girl's part. She insisted she wasn't having that baby without you. And she hasn't, in spite of the fact that the baby should have been born hours ago."

A small sense of relief washed over him. "You're telling me it isn't physical?"

Samuel shook his head. "I wish it was that simple. For whatever reason, and I'm guessing it's the stress, she isn't fully dilated."

"Dilated?"

"I don't know how it is with Centallian women, but on Earth, when a woman gives birth, her body makes a few temporary changes to allow the baby's safe passage into the world. That isn't happening fast enough with Amber."

"Is she in danger?"

"Not at the moment. But if the baby isn't born soon she'll need surgery."

"To remove the baby?"

"Yes. It's usually a safe procedure."

"*Usually?*"

"Her labor has gone on too long. Her condition complicates matters."

"Then you must not do the surgery."

"If that baby doesn't get here within the next ten or fifteen minutes, we may not have a choice."

He shook his head. "I will not lose her again." He returned to Amber and sat on the bed. Her eyes were closed, and damp tendrils of hair spilled across her forehead and cheeks. He brushed them back. "*Rishka*, open your eyes. I need to talk to you."

He had to wait for another contraction. She grabbed his hand and squeezed.

"Don't fight it, honey," her grandfather told her. "You know better than that. Pant. Don't push yet. Get on top of the contraction and ride it out. That's it. Good girl."

When the contraction ended, Rhyel was soaked with sweat. He needed to rub the circulation back into the hand Amber clutched, but she didn't seem inclined to let it go. That was all right with him.

"*Rishka*," he said, knowing there wasn't much time between her contractions. "We're having this baby now, you and I together. Keep your eyes on me, even when the pain starts—especially when it starts. Relax and let your body do what is necessary."

She tensed, and leaned forward, into the pain. He pulled the pillows from the bed and climbed in behind her, supporting her back with his chest, wrapping his arms around her, slipping his strong hands beneath the cover to rest on the tightening mound of her stomach, cradling their child.

"Remember what your grandfather told you," he whispered against her ear. "Don't fight the pain. You cannot leave me again. I want to see my son grow strong in your love."

Rhyel kept talking, kept Amber focused on what had to be done. She absorbed his strength, felt whole again.

Suddenly the doctor straightened. "Now," was all he needed to say.

She grabbed Rhyel, took a deep breath, closed her eyes, and pushed with every ounce of strength she had left. The baby slipped from her body, and she cried out in triumph. A high-pitched, disgruntled wail blended with her voice.

He folded his arms around her, his cheek resting against her head. His breathing was as harsh as hers.

"Our son's lungs are as strong as his mother's," he teased as he climbed out of the bed to give the doctor and nurse room to work. He bent and touched her lips with his. "I love you," he whispered before stepping around the curtain.

He watched Sonya bathe and dress his son and wrap the protesting baby in a warm blanket. She carried the squirming bundle to Rhyel, and he stared down in wonder at his son. Sonya tried to place the babe in his arms, and laughed when he vehemently shook his head.

"He won't break," she chided, before settling the child into his keeping.

He carried their baby around the privacy curtain. Amber was dressed in a pink cotton gown. Her red-gold hair spread out like a halo across the white, lace-edged pillow case. She had never been more beautiful.

She looked up and smiled when he walked over to place the baby in her arms. She did what every new mother does. She counted his fingers and toes. He watched, content, as mother and son became acquainted.

Amber's grandfather stepped out of the clinic, and closed the door behind him. A moment later a cheer arose in the great hall. A minute after that, Sam Donovan returned, Zitan beside him. "I brought someone to meet his grandson," the doctor told them.

Zitan's eyes never left the squirming bundle. "He is the image of Dzang," he told Rhyel. "Dzang also looked like your mother."

Rhyel nodded dutifully, looked down at his son, and wondered how the wrinkled, red-faced infant could resemble anyone who wasn't at least ninety years old.

"He's beautiful," Amber said to no one in particular.

Again, Rhyel nodded, this time, with more enthusiasm.

✧

"*Rishka*, wake up." Rhyel's voice was soft but urgent.

Amber came up from the depths of sleep as a swimmer breaks the surface of the water. When she opened her eyes, Rhyel was there. "Our son is impatient to greet his mother."

She gave her mate a brilliant smile. "Let me have him, please."

He sat beside her on the bed, and placed the tiny bundle in her arms. The baby gurgled, and turned his head to root against her breast.

"He's hungry," he said.

She fumbled with the buttons of her gown, fingers numb and awkward in her sudden shyness.

"Let me help." He loosed the buttons and brushed the material back, exposing her breast.

The baby's face touched her warm skin and his hands and feet pumped the air in his eagerness. His mouth puckered and he whimpered.

She wanted to cry with him.

"It's okay, sweetie," she crooned.

Rhyel helped support his head as she guided his smacking mouth to her nipple. He clamped down hard, rested his tiny fist on the side of her breast, closed his eyes in bliss, and began suckling.

"Your grandfather and my father are arguing over whose side of the family our son takes after."

"He looks like you," she said quietly.

Rhyel touched the tiny hand at her breast, and the baby curled his fist around his father's finger. "Have you considered a name for our son?"

"Before you returned for me, I thought about naming him after my father. I'd still like to, if you don't mind."

"What was your father's name?"

"Jonathan."

"Jonathan. It is a strong name. I like it. We will call him Jonathan, and when we have a daughter, we will name her Solaange, for my mother, if it is agreeable to you."

"I'd like that."

He lifted her hand to his lips. "I need to tell you something."

He sounded grave. She shuddered and pulled Jonathan closer. "Tzorik?"

"Tzorik is dead. I will explain the circumstances when you are rested."

"Is Valdon all right? He lost his son."

"Tzorik's actions devastated him, but he has the council's and the people's support." He touched the top of their son's head. "*Novaria* is gone. I... I couldn't save her."

She nodded. "I know. I watched her go down. I... I thought I'd lost you." She looked at their son, realized he'd stopped nursing, and pulled her gown closed.

She lifted the baby to her shoulder before asking, "What about the Guardians on Earth? Will they be okay?"

His eyes reveal his regret. "There is only one—Keeso. We have no way of retrieving him. We left a small shuttle behind on our last trip, but shuttles are not interstellar crafts. He can't make it home on his own."

"What will happen to him?"

"Eventually he will know something has happened to prevent us from returning. He has established an identity on Earth, and is accepted by his acquaintances. The gold we delivered will sustain him. He can make a life for himself on your world, but I fear it will be a lonely one. The possibility of genetic incompatibility is too great to chance taking a mate."

She touched his cheek. "I'm sorry about your friend, and I know how much *Novaria* meant to you."

He kissed her palm. "*Rishka*... we are stranded, too. We can survive without Earth, even flourish eventually." He took a deep breath. "But I can never take you home."

She blinked away the tears that blurred her vision.

He saw them and groaned. "Forgive me, *Rishka*."

She tried to smile and her lips trembled. He was her world, her soulmate. Without him she was only half alive. She leaned forward to touch her lips to his.

"I thought you understood," she whispered. "I love you. I am home."

Rose Sartin was born in Illinois, raised in Iowa, and has spent most of her life in the Missouri Ozarks. She and her late husband, Gary, raised two daughters, Melissa and Angela, and a son, Eric, while building businesses as beekeepers, leathercrafters, and managers/tour guides in a show cave. Ms. Sartin is also proficient with the mountain dulcimer, performing in radio, television, and documentaries. Today she lives in their family home on an Ozark ridgetop that overlooks the Mark Twain National Forest. She is currently finishing the second and third novels in her Honor trilogy. Her life is filled with family and friends, music, good books, and plotting adventures for characters who show up on her mind's doorstep.